Uncomfortably Dark Horror
Presents

The Baker's Dozen

Published by Uncomfortably Dark Horror

Edited by Candace Nola

Foreword by Jeff Strand

Cover Design by Don Noble

Interior Title Sketches by John Kostov Designs

"Demonic Donuts" by Lisa Vasquez

Limited Edition Hardcover available exclusively on

Uncomfortably Dark.com

Paperback and eBook available on Amazon.

Dedication

This anthology is dedicated to each one of the people that made it happen. Each one of you have my deepest admiration, and respect. Thank you for welcoming a new writer into this industry with open arms and for taking a chance on making my dreams come true.

To my usual suspects:

To Charity-Thank you for pushing me until I gave in.

To my kitty, my puddin', and my sir-You are my legacy, the reason I exist, the reason I write.

To my mom and my dad-who always knew.

To V.T.- You will be on every dedication, until I no longer exist. I know you are watching.

Special thanks to M. Ennenbach, Rowland Bercy, Jr., Ruthann Jagge, Eric Butler, James Carlson, and the House of Stitched family.

Early Reviews for the Baker's Dozen!

"The Baker's Dozen collects all of the ingredients for something delicious. You won't want to eat it, of course, because there's nothing safe or healthy found in these pages. But it's a feast for your eyes and your imagination you won't soon forget. Just try not to choke." -Nikolas Robinson

"A delicious assortment of horrors concocted by some of the genre's best!" - James G. Carlson, author of MIDNIGHT IN THE CITY OF THE CARRION KID

Table of Contents

Foreword
By Jeff Strand

Welcome, food lovers! It's time to snuggle up with your favorite baked treat and enjoy *Uncomfortably Dark Horror Presents: Baker's Dozen*!

Actually, don't. Put that treat away. You don't want to associate it with the book you're about to read. It would be a real bummer to ruin future chocolate-filled croissants because you take a bite and then suddenly an image from this book comes to mind, and you're all like "Ew! God, no!" and you spit out what would otherwise have been a delicious, flaky, buttery, chocolatey croissant.

When I was asked to write the foreword to this anthology, I assumed that "horror stories about baking" referred to stuff like burning a cake right before your mother-in-law comes to visit. Can you imagine? You're trying to impress your mother-in-law, who has never thought you were worthy of marrying her offspring, and when she gets there the whole house smells like burnt cake! How embarrassing! She looks disappointed, but she also has this smug expression like she *knew* you were going to burn the cake, because you're a terrible cook who can't do anything right in the kitchen. What a fucking bitch, right?

If you're offended by my use of the F-word and the B-word, let that be a warning that you are probably not the target audience for this particular book. These pages are not filled with lighthearted tales of kitchen mishaps. As it turns out, "Uncomfortably Dark Horror" wasn't a typo. These stories are *messed up.* They're twisted and gross and the authors involved—including me—should be ashamed of themselves for the evil they've unleashed upon the literary world. It honestly worries me that one or more of these morally bereft monsters might someday be in a position to served baked goods to the public.

Don't get me wrong—the stories are great. They're also remarkably varied in the ways they'll ruin baking for you. If you think this is going to be thirteen stories about making human organs into a pie, you'll be pleasantly surprised by the imagination contained within. All I'm saying is, don't watch *Jaws* before swimming in the ocean, and don't read this book when you have freshly baked chocolate chip cookies cooling in the kitchen.

You've been warned. And you've probably ignored the warning, because you're a rebel who plays by their own rules, so at least try not to get crumbs all over the book.

Demonic Donuts

PRETZELS OF GOD

CHRISTINE MORGAN

Pretzels of Gods

by Christine Morgan

Brother Jehan.

Everything a good and proper monk should be. Devout, pious, obedient, hard-working, selfless, humble, dedicated. Adhering effortlessly to his vows, making no complaint or lamentation. Not even over the celibacy, which has proved the sinful downfall of many a clergyman ... few of whom faced the constant temptations directed Brother Jehan's way.

He was young, fit, healthy. Tall of frame, muscular but lean. Thick of hair -- where not tonsured, which patch of unblemished scalp he kept smooth, not only having it trimmed and shaved weekly by Brother Ashton, the monastery's barber, but scouring it free of stubble as part of his daily morning ablutions. Dark of eye and fine of feature. Handsome, almost too handsome, almost pretty.

Oh, how the women gazed, fawned, all but swooned over him! Village girls and their mothers. Merchants' wives. Noble ladies. The abbess herself, ancient battle-axe that she was, doted upon him like a favored pet, and merely chortled indulgently when the novice nuns in her care blushed and fluttered in his presence.

Indeed, he could have had his pick of them, any or all. Yet, he remained as if oblivious to the intent of their attentions. Perfectly polite. Perfectly chaste.

Not once since his arrival had he availed himself of the services of Sister Ermengarde, whose task it was to supply relief to those monks in peril of sinful self-abuse. This, she performed with her left hand, as brusque and perfunctory as a nurse, with no other contact or conversation. It was, therefore, not congress of a lewd or wicked nature. Merely a matter of physical release, no different than lancing a boil. And it certainly was naught to do with Sister Ermengarde, nearly as old as the abbess, whose fingers were more akin to an owl's gnarled talons and whose weathered palm chafed with each well-practiced stroke.

Brother Jehan never visited that discreet chamber set apart from the cloister, that strange mirror of sorts to the confessional booth. He seemed as oblivious to the temptation of self-abuse as he was to the bevies of blushes, batted eyelashes, and 'accidental' brushings-against or bumping-into which so often happened.

His sole deviation from the monastic routine was to rise early of Sunday mornings, go to the bakery-house adjoining the kitchens, and make pretzels. Every week, he did this, every week without fail. Always the same amount, seven trays of seven pretzels apiece, the holy number times itself for a total of forty-nine. No more, no less. The cost of the ingredients and surplus wood for the oven, meager though it was, he paid for from his own monk's wages ... meager though *they* were, poverty being another vow to which he diligently adhered.

Brother Jehan.

Pious, handsome, polite, humble, dedicated, hard-working Brother Jehan.

How I loathed him!

How I hated him, him and his piety, him and his handsomeness, him and his perfection!

Him and his damnable pretzels!

For they, too, were perfect.

Perfect!

Oh, anyone could make pretzels, of course. And we did, particularly when the Lenten season came on. We mixed the dough, divided and worked it, formed it into the twist-knot representative of enfolding arms, dipped each briefly into the boiling solution of water and lye, daubed with oil or egg-wash, sprinkled with salt, and baked them. Pretzels. As simple as simple could be. There should hardly be, from one to the next, much difference. A pretzel was a pretzel, was it not?

So, one might think, had one not witnessed the flawless fruits of Brother Jehan's labors. Other pretzels made by other monks would show variations, the thinness of the doughy ropes, the formation of the knotted twists, the coloration of the crust. It was only to be expected.

And yet ...

And yet, somehow, his were always perfect. Always as uniform as coins struck fresh from a mint or cast from a mold. Of a size and a shape and a thickness so as to be all but identical. With a tawny dark-golden outer crispness of crust, the salt so evenly dusted each grain might have been precisely placed. The inner texture was always just slightly soft, slightly chewy. The taste was rich and yeasty, with a hint of sweetness, and an elusive tanginess somehow unidentifiable but irresistible.

It made no sense!

We all used the same bakery, the same ovens, the same trays! The same flour and water and lye and salt! The same recipe, followed to the letter -- and as monks, this, *to the letter*, we knew how to do; hours spent copying manuscripts by candlelight made sure of that! We'd observed his technique, practiced it with painstaking imitation.

He *didn't* secretly add anything to his dough; I had watched him closely enough, watched him like a hawk! I had searched the cell where he slept, searched every inch and nook and cranny of the bakery-house, examined the implements and equipment with a scrutiny normally reserved for the most important documents. I'd thought it must be, some clandestine sprinkling, something in the oil, *something*, but I found nothing out of the ordinary at all.

The technique, then, it *had* to be. A trick of the wrist, a flick of the thumb. His was a deft artistry unparalleled among our numbers, his speed such that it appeared he spun each wad of dough from ball to rope to twist-knot as if conjuring pretzels from thin air. Try as we might, none of us could match his pace or duplicate his results.

When asked, during the hours we were not bound by our vows of silence, he had no satisfactory answer. A knack, he'd explain with an innocent shrug. No one had taught him this skill. He simply came by it. Perhaps a gift of God's will, not that he would presume to know the mind of the Almighty. It just *was.* It just was, and he accepted it with gratitude and grace.

Why, then, one might wonder, did he not make more use of it? Why only of Sundays, and only forty-nine? When he could be at it all day, every day, turning them out by the hundreds, by the thousands?

To this query, Brother Jehan's response remained as vague and unsatisfactory. He felt a rightness to it, the seven trays of seven pretzels, once every seven days. To do more struck him as taking advantage, somehow, of cheapening and rendering commonplace what should be kept special.

Not only did he, the insufferable piece of sheep's shit, lack for sins such as vanity and lust, but pride and greed as well. And ambition! He lacked ambition! Rather than aspire to a higher station within the Church, to become abbot or cardinal or archbishop someday, he was content to while away his life as nothing more than a lowly monk.

What a waste! A waste of so many advantages; the rest of us only dream of being as fortunate, as favored!

Those pretzels, perfect and delicious as they were, better than any to be found elsewhere, could be sold at a tidy profit! To the betterment and benefit of us all! As we monks did with the apricot brandy we distilled and bottled, as the nuns did with their cakes of herbal soaps. Why not sell the pretzels as well?

And sell, they *would*, I assuredly knew! I'd heard as much from several sources. Such pretzels might even make a name for us, put us on the map, bring people from miles around, establish us along the paths of pilgrimages! Our donation boxes would overflow with silver! The local lords would be generous with their patronage! We'd be rich! We'd be famed!

But, to these suggestions as well, Brother Jehan's responses left much to be desired. He was, if anything, aghast at the very idea.

So, the perfect pious darling of abbot and abbess and everyone else had his special Sunday mornings in the bakery-house, to produce his seven trays of seven pretzels. No more, no less.

Which were then, as if for the sole purpose of further chafing my backside, dispensed freely to grubby little children. Some came from the orphanage, brought by Sister

Berthe each week for sermon-schooling. Others were peasant brats and village urchins, lured by the prospect of a warm and fresh-baked treat. Of those lattermost, I was convinced that more than a few had taken their prizes and sold them about the marketplace, the wretches!

Tell this to Brother Jehan or the abbot, though? They'd wave it off as if of no consequence. The pretzels were a gift, a reward for attendance and good behavior; what each child chose to then do with them was their own concern.

Maddening. Purely maddening. To see them, to watch them run off down the lane, all ragged clothes and dirty faces, waving perfect golden pretzels overhead ... when there were folk who'd pay good money ...

Perhaps my sentiment was uncharitable. After all, they were orphans and urchins, without much else to look forward to. Who was I to begrudge them a simple pretzel as the sole bright spot in their otherwise drear and dismal lives? I would not pry the damned things from their filthy fingers!

I maintained, only, the belief that we were missing out on a rare opportunity, squandering a valuable resource. Even if he baked just a dozen or two every day, instead of toiling at other chores, we'd all see benefit of it.

How was it I alone thought this way? In many other aspects of our monastic life, matters were given practical as well as ecclesiastical consideration. If Brother Reinhart gave lighter penance to those who slipped him a few coins … if Brother Sebastian, in his travels about the countryside, hawked the occasional 'relic' here and there … what of it? We were, none of us, perfect.

Except for Brother Jehan.

Pious, perfect Brother Jehan.

Wrong although I knew it was, my own dark sin to bear, my hatred for him grew stronger week by week. I began making subtle investigations, hoping to unearth *some* unsavory truth, some hidden secret from his past. Something, *anything*, to prove him as weak or flawed as any other man.

Oh, I knew the story, of course; we all did. It passed from mouth to ear, often in hushed or even reverential tones, when newcomers joined our numbers. Among the nuns and novices, especially, as if to further dissuade the smitten … for what little good *that* did. If anything, it just added to their interest, and Brother Jehan's own demurrals further heightened his allure and mystique.

He claimed to have no recollection of the incident, having been at the time just a babe. He knew merely what he had been told by others. Even his own parents, also of modest and humble nature, had not gone so far as to presume full divine intervention, miracles, or angels. A 'figure of shining light' was all they would describe, on the rare occasions when they spoke of it at all.

It did make a good tale ... the poor peasant family, a sudden early frost sending everyone of working age out into the fields in a desperate rush to harvest what they could of their pitiful crops, leaving the youngest alone in his cradle ... an ember rolling from the hearth, the hovel swiftly engulfed, the child wailing in terror, the desperate mother plunging into the raging conflagration ... and then, out of the smoke and flame, a figure of shining light, little Jehan enfolded safely in its arms. Not a hair upon his head so much as singed, not a single blister marring his tender skin.

Anyone else might have made the most of it, such fame. Word spread far and wide. Neighbors were far quicker to cite the Almighty; the babe was surely blessed, God's chosen! He must be special, destined for some greatness! Yet, his parents remained modest and humble, seeking no profit or gain, merely thankful beyond measure their son had been spared, their family left whole.

As he grew from infancy to boyhood, the village priest persuaded the family to render Jehan into his own tutelage, there to learn to read and write, to study the Scriptures, and to prepare for a future in the service of the Church. Some few years and a well-placed word to the priest's old friend the abbot later, Brother Jehan joined the monastery.

Where he ... made pretzels.

Only on Sunday mornings.

25

Seven trays of seven pretzels each. No more, no less.

To be given to orphans and urchins as a treat for their sermon-schooling.

Pretzels.

The most delicious, perfect, flawless, golden pretzels, which could have been baked by the dozens and sold for a fine profit, enriching both the monastery's coffers and reputation.

What absurd manner of glorious God-granted destiny and purpose was *that*?

If, in fact, so it was ... the 'knack' by which he made them having been bestowed upon him when the 'figure of shining light' rescued him from the burning hovel ... why so limit it?

These thoughts, I pondered as the weeks went by. My investigations turned up nothing, nary a whiff of shame nor scandal. Perfect, pious Brother Jehan had never, it seemed, cast a lewd look upon a woman, done harm to anyone, or uttered an unkind word. He did not drink to excess, nor gamble. What pittance of his meager monk's wages did not go toward his own basic upkeep and the making of the pretzels, he, dutiful and ungrudging, sent home to his peasant parents.

My hatred seethed. My resentment grew. I hid it well, however.

Even when I saw the kindly affection with which Sister Berthe regarded him while he dispensed the precious fresh-baked treats to her orphan charges ... even when the abbot singled him out for introduction to and dining with a visiting bishop ... even when the newest novice, pretty Sister Lisetta, who, under other circumstances, still would not have given the likes of *me* a second glance, sighed with hands clasped to her bosom in sweet maidenly yearning as he passed by ...

Oh, yes, I hid it well.

More and more, I found myself wondering about this so-called 'figure of shining light.' My musings turned toward darker, sinister suspicions and speculations. Suppose it had, in truth, been no angel after all, despite what the neighboring peasants and village priest believed? Suppose Jehan's mother had witnessed ... something
What else, *who* else, was described as a 'figure of shining light'? Whose very *name* meant something very similar?

Should such be the case, would it not explain Brother Jehan's reticence to discuss his uncanny fortune and favors, his uncanny gift? Might he not be playing a greater ruse upon us all than anybody knew? Were the pretzels, and the ease with which he crafted them -- had not I myself phrased it as 'conjuring'? -- not any sort of Heavenly handiwork at all, but the precise opposite? Had he, as an infant. been carried through the very fires of Hell, its influence permeating his entire being? Infusing itself into the pretzels, imbuing them with evil? To corrupt the weak-willed innocence of helpless children? And taint the souls of good, Godly monks and nuns?

Of course! It had to be! It *must* be!

And only I, not taken in by his guise of pious humility, saw it for what it was! My hatred was not a sinful failing but salvation! I, and I alone, could stop this wickedness! By exposing his true nature, and the vile mischief he was perpetrating ... well, we'd see who *next* was invited to dine with the bishop, wouldn't we?

I did not bother trying to sleep Saturday night, just made a pretense of it until the monastery was filled with slumber. Quiet as a phantom, I slipped from my pallet and made my way along the darkened halls. Enough moonlight filtered in to aid my passage, while shadows cloaked the courtyards to conceal me from any wakeful eyes while I crossed to the kitchens, past the pantries, and into the small bakery-house.

There, I hid myself, to watch and wait.

There, in defiance of my best intentions, drowsiness overtook me. I woke with a start sometime later to the unfamiliar confines of the cabinet where I'd hidden, to hear the sounds of routine activity and see a warm glow through cracks in the door. I smelled yeast, the dough already rising. I smelled the acrid steam of lye mixed with water.

Creeping to the door, I peered out and saw, as I'd expected, Brother Jehan. Solitary, as he often was, going about the business of his pre-dawn pretzel making. He had the oven stoked and heating, the cauldron simmering toward a boil. Seven trays sat stacked and ready. On the long table, he spread a thin coating of oil with a horsehair brush. The salt-pot stood nearby, an amusing glazed-clay novelty in the shape of a rotund, beatific, jolly monk.

I'd always hated that thing, too, albeit for different reasons. The chubby cheeks, the simpering smile, the fat and well-fed belly. Furthermore, something about lifting the top of his tonsured head off to get at the salt struck me as inappropriate, if not outright sacrilegious.

Brother Jehan, by contrast, moved about the room lean and agile, neither smiling nor frowning, but with an expression of serene purpose. He did not hum, chant, sing, talk to himself, or pray. He rolled the dough into ropes, then with that deft flick of wrist formed the ropes into twisted knots -- enfolding arms, they were meant to symbolize, just as the enfolding arms of that 'figure of shining light' had been said to shelter him from the consuming flames -- dunked each for a brief immersion in the boiling lye-water bath, and placed them in neat arrangement on the trays.

The longer I watched him, the more closely I scrutinized him, the handsomer and more perfect he seemed ... and the more powerful my hatred and conviction grew.

Who else, after all, had been depicted as uncommonly handsome? Fairest among all the hosts of

Heaven, before the outcasting and ignominious fall from grace? Why, for all I knew, the *real* Jehan might have died in the fire so many years ago, with another stepping in to take his place! Walking among us, mocking us, defiling our holy order!

As the contents of the cauldron had reached full boil, so too did my hatred, erupting into rage. I burst from the cabinet, driven by my fury, taking Brother Jehan by surprise.

He had just begun rolling out another rope of dough when I sprang upon him. It dropped from his hands to the oiled tabletop like a pallid worm. Before he so much as had the chance to cry out, I seized him and forced his head into the cauldron.

The pretzels, when thus baptized, were submerged for no more than a count of ten or twelve. Brother Jehan, I held down much longer. Although he resisted, although he was the younger and fitter of us both, I overpowered him easily, with a strength which barely seemed my own.

Boiling lye and water scalded me to the wrists and splashed well up my forearms, but I felt no pain. The acrid scent of the steam took on a deeper, heartier note, reminiscent of a broth of chicken, or stewing pork. Frothy pinkish-yellow foam bubbled and burbled to the surface.

In the extremity of our struggles, trays went flying with a clatter. The rotund little salt-cellar monk tipped over, cracked, and spilled its gritty contents across the oiled table. The cauldron swung wildly on its iron tripod, and I regained enough presence of mind to realize the clangor it would cause if it struck the floor. I yanked Brother Jehan's head up from it by the sodden wool cloth of his cassock. He reeled back limply, flopping against me in a loose and heavy deadweight.

He may not have cried out, but when I saw his face, *I* almost screamed. The lye had already begun dissolving his skin. The flesh beneath hung loose, sloughing as if half-melted from the bone. His eyes bulged opaque and blindly clouded from their sockets, poached like runny eggs. As the caustic liquid streamed from his slack, gaping mouth, I saw he'd either swallowed or, drowning, inhaled it ... his tongue was whitened, puffy ... the linings of his throat dangling in filmy wet cobwebbing and threads.

I may have managed not to scream, but a strangled noise of revulsion did escape me. It almost became a cackling laugh -- not so handsome, now, was he? -- but, before it could, and before I could let his body fall, he convulsed to thrashing, flailing life. His hands, nearly as ruined as his face, groped for purchase at my cassock. A vile spray of breath and lye-water steam gusted from his softened, peeling lips. Perhaps it was meant to be a scream, perhaps a plea ... but the scalding solution must have dissolved his voice box, rendering him mute as well as blind.

In a panic, perhaps in a raw and atavistic horror, I drew again upon the surging strength that barely seemed my own. Handling him as if he weighed no more than a child's rag doll, I hefted him and turned and, without hesitation, pushed him headfirst into the oven.

He only went as far as his shoulders, but it was far enough. I held him there until his wild movements became spastic ... then sporadic ... and then stopped. His hair and clothes had begun to smolder. The aroma of roasting meat wafted in the smoky air.

My mad, cackling laugh manifested after all. I felt insane, maniacal, yet also somehow triumphant and exalted. Where, now, was any 'figure of shining light' to enfold him safely in its arms? Where, now, was his piety, his perfection?

I hauled him backwards, and, spying the scatter of salt-crystals spilled from the broken crockery monk, rolled him face down in it, encrusting him from brow to chin and ear to ear. I laid him out on the bakery-house floor, in the posture of a martyred saint upon a bier, palms pressed together in an attitude of prayer. Unbaked pretzels, I arranged around his head in a corona. I laughed, and cackled, and cackled, and laughed, until I must have taken leave of my own senses.

When I revived, only mere moments had passed, but so had my madness. In its place came instead a deadly clarity, a deadly calm. I could not let him be found this way, in such grisly tableau. It would have to appear an accident. A mishap, a terrible tragedy, such a woeful loss unto us all.

Hastily, I disarranged the scene and did what I could to give the impression of him having slipped, somehow badly splashing himself from the cauldron, and then, blinded by pain and confusion as well as his poached-egg eyes, blundering about knocking things over until he stumbled headlong into the hot oven. The results to me looked absurd, farcical, but at least did not speak outright of murder.

Furthermore, as the passion of the act faded, my own pain began asserting, my scalded hands an agony surpassing any I'd ever known. I held them before my face, staring as if these reddened, swollen bundles of weeping blisters belonged to someone else. For a moment, I imagined it would hurt less to sever them at the wrists. But the prospect of holding a cleaver ... and even could I chop off one, how would I then chop off the other?

Nor was there the time. I rushed back the way I'd come, aware of the waning shadows as pale dawn approached from the east, and of candles already alight in the windows of early risers. Once in my solitary cell again, I -- despite the sheeting, consuming pain -- exchanged my stained and damp cassock for another. My hands, I swathed clumsily in bandages. Should anyone ask, I'd say it was a rash, from weeding the stinging nettles that encroached upon the gardens.

I doubted, however, anyone *would* ask. I drew scant enough attention as it was, and once the gruesome discovery was made, all other matters would go unnoticed. I had only to carry on as if another normal day, doing nothing to stir suspicion.

To my fortune, little in the way of manual labor was required of a Sunday. Hiding my bandaged hands within my voluminous sleeves, keeping my head bowed and my hood drawn up, I went solemnly to morning services.

My nerves were taut as bowstrings, my ears keened for the initial outcry and alarum. My hands throbbed like twin pulsating organs of their own, matching the anxious canter of my heart.

Morning services went on, but the outcry and alarum did not come. I shifted, seeking an unobtrusive view in the direction of the bakery-house ... to no avail.

Had no one found him? Had no one gone to offer their assistance in the pretzel-making? Had no one noticed his absence? Or was that, too, overlooked with indulgence? The *rest* of us might be expected to leave off whatever we were doing to attend daily prayers; not so for perfect Brother Jehan!

I dared not, however casually, broach the subject. I did not ask if anyone had yet or not seen him. It wouldn't do to have myself linked to him in even the slightest way. Although brothers in the order, brethren of the cloth, we could hardly be called friends, any sudden show of concern on my part might seem curious.

So, fidgeting, chanting the required responses by rote, I waited.

And waited.

And began to wonder if the entire affair had been a dream, some fevered machination of my sleeping mind ... though the very real and scalded agony of my hands assured me otherwise. It had *not* been a dream!

Then, from the corner of my eye beneath the edge of my hood, I saw Sister Berthe, leading her orphan charges from the chapel where they had their sermon-schooling toward the sunny, grassy sward outside the bakery-house. There, they'd customarily receive their Sunday pretzels, and be allowed a span of time to run and play before returning to the orphanage.

I saw, also, some of the usual raggedy, grubby urchins trailing along, as well as one or two peasant children from the village.

Dismay clutched at my chest. Were *they* to find him? Kindly Sister Berthe, and these youthful innocents? Were they to be first upon that morbid spectacle of horrific death?

But *then* ...

My mind reeled with incomprehension.

For there came Brother Jehan. Wheeling, as he always, did the cart upon which stood the branch-spoked pretzel-rack. Laden, as it always was, with its twist-knots of perfect golden pretzels. Forty-nine of them, fresh from the warming-trays.

Or ...

Was it Brother Jehan?

The approaching figure was of the same height and build, but moved at a slower, faltering pace. With his head bowed and his hood drawn, as my own were, I could discern nothing of his features.

I had, without cognizance, pushed through the ranks of praying monks, eliciting sternly disapproving looks, which I ignored. My gaze was fixed upon the hooded figure -- Brother Jehan rarely wore his hood; of *course,* he wouldn't! -- and the excited children clamoring for their rewards ... and upon Sister Berthe, who had hesitated in her stride, sensing something amiss.

He raised his head then, letting the hood fall back.

Revealing his face. Revealing the ruined, suppurating nightmare of his face.

The world went silent. The world went numb. Each orphan and urchin stood as if rooted to the spot. Sister Berthe had become as a statue, paled to alabaster, one hand raised in warding and the other curled around her rosary.

From my fellow monks came gasps and cries of shock. Somewhere nearby, a novice -- pretty Sister Lisetta? -- screamed. Other nuns added their voices in a horrified choir.

Heedless of it all, Brother Jehan went among the children, dispensing pretzels one-by-one. These were taken hold of by tiny, tremulous fingers, while chins quivered, and tears ran from unblinking eyes. None of them brought the pretzels to their lips, merely held them in their shaking grasps.

No one else seemed able to move or intervene. We could only watch his slow and faltering progress as he made his way from one child to the next. When he reached Sister Berthe, he paused to offer what may have been meant as a sad smile but was instead a hideous ghoulish leer. She shuddered and crossed herself, rosary beads tangled around her slender fingers.

With a sorrowful nod of understanding, Brother Jehan moved on, until he'd given a pretzel to every child. The last was a peasant boy who'd wet his breeches, but accepted it, nonetheless. The children stood weeping, holding their goodly rewards for attending their Sunday sermon-schooling, holding them as if they had never seen pretzels before and did not know what to do.

A lone pretzel remained. It hung upon the branch-spoke, the final fruit of a strange tree. Brother Jehan plucked it loose. He turned. He came toward the group of monks ...

No.

He came toward *me*.

With slow, inexorable purpose.

I wanted to run, to flee as fast and as far as my legs could carry. I wanted to attack him, strike him down before he could fulfill whatever might be his grim intention. I wanted to fling myself to my knees before him, confess my sins, beg forgiveness.

I did none of these things.

When he stopped before me, and held out the perfect, golden pretzel ...

I took it.

With everyone looking on, including Brother Jehan's blind and awful eyes, in the sight of God and all His works, I extended my bandaged hand and took the pretzel.

Which crumbled to ash and soot and sawdust like damnation at my touch.

APPLE PIES AND DIAMOND EYES

CHRIS MILLER

Apple Pies & Diamond Eyes
By Chris Miller

Karen Waters has a mini-van full of teenaged girls and a head full of indignant reproach. Chesterfield Bakery is only a few more blocks away, but when she'd called ahead about the apple pie she was to pick up for the end of season Cheerleader's party—her daughter Amanda and her friends in the back had all cheered their local Panthers to a disappointing end that hadn't made the playoffs—she'd been told by the woman who answered the phone that the pie *might* not be ready by the time they arrived.

After all, the initial order had stated a twelve PM pickup time, and it was only ten-forty-five. Well, none of that was Karen's fault; she wasn't the head of PTA—that condescending, poorly aged Barbie Doll Wynona George had been elected for a third time now—and *she* hadn't moved the time of the party up an hour. Pies needed time to cool, the lady had said, to which Karen had responded, "I *knoooooowww!*", and their conversation had deteriorated from that point forward.

The girls in the back are on their phones and giggling. One of them is talking about her boyfriend, who hasn't called or texted her in over twenty-four hours now, and *what was up with that?* Amanda suggests maybe he's talking to Courtney Owens. Says she's seen them in study hall chatting a lot. The first girl, Olinda Aguilar, scoffs at this, but Karen can see her in the rearview. She's upset. Great. An upset teenager always leads to *more* upset teenagers, and she has no patience with adolescent crises.

They know nothing of having a *real* relationship, nothing about living with and marrying a man and then getting divorced twenty-seven years later while their husband saddles up with a girl maybe five years older than the girls in the back. She wants to shout at them, but she saves her frustration for the woman at the bakery. *Oh,* was that woman ever going to get it from her. A piece of her mind and then some.

She turns the van onto the street and Chesterfield's Bakery is a couple hundred yards up ahead on the right. Karen's fingers are wrapped tightly around the steering wheel, and she can feel the pressure mounting in her. Always like that aging *hag* to pull a last-minute change and throw everyone else's life into chaos. And does she care? No, she does *not* care. She does not care that other people have lives, other people have schedules, other people have pies to pick up at specific times. She's going to get an earful too, if Karen has anything to say about it.

And brother, she has *lots* to say.

"Courtney Owens is a total slut," Olinda says in the back as her thumb nails clack at the screen of her iPhone.

"Ugh, I hate her. I swear to God, if I find out he's been out with her, she's dead. Like in that movie."

"Which one?" Brandi Murkowski asks. Karen hates her voice. It squeaks. And her parents allow her to wear the most revealing clothing. Another stripper in training.

"Which one what?" Olinda responds, not looking up from her phone.

"I think he's probably just bummed about the playoffs," Amanda says, and Karen almost barks a scoff of her own. She's met that boy. If there's talk of him with another girl, you can bet he's doing the dirty with her. Not even eighteen yet and having *relations.*

The moral ambiguity is repugnant.

"He doesn't give a shit about the playoffs," Olinda says then gasps as she looks up to the rearview. Karen's eyes are already on it, stern, round, and sharp.

"Not in *my* car, young lady!" Karen snaps. Olinda apologizes as Karen nears the bakery.

"I mean which movie?" Brandi asks, as though *profanity* is nothing to get worked up over.

Olinda looks up from her phone for a second and shrugs.

"Pick one," she says. "I don't care. Ugh, *why* isn't he calling me back?"

Her thumbs are tapping away again, and Amanda is trying to assure her there's a reasonable explanation and Karen is going to have to have *another* talk with her daughter about boys and relationships and *the only thing they're after.*

A phone rings. Olinda answers.

"What the hell, Chad?" she answers.

"What's he saying?" Brandi asks. "Put it on speaker!"

"Do *not* put it on speaker!" Karen growls, her short cropped and combed over hair—spiked in the back, of course—waggles as she speaks, though the extra stiff hairspray she used this morning holds things firm.

Brandi and Amanda lean in close, listening, mouths and eyes open wide.

"Whose voice is that?" Olinda asks angrily. Brandi leans back, shaking her head and putting her hands up.

"I told you he's been talking to that girl," Brandi says.

"It could be his mom," Amanda offers, but without any conviction.

That pie better be ready, Karen thinks, gritting her teeth in a snarl.

"You are *such* an asshole!" Olinda says into the phone. "You don't get to ignore me; we're in a *re-la-tion-ship!* People in relationships call each other—"

"Young lady, I already warned you about that kind of language once," Karen growls. She could *kill* Wynona George for changing things last minute. She wants to slap these girls. Even Amanda, just for good measure.

"Oh, my God, he *hung up!*" Olinda says, paying Karen no attention. "Said he's *'dealing with some heavy shit'*, needed a break. Ugh!"

Karen slams on the breaks and the van screeches to a halt in front of the bakery as a man in a hoodie steps out, rubbing at his nose and scratching the side of his face. Karen instantly pegs him as a junkie, but she ignores him as she turns around to the girls in the back, her makeup cracking near the eyes as they bore into the teenagers.

"I said *stop* that sort of language!" she hisses. "I am *sick* and tired of young ladies your age talking like cheap whores and acting like some high-school relationship has even the *remotest* resemblance to a *real* relationship! *IT DOESN'T!* He probably *is* cheating on you, Olinda; he's a male. That's what they do. Get used to it."

All the girls are staring at her, wide-eyed and thin-lipped.

"And another thing," Karen says, waving a finger in the air, "if I hear just *one more* swear in *my* car, you're walking the rest of the way. Don't think I won't call your mother!"

Olinda slumps low in the seat and Brandi and Amanda join her.

"Yes ma'am," she says quietly before returning to her phone.

Karen jerks herself around in the seat and throws the van into park, seething. She's good and worked up and the lady in the store had better *hope* there is a manager to speak with.

She slams the door and marches with the unintentional waddle of indignation towards the door of the bakery, whose bell announces her entrance. There is an old woman behind the counter wiping her hands on a towel. Karen marches towards her, passing a black backpack on the floor next to a table.

No one else is in the bakery.

***

Perry Fuentes puts the tiny scoop to his nostril and sniffs. An instant mule-kick is delivered to his chest, and he loves it. Nerves tingle, synapses fire, and he shakes off a shiver before checking his watch. Two minutes to go. He's in an alley and can see Jefferson's Jewelers across the street. Two employees inside. A hot chick in a tight skirt and button-down shirt and a guy in a full suit with blond tips in his hair who probably smells fantastic.

Perry checks his watch again. Barely thirty seconds have passed since the last time. He opens the bag, checks the contents. At one minute till, he's supposed to flip the switch, drop the bag in the shop across from the jeweler, and get the hell out. The switch is nothing special, just a metal toggle. There are no lights—they hadn't bothered to wire them in—so there's nothing to indicate if it's on or off.

Fifteen seconds to go. Erica and Lance should be ready. Perry feels like he's ready. Is there time for one more sniff? He checks his watch and sees there isn't, but he's quick and pulls the vial out and gets a snort, then he's off to the shop.

He walks in and sees an old woman behind the counter with a kind smile.

"Hey there," she says as he stands nervously in the doorway, the pack over his shoulder. "Can I get you anything?"

Perry freezes. He doesn't know what to say. Her face reminds him of his Gam-Gam. Not like they're twins or anything, but something about her...maybe the eyes. They have that same crystalline quality Gam-Gam's had, a sparkling blue, something you felt you could swim in.

"I've got pies, danishes, scones..." the lady is saying as he lets the pack slip from his shoulder to the floor. "Fresh coffee if you're in the mood for a cup."

Perry finally manages a smile, and the woman cocks her head.

"Honey are you okay?" she asks.

It's more than the eyes. Her hair, it's *identical* to the way Gam-Gam had styled it. Exactly the way it had been when he and Lance had looked at her for the last time at her funeral.

"You…" he starts and clears his throat. "You remind me of someone."

It's sitting on his chest like an anvil. The weight is crushing. All he can see is Gam-Gam's face on the lady, projected from his mind. She had raised he and Lance. Their mom had been a junkie and was likely dead and their dad hadn't been the fatherly type, vanishing before Perry had been born. But Gam-Gam had stepped up and done the best job she could for them both.

And he'd still ended up like his parents.

"Well, maybe I've got one of those faces," she says, reaching for a towel and smiling warmly at him.

He coughs a small laugh and says, "Maybe…I'm sure that's…"

A glance at his watch almost gives him another mule-kick to the chest, but not one he likes. He glances over his shoulder, sees Erica and Lance moving out of the alley across the street.

He looks back at the woman for a second, mouth moving, but then turns for the door, telling her he'll be right back, as though he's forgotten something. As he exits, a van screeches to a halt and his body jerks, startled. Then he rubs his nose and scratches his cheek as he moves. He can hear the woman in the van shouting something. Young girls in the back. He hopes they stay in the van.

The lady gets out and marches into the bakery, her teeth bared as he glances back at her. He hears the bell over the door as she goes inside. He'd hate to be on the receiving end of her wrath, God help whoever married *her*.

He does another snort. Gets another jolt. Feels it in his eyes. It's good stuff. If things go like they're supposed to, he'll be able to afford mountains of the stuff. He's done his part, now it's all on Erica and Lance to get the Diamond Eye. He thinks of that old lady, the one that reminded him of Gam-Gam. He can't get her out of his mind. It's unnerving. What would she say if she were here?

Another twist of his vial and the scoop is in his nostril. He takes it in. Feels the kick. The tingle. The rush, blood soaring through his veins, and he's forgetting all about Gam-Gam now and little old bakers who look like her, focusing on just what he's going to do with his cut from the—

He's fifty yards down the street when he realizes he never flipped the switch.

***

Lance Fuentes plunges his tongue deep into Erica Rosen's mouth and drags it over hers. She moans. He grunts. They pull away, eyes wild. They're wearing black ski masks, but they're pulled up like toboggans on their head right now. Lance checks across the street, sees Perry going into the bakery.

"You ready, baby?" he asks as he pulls the Glock from his waistband and holds it at his side.

She smiles, licking her lips seductively, and grabs the back of his neck to pull him in for another kiss. When she pulls away, she winks.

"Do I have diamonds in my eyes?" she asks with a flutter of eyelashes as she pulls a Glock of her own.

Lance checks his watch. "In less than sixty seconds, we both will."

He grins. She grins. They kiss again, hungry, consuming mouthfuls of face and tongue. They pull away and shiver, still smiling.

They start onto the sidewalk, Glocks low by their sides. A van screeches to a stop in front of the bakery, then the bell dings and Perry is out and heading down the street. When the woman from the van goes marching inside, they pull their masks down over their faces, two storefronts down from Jefferson's.

"Stick to the plan," Lance says. "Keep them on their heels, don't give them a chance to react. In and out, just like we talked about."

Erica nods discreetly and rolls her shoulders.

"I'm gonna fuck you so hard later."

Lance smiles behind his mask as they enter the store, shouting and raising their guns. Neither notices Perry sprinting back down the sidewalk across the street towards the bakery.

***

Karen throws the door open, her teeth clenched, but still concealed for the moment. The *nerve* of some people. Annoying kids playing at relationships, PTA Queens tossing structure and planning to the wind, bakers who don't *want* to step up and do what needs doing. Karen has learned through the school of hard knocks that when a customer finds themselves in a bind, *you*, the service provider, are *also* in a bind, and you move Heaven and Hell and shift Purgatory around a little to make sure your customer leaves satisfied.

But not the woman who had answered the phone earlier—no! —*that* woman clearly didn't see Karen's crisis as her own. Well, Karen Waters had a thing or two say about that.

An old woman is looking up at her, putting on a smile when Karen's laser eyes begin boring into her. When she doesn't incinerate immediately, Karen lets loose.

"I'm here for an apple pie," she starts as she marches to the counter. "I called before, I am running late, so—"

"Missus Waters," the old lady says nodding, the kind smile shrinking. "Yes, you moved the order up. It's just out of the oven and cooling, if you can wait another fifteen minutes or so—"

Karen throws her hands in the air and her spray-cemented hair waggles. "I could have guessed, can't get anything done in this world anymore. I don't *have* fifteen minutes to wait. I've got a van full of teenaged cheerleaders, two of whom are of questionable repute, and a party to deliver them all to in less than half an hour. I told the person on the phone I needed the pie to be ready!"

The older woman nods, slinging the towel over her shoulder. "Yes, I took your call. Baking takes time, cooling takes time, I'm working as fast as I can. You did change the pickup time with almost no notice at all."

Karen's teeth make their appearance and then her jaw begins to lower. Her eyes grow. Her hip kicks out to one side and her hand perches atop it.

"I'm not interested in excuses," Karen hisses, "I want *results.* Where's the manager?"

The woman laughs. Actually, *laughs.* Liquid magma fills Karen's face.

"You're looking at her, honey," the old woman replies, attitude populating her face.

"*You?*" Karen scoffs and crosses her arms. "Well, I'm sure the owner of this establishment would be pleased to know just how poorly their management is running their business. I want the owner's name! Get them on the phone, now!"

There are snaps from Karen's fingers. The woman slaps the towel down on the counter.

"I'm manager, owner, sole-proprietor," the woman says calmly. "So, if you'd like to leave a suggestion, there's some cards and a box right by the front door. Feel free to fill one out, I'll take it under consideration."

Karen's blood boils. Her skin ripples. Scoffs come in irregular triplicates as she looks around the empty room for someone to share in her astonishment about her insulted pride but finds no face.

"I have *never* been so insulted," Karen seethes. "You can bet your bottom dollar you'll never get another one of mine! And I know people, lady! *Lots* of people! They're going to hear—"

"I don't give a baboon's blue ass *who* you know, woman," the old lady says, still cool as a cucumber. "But I do want you out of my shop. I don't want your business, and you tell any*one* you like any*thing* you like. This bakery has been around longer than you, lady. Now, take a hike."

Nuclear crimson is spreading over Karen's face when the bell dings and someone comes inside behind her, but she doesn't turn. She's frozen in indignant fury. Not even when she hears the panicked breathing, or the frantic scratching does she turn. The old woman, however, looks over Karen's shoulder and her face softens, confused.

"Darlin'," she asks, "is everything all right?"

"Um," a man's shaky voice says, and Karen glances back to see the guy who'd left just before she came in, fiddling with a backpack on the floor.

"Don't buy anything from this *rude* woman!" Karen says to the man, who is now digging inside the backpack and ignoring her.

"Fuck, fuck, fuck," the guy is saying and Karen's rage soars to new heights.

"This whole world is going to *poop!*" Karen says.

"You leave him be!" the woman behind the counter says.

Shrieking sirens erupt from across the street, bells ringing and whining and whirring.

"What th—" Karen starts.

"*Oh, fuck me!*" the man with the filthy mouth says.

Then there's a gunshot.

***

The cute girl with the form fitting blouse and skirt is screaming. The blond-tipped guy is *also* screaming, though in a higher pitch. Both are making other sounds, but if they're words, Lance can't make them out.

"*Shut up!*" he shouts then glances at his watch. It should be going off. Right now. Maybe their watches weren't sync'd up as tightly as he thought they were. But any second now and the distraction will go off and those diamond eyes on display would be in their hands and—

Wailing, nerve-shattering sirens go off, lights blinking from corners. Somewhere, a bell is ringing, like the old-style alarm clocks. Lance's body jerks and he ducks instinctively. His eyes are darting. He's panting.

"What the fuck happened?" he shouts as it occurs to him the bakery is still not in cinders, and everything is utterly going off the rails.

"That bitch hit the alarm!" Erica shouts.

"I swear to *God*, I didn't touch anything!" the guy with blond tips says. Lance thinks he's English. "Just take what you want and go!"

Lance looks back across the street, seeing the van in front of the bakery, now with three young girls looking out the window at them. To a one, their eyes are wide, and their phones are out, no doubt filming for social media distribution or '*Going Live*' at that very moment.

Fucked. The whole thing is fucked. Perry fucked up the diversion, probably running powder up his septum.

He looks back at the display case with the diamond eyes, which seems to watch him with disinterested beauty. He busts the glass with the butt of his pistol and starts grabbing them, sifting through the shattered glass.

"Oh, dear Lord, me!" Blond-tips whines as a phone starts ringing, just loud enough to cut through the chaotic din of the alarm system.

"Don't you fucking dare!" Erica is shouting as Lance looks up and sees the cute girl reaching for the phone *despite* the loaded weapon aimed at her.

"Lady, just— "Lance starts as he grips the diamond eyes in his fist. But he is cut off when Erica's gun goes off and the cute girl isn't so cute anymore. She's thrown back into a splash of her own gore, head rocking back before she slides down bonelessly to the floor behind the counter.

Blond-tips has found a new register to explore his screams with and his hands are to either side of his face while he screams.

"Stacy?! STACY?!"

Stacy doesn't say anything, and it takes Erica grabbing his arm to pull Lance from his shock.

"Your brother fucked us," she's saying as she drags him towards the door. "I'll fucking kill that worthless son of a—"

She stops and Lance stumbles up beside her on the sidewalk. The sirens are loud. The bell ringing is loud. The phone is loud. *Blond-tips* is loud. Lance follows Erica's eyes and she's staring right at the young girls in the van, all still filming, all now screaming themselves. He can hear their muffled voices through the din.

"Come on," Lance says, tugging at her as sirens of another kind come alive in the air, not far away, "we have to move!"

Erica isn't moving. She's snarling through her mask's mouth opening, and she begins to march towards the van, her Glock coming up slowly.

"Jesus Christ, Erica!" Lance shouts, rushing to stop her.

***

Van Lady with the stiff hair is shouting. The Gam-Gam twin is shouting. Perry is being told he has a filthy mouth.

He doesn't disagree, but he's focused on fumbling with the goddamned switch in the fucking bag full of explosives and the switch he forgot to activate. Van Lady is kicking him now. He flinches away, trying to stay focused on his task. Sirens are going off. There's been a gunshot. The whole plan is in the toilet and he's wondering why he's even bothering with this stupid bomb he can't manage to make explode.

"Would you talk that way in front of your mother?" Van Lady hisses at him. "What if Jesus were here, huh?"

Perry stands, holding the bag. His eyes are big and red, and his nostrils are chaffed, and his lips are chapped and now there're police sirens coming.

"What the hell is happening out there?" Gam-Gam twin is saying.

"You just get my pie, woman!" Van Lady says over her shoulder.

"Fuck it," Perry says. "I'm out!"

He thrusts the backpack into Van Lady's flustered arms, her cheeks blazing with the fire of a thousand suns.

"I've had just about enough of you," Gam-Gam twin says as Perry turns for the door, astonished to see Erica marching towards the van outside and Lance rushing up behind her.

"What the..." Perry starts but trails off as he pushes open the bakery's door, the bell chime hardly noticeable in all the racket.

"Enough of *me?*" Van Lady screams in a perfectly curved pitch. Perry glances back and sees two astonishing things happening at once.

The Gam-Gam twin is throwing a steaming pie, the oven mitts on her hands telling him it's still piping hot, and it begins to tumble through the air. As it begins to fly, the angry Van Lady then rears back and hurls the backpack he had just thrown into her arms at the Gam-Gam twin.

"You'll hear from me on Yelp!" Van Lady says.

Perry's voice is caught in his throat as he watches the two items tumble through the air, passing by each other on opposite trajectories. He wants to shout. He wants to warn Gam-Gam who isn't Gam-Gam. He wants to *run.*

He turns back. Erica is raising the gun at the van. Lance is reaching for her, like he's trying to stop her. Perry hopes he does.

What the fuck is she doing?

A wet *clap* jerks his head back around in time to hear the muffled scream of Van Lady with the piping hot pie on her face, now dripping down her blouse as she stumbles backwards, indignation replaced with several hundred degrees of pain.

"There's your pie, bitch!" Gam-Gam twin snarls just as the backpack tumbles behind the counter and smashes into an open oven.

Perry almost has time to say, *"Oh, shit."*

Almost.

The girls are ducking down in the van, no phones visible now as Erica marches like a madwoman. Lance is right behind her, his fist still clenched tight around the diamond eyes.

"Erica, *NO!*" he shouts, but she gets a shot off before his hand can pull her arm down. The side window of the van explodes, and his ears are ringing. He looks and sees through the van, see's Perry in the door to the bakery, looking back. Sees a woman stumbling, arms whipping in the air. Sees another woman behind the counter, snarling.

And he sees a backpack flying into an opened oven.

The first police car slides onto the street as a blinding white light consumes all he knows, and the diamond eyes slip from his hand as his body begins to tear and lacerate from debris while the van flips over.

The last thing he sees is its roof rushing to meet his face.

***

No one was quite sure what set off the bomb in the end. When the police arrived on scene, screeching to a halt and jumping out with guns up with no one to point them at, they had found Chesterfield's Bakery aflame. A van was on its roof, three screaming teenage girls crawling from the wreckage. Something that might have been a charred corpse—which was later confirmed by the coroner—was slumped over the side of the upturned vehicle.

A screaming Englishman with blond tipped hair, Phil Abercrombie, had to be sedated by EMTs before he could tell the story of the two masked thieves who had come in and shot Stacy, his co-worker, in the head before taking their display jewels known as the Diamond Eyes.

"Why they call 'em that?" a cop had asked the medicated Phil.

Phil looked up from the back of the ambulance, a blanket draped over his shoulders, and blinked several times.

"Well, I imagine perhaps it's because they're shaped like eyes and made of diamond."

The cop had grunted, making a note on his pad and writing *'asshole'* next to Phil's name.

After the fire had been put out and the teenage girls were able to be interviewed, they had discovered the bodies of one Karen Waters and one Christine Chesterfield, known to her family and customers alike as 'Chrissy'. Both were killed instantly in the blast, a metal pan partially molten over Karen's face.

Beneath the van were discovered two more bodies, partially burned, but their deaths had come as a result of the van flipping over atop them and smashing their bodies flat. Emergency workers had a difficult time getting their remains scooped off the pavement after the van had been cleared, their bodies squished and partially melted to the road.

"Most confounding thing I've ever seen," Phil told another cop after the first had wandered off to question the young girls. "*Batshit* might be a better description. I don't think either of them had any idea what they were doing. But that woman, *she was crazy!*"

He told them how she'd murdered Stacy and that he'd seen her open fire on the van a second before the explosion. No bullet fragments had been found in the rubble, and it was speculated that perhaps her shot had inadvertently hit the bomb—there had been a blasting rod recovered, but the bomb squad had said the whole thing had been wired wrong—but they could never be sure.

The Diamond Eyes were never discovered, even with pictures of the jewels and Phil's help in searching for them. It should be noted, however, that after the investigation was closed, Phil Abercrombie suddenly moved to an island in the Caribbean where he enjoyed lounging on the beach and sipping cocktails with a young Mexican man.

"We've contacted your parents," a cop was telling the girls even as they were uploading the footage of the events to their Facebook pages. "Is there anything we can do to make you comfortable until they get here?"

Olinda looked up from her phone, her eyes puffy from tears. "I'm hungry," she said.

The cop winked, snapped his fingers, and said, "I think I can help you out with that."

He went to his cruiser and returned with a small package, which he handed to the girl. She looked down at it and smiled before tearing it open. Delicious. Savory. Full of sugar.

"Thank you," she said to the officer between bites. "I *love* apple pie."

PIEBIRD

RUTHANN JAGGE

Piebird
by Ruthann Jagge

Flora Corolla has lost all track of time. At first, she tried counting the seconds and minutes, matching the numbers to her ragged breathing. It's too hard now. Even the slightest air intake causes her eyes to flood with tears, and she can't wipe them away. Her skin is cold and wet. Her chest is tight and heavy, collapsing further inward with every breath. She tries focusing on a blackbird visible through a tiny crack but sees only a menacing shadow of death, inching closer with every movement of the creature's dark wings. Flora only has a short time remaining to absorb life.

***

The Corolla Pie Shop is famous for its pies. Two previous generations of skilled bakers left a legacy of recipes and baking secrets to Vito Corolla, the shop's current owner.

Renowned not only for unique pie fillings, such as honeysuckle blossom and cherry tomato, but also for the flaky and tender pastry said to melt in your mouth at the first touch of a fork. Evidence of traditional skills only a few ever master to perfection shows in every pie they produce.

Vito, his wife Cora, and their only daughter Flora, age 19, rise early and walk three blocks together to their bakery in the Hamlet of Leaven. It's a picturesque setting in a valley surrounded by mountains. Travelers on their way to more notable destinations frequently include Leaven on their path, eager to sample the famous baked goods made by the Corollas.

Life is peaceful in Leaven. Most of the residents work hard and have what they need. The strict local Magistrate has the power to evict anyone living a questionable lifestyle. Serious crimes are unusual, but they result in swift and harsh punishments intended to deter others. Some claim it's a peculiar place, with quirky customs and archaic laws, but those who live here are content.

The Corolla family is proud of their heritage. Vito and Cora laugh together as they work elbow to elbow, rolling out dozens of crusts every day. The couple's movements are precise; each of them knows how to form the perfect shape and thickness, making sure the dough fits inside the dented copper tins, original to the first owners of the shop. These tins, polished every night before closing, braved the ocean along with Vito's grandparents, and the Corollas believe they are responsible for the pies' delightfully fluted and golden-brown edges.

Their pride outweighs any substantial income, and no other bakery can beat The Corolla Pie Shop at the annual competition held in Leaven every October.

***

A brass bell attached to the door of the shop jingles. The first customer of the day. The air rushing in is crisp with hints of Autumn.

"Good morning, Louis, what's your flavor today?" Vito greets his customers, grateful for another day of business. A small man enters the shop, supporting his frail body on a gnarled walking stick. He wears a patch of black leather tied with string over a missing eye. There's a small gold star on the patch, and it matches the twinkle in his other blue eye. Louis was attacked by blackbirds one day while walking in a cornfield. They are a nuisance in Leaven, flocking to the hamlet because of the many fields. Louis is simple, without a home or family, and prefers to wander the streets most days. Kind folks look after him, leaving clean clothes on their line and making sure he has food. In bad weather, Louis likes to curl up in the back of the warm Pie Shop, and the Corollas welcome him. He flashes a wide toothless grin and nods his regards to Vito. No one's ever heard him speak. There's always a pie waiting for him to enjoy as well.

"How about a bite of red pepper/chocolate, fresh out of the oven?" Cora offers a taste of her newest flavor, handing the man with sparse grey hair a napkin. "This combination came to me in a dream, not too sweet with a slight tickle." The Corolla fillings are seasonal, and when produce and flowers become scarce in the colder months, Cora boils up brandy and spices, adding in finely chopped scraps of meat and dried fruits. Freshly ginger root is the secret to her tasty mincemeat pies.

Louis pops the small piece into his mouth. His good eye sparkles when he gives Cora an exaggerated thumbs-up. She is delighted; Cora counts on Louis to advise if her combinations are delicious.

"I'm glad you approve. It's supposed to storm this week. I'll tell Flora to leave the back door unlocked, along with an extra blanket just in case. You can help yourself to plenty of pie too." Cora winks, guiding the harmless man out the door. She's fond of Louis. Everyone is. He nods his thanks, patting Cora's arm as he heads out for his daily stroll.

Flora Corolla works by herself in the small cooling room at the rear of the building. Her tasks include taking pies from the oven with a wooden paddle and carefully washing the baking utensils and tins. She's also responsible for the best-kept secret of the family's success, pulling the small ceramic piebird out from the center of each one at precisely the right time during the cooling process, preventing the crust from collapsing. The juicy pastries sit in a row on a long table right out of the oven.

"Swooooooooosh." Flora leans over, listening to the steam coming out of each small ceramic beak, like the peaceful breathing of a sleeping child. It's time to remove the bird. She carefully places the pie on a perforated tin shelf inside a tall pie safe to rest. Her method never fails. The pie birds are sticky with juice and crumbs, so Flora carefully washes and dries each one to prevent them from cracking. They are charming and unsettling at the same time, with their beaks frozen open in permanent screams.

Vito Corolla keeps a supply of the small ceramic birds with pointed peaks on hand, made to his specifications by a local potter. His grandfather, Dominick, discovered the original one accidentally when Vito's sister popped her hollow pine dove into a pastry. She insisted her favorite toy be "baked in a pie" like the nursery rhyme. The bird allowed the steam to vent the rising dough, and the result was a perfect pie free of bubbles and creases. It's now an essential tradition in the Corolla family process.

The young woman prefers spending her time alone with only her parents for company. She pretends not to notice the thick red ropes of twisted skin on the side of her face, reflecting at her from the polished metal of the pie safe. As a child playing in the shop while Vito and Cora baked happily together, Flora accidentally fell on the hot metal grate used to prop up the pies as they bake in the crumbling brick oven. Heavy scarlet lines crisscross deep into her skin. Some claim she bears the mark of a witch.

She blames her parents for her scars, but Flora keeps her despair and anger to herself. She hides her resentment beneath the surface, much like the steaming crusts hold the hot fillings captive in her pies.

Her parents believe Flora will never find love, but she has a plan.

"The Dance of the Pies" is an anticipated event. Leaven hosts an annual pie tasting competition on the third weekend of October. It's also an opportunity for young people living in this rural area to gather. There's food and music, and bakers bring their best recipe to determine who makes the most delicious pie. This competition is friendly but fierce.

Eligible young women also bring their pies to the party. The baker who wins the contest selects the best of them for "The Dance of The Pies." The chosen pies decorate a table covered with a white cloth. When the music begins, single men stroll around it, waiting for the music to stop. Then they sample the pie in front of them. If they approve, the men dance with the name of the young woman who made it, hiding beneath the tin. Many couples pair off because of the kiss encouraged at the end of the dance.

This years' celebration will take place in one week.

Flora has been practicing a recipe of her design for the upcoming party. She believes her new flavor is so mouth-watering, no one will deny her skills. The hard-working men of Leaven value good cooking, and perhaps one who enjoys eating will look beyond her appearance.

 She lingers at the shop after her parents leave at sundown, peeling and chopping the ingredients for her filling. She carefully mixes flour, salt, and water with cold lard, then rolls out her crust to an even thickness. She intends to do this every night until her pie is flawless.

Flora bakes each of her pies with her favorite piebird. It's a warbler coated with a shiny brown glaze. She likes the way it feels in her hand when she places it firmly into each of her creations, cooking them one by one. They bake rapidly in the always hot oven. A thin curl of steam lets her know it's ready. Once it's cool enough to eat, the young woman indulges in a slice or two, thoughtfully considering the texture and flavors, but she's not alone.

An oversized black cat is sitting on the windowsill. The animal recently showed up at the pie shop, perhaps a stray. Flora hasn't seen it during the day when the Corollas are busy baking and customers come in and out, but every night while she practices her recipe, it's there on the shallow ledge staring in. She feels it watching her every move. Licking away the crumbs on her hand, Flora unlocks, then pushes the small pane of glass open,

"Hello cat, would you like a taste of my pie?" The cat's deep red oval eyes narrow as it considers her question. Flora holds out her folk with a morsel of pie still hanging from it, expecting the animal to take it.

"Your pie is bad. I can make it better." A low voice rumbles in the room. Flora jumps back away from the window, unable to believe what she's hearing.

"I know how to win a husband." Raising a paw, the cat swats the fork from Flora's hand, leaving behind a thin red steak of blood. The girl wants to run and hide, but she also wants a man to notice and love her.

"Give me a bird." The cat's head tilts to one side, eyes moving around the room. Picking up one of the small ceramic pie birds, Flora cautiously holds it out in the palm of her hand. The cat licks at her blood. "No foolish girl, a real bird. I want my dinner tomorrow."

Flora is terrified as she watches the cat leap from her sight. She quickly cleans up and scrambles home, wondering if she's losing her mind. She has terrible thoughts some days. She resents her parents and her scars, and most of all, her sad life in the pie shop. Maybe the cat is a sign of good luck, an omen. Perhaps she will bake an irresistible pie, and a man will take her away from Leaven to be happy with him forever.

The next night, as Flora finishes rolling the dough for her practice pie, she hears the fluttering of wings. Glancing up, she sees a blackbird perched on the top shelf of the pie safe. It screeches, mocking her.

"Shoo, go away. You'll soil the shelves and make extra work for me." Flora snaps a linen towel at the bird. There's a tapping sound; the cat is back. She opens the window.

"What do you have to eat?" The mysterious voice fills the room.

"I haven't finished making my pie tonight. Tell me what to do, and I will bake it for you to taste." Flora's mouth is dry.

"Give me the bird. Use your knife to kill it. Mix the blood and the meat into your filling. Bake it until your fake bird screams." The voice is louder. Flora's hands shake as she wipes them on her apron.

Standing on the flour sacks piled high on the floor, Flora uses the linen towel to capture the blackbird, snatching it quickly from the shelf. The cat watches as she twists its neck leaving the body limp. Working carefully, she removes the feathers, gagging at the foul smell of the wild bird.

"I want to taste blood."

Flora's ears ring with fear at the deep voice, but she continues. Grabbing a sharp knife hanging on the wall, she punctures the carcass, draining blood into a small bowl. Flora chops the meaty flesh into pieces, then mixes the mess into the pie filling she's working so hard to perfect. It's a hearty mixture of fruit, ground vanilla beans, and apple cider, and the remains of the bird blend in well with the mince. She fills the crust and places another pastry on top, carefully sealing the edges. Flora frantically pushes her pie bird into the center, and as it bakes, she cleans up her worktable, avoiding the eyes of the cat.

"Swooooooooosh." The pie is perfect but still hot. She removes the ceramic piebird. It's ready to rest on a shelf to cool.

"Bring it." The guttural voice fills the room. Flora is shaking and struggling to breathe. Using the wooden paddle, she carries the hot pie to the window.

The cat pounces, tearing into the pie with its claws, feasting on the steaming crust. It buries its head deep into the layers of pastry. Mouth and teeth stained red with the horrible filling.

"Eat it." The voice commands Flora. Despite her disgust, she dips a finger into the ruined crust, gingerly placing the gooey mixture in her mouth. It's the most delicious pie she's ever tasted.

"Tomorrow, kill two birds." The cat jumps down, disappearing into the dark.

Flora's heart races as she hurries home. She doesn't understand what's happening. However, the revolting pie is the best she's ever tasted. Flora rubs her scars with fingers covered in fresh manure while praying to any being who will listen. She does this ritual every night, hoping to erase them. Her parents sleep in the next room, and she decides they must never know about the cat. They might think she's insane.

Flora goes through the motions during the day at The Corolla Pie Shop. Vito and Cora are working extra hard as they prepare for the competition. The pair intend to enter their most popular pie, "The Pumpkin Queen," a secret blend of pumpkin and squash grown locally in Autumn and soaked overnight in mead. The smell of the trial pies baking draws more customers. Cora shares samples, clapping her hands when visitors rave about the pie. The confident bakers expect to win again this year.

Every evening, the black cat with red eyes watches as Flora makes her pie. She works faster. She's perfected her technique but spends more time making the distinctive filling.

"Five. I want five birds tonight." The voice is louder now. As soon as her parents leave, Flora opens the back door, allowing the blackbirds entry to the bakery. She captures them as they nibble crumbs, twists their necks, then quickly chops up the bodies to mix into her filling.

"Swooooooooosh" Tonight's offering is ready. Flora scoops out a steaming portion for herself, no time for the pie to cool, and puts the rest on the windowsill in front of the demanding cat. Flora savors her pie, sticky with rich meat from the birds.

Licking its messy paws with a snake-like tongue, the cat leaps from the window. It's drizzling, and the mist hits Flora in the face as she slams the window shut. It's almost time for "The Dance of the Pies," and Flora believes her entry will be irresistible with the help of the cat. Laughing with anticipation, Flora skips home.

The rain is heavy the following day when the Corolla family makes their way to the shop. Brisk winds ring the brass bell on the door repeatedly, but there are few customers today.

"Flora, we're leaving early, your father and I are weary, and the competition is tomorrow, rain or shine." Cora holds her special pie, carefully packed inside a weathered wicker basket. "Lock the front door. Don't accept customers but leave the back door open if Louis needs shelter. There are unsold pies for him to enjoy. Be safe on your way home if it doesn't let up." Cora and Vito huddle together and under a large umbrella as Flora closes the door behind them. She turns the lock, ready to make the night's pie, but first, she needs to tidy the bakery and wash the utensils.

Washing the ceramic pie birds with soapy water, Flora lines them up to dry, noticing a small crack in her favorite brown bird. She's used it so much it's fragile from the heat of the oven. She opens the back door, and although the wind threatens to slam it shut, the downpour has slowed.

Flora ties the door open with the strings of an apron and waits. No blackbirds are circling in the grey sky. None fly in, attracted by the warmth of the bakery and the many crumbs. She will make her pie for tomorrow without them, hoping for the best. Someone is banging on the door of the shop. She hurries to open it, draping a linen towel around her neck to hide her scars.

The black cat is at the door. It scampers in, scratching at the girl's ankles.

"Where is my dinner?" The voice pierces the room. Flora covers her ears. Red eyes glare at her, and she cringes, moving fast into the back room, away from the creature.

"I can't make you a pie; there are no birds." The cat is menacing. As she steps backward, her foot hits something hard, and she drops to her knees. Louis is on the floor, curled in a fetal position, his head bleeding profusely from a gaping wound.

"Louis, what happened to you?" His one good eye is cloudy, the usual twinkle gone, and his skin is pale. Flora slaps her hand over her mouth, muffling a scream, and tries to prop him up, but she can't catch her breath. Panicking, she dabs at the flow of blood with the linen towel. His body flops like a ragdoll and lands hard on the floor again.

Flora sees razor-sharp teeth for the first time as the cat gnaws on the dying man's hand. It is resting on its haunches next to Flora, lapping greedily at the blood.

"I want him for dinner. Make me a PIE" The beast's hideous words echo in the small room. The black abomination tears at Louis's throat with claws and fangs, shredding his skin. "Make my pie, or I will eat YOU!" Mouth full of streaming gore, the cat sinks its teeth into her hand. Flora screams.

"Use your knife." Shaking her head in denial, Flora shakes as she removes the sturdiest knife from the wall. Stuffing the towel into her mouth, Flora slices a bit of skin from one of the dead man's fingers.

"I WANT HIS HEAD." Flora's tears fall uncontrollably. Her hands and lips tremble. Wincing, she plunges the knife into Louis' neck. The cat laps up every drop of blood as it falls, nipping hard at her when she hesitates. The girl is nauseous and dizzy. Only the towel between her teeth holds back the bile. Flora gags holding Louis' head in her hands. Not one spot of blood stains the floor. Sweating profusely, she drags the headless corpse to a corner, piling sacks of flour on top of it to hide her shame.

"Make my pie." The red scars on Flora's face are livid. Her heart is racing. She sees nothing but swirling colors in front of her eyes through her hysterical tears as she prepares the head for the filling. There's more than usual in the bowl. The cat is curled on her worktable, sucking and chewing on the remains as she works. She throws bones and unspeakable pieces into the oven as she places her pie to bake.

"Swooooooooosh." Flora's brown piebird signals it's ready to eat. She places the pie on the floor opposite the cat. It has a round distended belly.

"Taste it."

"I cannot, I CANNOT." Flora's stomach lurches, but the cat bares feral teeth, ready to lunge at her. She sinks a fork into the pie, choking as she gulps down the steaming bite.

It's incredibly delicious. The crust is rich and the filling moist, with a perfectly balanced flavor of sweet and salty.

"This is a husband pie." The cat hasn't touched the piping hot mess on the floor. The creature from hell prances over to the open door and vanishes.

Flora feels her mind slipping away as she spoons the remainder of the filling into another crust. She's extra careful with this pie, smoothing the crust and pinching the edges with moist fingers. Pushing her piebird into the center, the girl composes herself as it bakes.

"SQUAAAAAAK." A shrill sound fills the room from the beak of the piebird as her prizewinning pie cools. Flora plucks it out. The crack in it is wider now. *It must be why it sounds different.*

She dismisses the noise. Her pie is golden, baked to perfection, and Flora knows it will win her a man. She erases the ghastly night from her mind entirely as she locks the door behind her.

It's humid and damp at sunrise, but the rain has stopped. A large canvas tent stands in the center of Leaven. The first visitors arrive, balancing woven baskets containing pastries. By the afternoon, folks are ready for the excitement to begin. Vito and Cora are pleased to see old friends praising their children and their entries. Their pie sits in an elevated glass dome in the center of a long table, distinguishing them as the bakers to beat.

Flora puts on her best skirt then stops at the shop on her way to the tent. There's an unusual smell as she opens the door. The girl ignores it, anxiously wrapping her pie in waxed paper to keep it fresh. Sliding her brown piebird into her pocket for luck, she neglects to fasten the door behind her as she hurries off.

"It's time for the judging of the pies. Has anyone seen Louis?" Vito Corolla motions to the chairs on either side of the table, each with a paper and pencil. The kind soul is always happy to be included in the festivities. "Well, we'll have to start without him. May the best baker win." Vito is eager for another victory.

Cora and another woman serve thin slices. At her mother's request, Flora pours glasses of cold milk, avoiding eye contact. The judges eat quickly, taking small bites, and then write their favorite baker's name on the paper.

When they are ready, Vito collects the folded notes, and the bakers form a circle. Vito squares his shoulders as he announces the winner.

"JOHN MILLER bakes this year's best pie." Vito's voice cracks slightly. Cora's mouth drops open, but she claps and kisses the cheek of a woman standing close.

Flora knows her parents are trying hard not to be jealous, but she hides her feelings daily. She feels nothing for them today. It's her time to shine.

"Ladies, it's your turn." John Miller smiles broadly as young women nervously place their offerings on the table. Flora's pie stands out, embellished with a heart of red dough. John nods at her pie along with several others. Flora nervously fingers the smooth ceramic piebird in her pocket. The pastries are displayed on a white cloth as the young men tease each other, anticipating "The Dance of the Pies" Several of them wink at the blushing girls, waving their forks in the air. Flora keeps her head down.

A waltz fills the tent. The males move to the rhythm with exaggerated steps as they circle the table. Suddenly, the fiddles stop. Pointing with glee at the pie in front of them, they all dig in, stabbing with their forks, bringing up generous mouthfuls to taste as folks cheer them on.

"Damn, now, THIS is a pie." Colin Wayne, a good-looking young man with black hair, smacks his lips, enjoying Flora's pie. She feels her face grow hot. She finds him attractive. Then Colin coughs, spewing pie on the white cloth. "What the HELL?" He coughs again, pulling out a black string, struggling to chew. *Pfffffhat.* A mangled glob of black leather falls from his mouth, dripping with red filling. It lands on the white cloth. A gold star on the leather is visible. Colin Wayne clamping his hand over his mouth runs from the table. Others press forward in shock and disgust. They lift the pie to reveal a name. Flora Corolla.

"He's dead. Louis is DEAD." Robbie Alcott, a farmer late to the scene, cries out. "The door of The Corolla Pie Shop was open as I walked by, and there was a cat, a MONSTER black cat, on the floor, eating poor Louis' body with no HEAD." Several women in the gathering scream. "I swear the cat snarled at me to LEAVE." Robbie stuttered as he spoke, holding his hand over his heart.

Vito and Cora Corolla try making their way to the table, but other bakers hold them back. The Magistrate orders his men to tie Flora's hands. She's barely conscious as they drag her from the tent. Her hopes for a husband are gone; she sees only the swirling colors again. The once friendly gathering spits at the Corollas, yelling obscenities, throwing handfuls of the disgusting pie at them as they limp away.

The sobbing couple staggers to their shop, holding each other for support. It's empty. The cat and the headless corpse are gone. They cannot bear the shame of Flora's crime. No one will ever enter their shop again. Vito pours oil as Cora places waxed baking paper on the floor of their legacy. He stokes the oven to a roar, using the wooden pie paddle, then lights the floor on fire. They hold hands, leaning in for a last kiss, as flames consume The Corolla Pie Shop.

Flora is guilty. The residents of Leaven demand immediate justice for the heinous crime, the death of a beloved community member. She stands in the middle of the crowd, oblivious, her red scars raw and angry, whispering to the ceramic bird in her pocket.

"Flora Corolla. There is no doubt you are guilty of murder." The Magistrate's voice rings in her ears. "There is only one punishment for such a despicable crime, as described in the laws of Leaven. Your sentence is immurement. At sunset, you will be walled in while you breathe, never to be released from a prison of stone." Some in the crowd gasp. It's a punishment only whispered about as a dire warning.

The girl shows no emotion, saying nothing to save herself. Flora's thinking of the black cat, wondering why it came to her. Were her resentment and desire so strong, she conjured the animal? The Magistrate tells two masons to prepare, and they nod in agreement, they will avenge Louis.

They take Flora to a rock wall on the west side of Leaven. Her feet are bound, and a coarse rag is tied over her mouth, muffling any screams. In her mind, Flora is dancing the waltz with Colin Wayne. She is held in an upright position by the Magistrate's men as the skilled masons construct a tight wall on each side of her. They move to the front, ready to tie her hands, preventing her from striking at the rock. One of them notices something in her hand. It's the brown glazed piebird.

"Should I leave it, Sir?" A mason points to the small piece of ceramic.

"She deserves no comfort in this life or the next." The Magistrate pries it from Flora's fingers, examining the hollow bird. Only the girl's face is visible now. Rock and rough mortar surround her. Running his fingers over the girls' atrocious scars, he laughs.

"I suspected you are a witch. You have the mark." The brutal man shoves the piebird deep into Flora's mouth, her eyes filling with tears at the pain. "Take your last breath with the devil bird you used to torture Louis."

The masons' chip rocks, fitting them precisely in place to cover Flora's face. Only the pointed beak of the piebird remains visible, screaming out from her prison wall.

"Swooooooooosh."

NEXT BEST BAKER

JEFF STRAND

Next Best Baker
By Jeff Strand

"Congratulations, bakers, on making it to the final four!" said Edgar, clearly reading off the teleprompter. "The standards are getting higher and higher, and the judges will expect your very best performance. For today's challenge, you'll be asked to make a cake. It can be any kind of cake you want, but you must incorporate these four mystery ingredients."

Tiffany, Cyrus, Helga, and Mark, standing side by side in their white aprons, braced themselves for the big reveal.

Edgar walked over to the table. He pulled off the first cloth. "Carrots."

There was a close-up of Tiffany as she nodded.

Edgar pulled off the second cloth. "Pistachios."

A close-up of Cyrus as he nodded.

Edgar pulled off the third cloth. "Mint."

Helga frowned. Mint? With carrots and pistachios?

"And finally," said Edgar, pulling off the fourth cloth, "dog shit."

Mark's face fell. This was not going to be an easy challenge.

"You have one hour," said Edgar. "Starting...now!"

The bakers rushed into the pantry as the camera crew followed each of them.

"The carrots are no problem," said Tiffany. "I don't want to play it too safe and go with carrot cake, but there's a lot of potential there. And the pistachios are easy. I'll grind them up and use them as a topping. The mint is going to be tricky. I can't just use it as a garnish—the judges will see right through that. Maybe a hint of it in the frosting. I'll figure it out. The ingredient I'm most worried about, obviously, is the dog shit. There's no good flavor profile that includes it. But we're in the semi-finals, and I'm going to prove to the judges that I deserve to be the world's Next Best Baker."

"I think we're all concerned about the dog shit," Cyrus told the camera. "Nobody wants that in their cake.

It's certainly not something I'd ever order in a bakery. I honestly don't know what I'm going to do—this is definitely the hardest challenge so far."

Helga tossed a mango and an orange into her basket. "I'm hoping that strong fruit flavors in my cake can offset the dog shit. It would be a different story if they gave us something more delicate, like poodle shit, or something whimsical, like pug shit. But ours looks like it was dropped on the sidewalk by a St. Bernard. This could be Cujo shit."

"Could it be worse?" Mark asked. "I suppose. It might have been spoiled ingredients, or rat poison or something like that. I knew they weren't going to make it easy for us, but I was anticipating something like canned green beans. Mushrooms. Maybe veal. Whoever wins this challenge deserves the crown, because it is very, *very* difficult to bake a tasty treat that includes dog shit."

The bakers hurried out of the pantry, went to their individual stations, and frantically got to work.

* * *

"All right," said Edgar. "It's time for the judges to taste your creations. Tiffany, bring up your cake and tell us what you've made."

Tiffany carefully brought her cake up to the judges' table. "I made a carrot cake with a light mint frosting and a layer of pistachios sprinkled on the edges."

Kevin, one of the two judges, frowned. "Carrot cake, huh? Sounds like you played it safe. It's fine to keep it simple, but if that's the case, you'd better deliver perfection."

Kevin and Meredith each took a bite.

"It's actually quite good," said Meredith. "I didn't think the frosting would work, but it's just a hint of mint flavor and rather refreshing. The cake itself is perfectly baked. I do wish that the dog shit was a bit more subdued— it doesn't really blend with the other flavors. But overall, an excellent cake."

"Yes, I agree," said Kevin. "The cake is moist and delicious. Well done."

Tiffany, beaming, returned to her station.

Edgar called up Cyrus, who brought his cake to the judges' table. "I made you a triple dark chocolate cake topped with raspberries."

Kevin took a bite. "Oh, wow, that is *rich*."

Meredith nodded. "I could never eat a full piece of this."

"Right," said Cyrus. "I wanted to make something decadent."

"Decadent is fine," said Kevin. "The problem here is that you've overwhelmed all of the other ingredients. All I can taste is chocolate, and that wasn't even one of the four challenge ingredients. Where are the carrots?"

"I blended them up into the batter."

"And the mint?"

"Blended."

"Pistachios?"

"Blended."

"Dog shit?"

"Blended."

"The cake is good. I'm just not convinced that it meets the requirements of the challenge. You were supposed to find a way to incorporate all four of the ingredients into the cake so that we could tell they were in there. There's not even the faintest trace of mint flavor here. Is this a perfectly fine cake? Yes. Is it going to get you through to the finals? I'm really not sure."

Suitably chastised, Cyrus returned to his station.

"Helga, bring up your cake," said Edgar.

Helga placed her cake in front of the judges. "I've made you a fruit cake. Not a fruitcake, but a cake with lots of fruit." Everybody laughed. "You'll find orange, mango, grapefruit, peach, cherry, and blackberry flavors in here."

"Ambitious," said Meredith. "But it almost sounds like it could be too much."

Kevin and Meredith each took a bite.

"That's absolutely delicious," said Kevin. "You've really come a long way in this competition. The fruit flavors work perfectly together, and yet I still taste the carrots, pistachios, and mint."

"I agree, absolutely delicious," said Meredith. "One of the best desserts we've had all season. And I like how it has only the mildest flavor of dog shit, almost like an aftertaste. Very good work, Helga. I don't think you have anything to be worried about."

"And, finally, Mark. Bring your cake up."

Mark placed his cake in front of the judges. "I made you a dog shit cake."

"Excuse me?" asked Kevin.

"The entire cake is dog shit. We're in the semi-finals, and I wanted to take a risk. Go big or go home."

"A bold choice," said Meredith. "But I'm not sure it was the correct one."

"I'm confused by what's going on here," said Kevin, gesturing to the top of the cake. "Why are there carrot sticks arranged in a square?"

"That's supposed to be the fence," Mark explained. "The pistachio is supposed to be the dog, and the sprig of mint is supposed to be a tree in his yard."

"I see," said Meredith.

"I have to admit that on first glance I'm kind of underwhelmed," said Kevin. "It seems kind of sloppy and childish. Like you said, we're in the semi-finals. We admire risk-taking, but the risk has to be part of a well-thought-out creative decision. I don't believe this was. Maybe time got away from you, but I don't understand why you would think that decorating your cake with a carrot sticks dog fence was the right thing to do. The pistachio doesn't look anything like a dog."

"I drew eyes and a mouth on it," said Mark.

Kevin picked up the pistachio. "You did, yes. But that doesn't make it look any more like a dog. It could just as easily have been a happy pistachio. From an appearance standpoint, this is probably your worst effort all season."

"So, it's going to be all about the flavor," said Meredith. "If you want to make it to the finals, this cake will have to be absolutely stunning."

Kevin and Meredith each took a bite. Kevin grimaced.

"I'm sorry, but this doesn't work for me at all. Did you even add flour or sugar?"

Mark shook his head. "It's just dog shit, with a little butter."

"It's awful. I truly don't think you understood the challenge. Dog shit has an unappealing flavor, aroma, and texture. Your goal was to figure out a way to somehow incorporate that into a delicious cake. Going all-in on the dog shit was disastrous."

"I could not agree more," said Meredith. "It's a very bad cake. It tastes like something you'd serve to a lover right before confronting them with the fact that you know they cheated on you. Did you even try this cake before you presented it to us?"

"No," Mark admitted.

"Try it now."

Mark reluctantly took the fork that Meredith offered him and scooped out a bite of cake. He put it in his mouth, swallowed, and nodded. "It's not very good."

"You didn't even want to chew it, did you?"

"No."

"You've shown a lot of promise this season, but I really think you lost your way on this challenge. You can head back to your station."

"All right," said Edgar, "the judges will confer, and then we'll find out who's going to the final round of Next Best Baker!"

"There's no need for the usual drama and suspense," said Kevin. "One of the four cakes was clearly not at the level of the others, and I'd like that baker to do the right thing and step forward now."

After a moment, Mark stepped forward.

"Mark, we've been very impressed by your baking journey," said Meredith. "The dog shit cake was a poor choice, but you have a bright future ahead of you, and I want you to promise me that you'll never stop baking."

"Baking is my life," said Mark. "I'll never quit."

Mark gave the judges a hug, then left.

"In retrospect, I should've known that the dog shit cake wasn't going to be well-received," Mark told the camera. "I'm disappointed to have gotten so close to the end only to come up short, but I wouldn't trade this experience for anything, and I wish Tiffany, Cyrus, and Helga the best of luck."

* * *

"Welcome to the final challenge," said Edgar. "One of you will become the Next Best Baker. Will it be Tiffany? Will it be Cyrus? Will it be Helga? Or will it be somebody else entirely?"

The contestants glanced at each other, confused.

"Welcome *back* into the competition...Vincent!"

Tiffany, Cyrus, and Helga gaped as Vincent, who'd been the third person eliminated, walked onto the stage.

"Yes, Vincent is the winner of Next Best Baker: Second Chance, our web series where the eliminated contestants compete for their chance to get back into the kitchen! Vincent proved to the judges that he deserved a spot in the finals."

Vincent, who looked like he hadn't slept in a week, nodded. "The things I did to get back in... oh, God, the things I did...every time I close my eyes the images flash before me...it terrifies me to even blink..."

"Anyway, welcome back, Vincent. The four of you will be competing in your most difficult challenge yet. The winner will receive the title of Next Best Baker. Will it be Tiffany? Will it be Cyrus? Will it be Helga? Will it be Vincent? Or will it be...just kidding, it's going to be one of you four. Are you ready for your final challenge?"

Tiffany, Cyrus, and Helga said that yes, they were ready. Vincent stood there and twitched.

"For your final bake, you can make...anything you want. Cupcakes. Cookies. Bread. You're limited only by your imagination. Sounds pretty easy, doesn't it? Well, of course there's a twist. You have to bake it inside of a human head."

"For real?" asked Tiffany.

"For real. And you may think that I simply mean you'll need to bake it inside of a skull. Nothing so easy for your final challenge! I'm talking about a freshly severed head. But fear not, you'll have a bone saw and all of the tools necessary to complete the task!"

Crew members brought out bowling ball-shaped objects covered with cloth and placed them at each station.

"This is going to be awful," Tiffany told the camera. "Everything I know about baking will go right out the window. I can pour batter into its dead mouth, but how does that impact the cooking time? What if the smell of flesh permeates the flavor of my cinnamon roll? This has disaster written all over it."

"As a vegan, I find the whole idea very off-putting," said Cyrus. "I'm sure the owners of the heads signed all of the proper consent forms before they died, but no living creatures deserve to be the vessel for baked goods. It's morally repugnant. I'm not trying to be controversial here, but I don't believe that severed heads should be part of the process. I would actively boycott a restaurant that prepared their baked goods this way."

"Not gonna lie—I'm looking forward to the challenge," said Helga. "Unlike dog shit, human flesh has the potential to add pleasant layers of flavor. I've never tried it myself, but one of the most rewarding things about this competition is how it's allowed me to work with ingredients that I could never afford. Obviously, I'm going to bake something savory instead of sweet. I'm sure the other contestants are feeling revulsion right now, but I'm excited!"

"It physically hurts when I close my eyes," Vincent told the camera. "Closing my eyelids feels like there are red-hot needles underneath them, even though I know the needles are just hallucinations. I shoo away cat-faced insects. My blood is alive."

"Guess what, bakers?" asked Edgar. "From the very first episode, we warned you that this will be the most challenging season of Next Best Baker yet. And now we're about to prove it. Because the severed heads do not belong to anonymous strangers!"

With dramatic flourish, Edgar tugged the cloth off the first head. "Tiffany, say hello to your brother, Jacob!"

Tiffany fell to her knees in horror. "No! Jacob! He had so much to live for! He was going to be a realtor!"

Edgar walked over to Cyrus' station. "Cyrus, you've talked about how much you missed her while being sequestered during this show, and now you're reunited with—" he pulled away the cloth, "—your wife Diane!"

"*Noooooo*!" Cyrus wailed. "Tell me it's not true!"

"Oh, it's true," said Edgar. "That's why you should carefully read contracts before you sign them, even if they're really long. How are you feeling right now, Cyrus?"

"Devastated!" Cyrus began to sob. "She meant everything to me."

"Well then, you'll want to make sure her death was not in vain." He walked over to Helga's station. "So, Helga, whose face do you most *not* want to see when I pull away this cover?"

"One of my six children."

"They say that a parent can't choose their favorite child. But can you choose your least favorite? It is indeed one of your children's severed head under this cloth, but which one? Who do you hope it is?"

Helga wiped away a tear and thought about it for a moment. "Stephan."

"Let's see if your wish was granted!" Edgar pulled the cloth away. "Nope! It's Anton! That's certainly going to make things awkward with Stephan when you see him again."

Helga hurried over to the table and caressed her dead son's hair. "My dear, sweet, precious angel. I'm so sorry. So very sorry. Mommy loves you."

Edgar walked over to Vincent's station. "One left. Vincent, you've lost so much already. Whose head would finally destroy the final tenuous connection you have with reality?"

"Keanu Reeves," said Vincent. "He's a great actor and, I hear, a genuinely kind and caring person."

"Lucky for you, it's not Keanu. It's your mentor and father figure, the man who cared for you after your parents died when you were seven, the man who put you through college and was always there for you when things were at their darkest, the man who beat cancer three times only to die at the hands of a crew member with a hacksaw."

"Dylan," said Vincent, in a sad whisper.

Edgar pulled the cloth away. "That's right."

"What...what happened to his face? Where's his nose?"

"Dylan struggled more than the others. I apologize for his appearance, but that's part of the competition. So, you four finalists have one hour to bake a tasty treat in the severed heads of your loved ones. Your time begins...now!"

The contestants rushed into the pantry to gather their ingredients.

"Jacob's favorite dessert was always pineapple upside-down cake," Tiffany told the camera. "Every single night he asked our mom to make it, but we only had it, like, every couple of years. I'm going to make pineapple upside-down cake to honor his memory."

"Since we have to bake inside of the heads, I guess I do have one advantage over the others," said Cyrus. "Diane had a big mouth." He frowned. "Why did I say that? Why did I make that joke? That was cruel. Yes, she talked a lot, but that didn't mean I loved her any less. It's just that I'm going to miss her so very much that my mind isn't working properly." He took a few deep breaths. "Focus, Cyrus, focus. You can do this."

"Anton wasn't my favorite child, but he was up there," said Helga. "He wanted to be a police officer, and police officers love doughnuts—at least that's what the comedy shows say—so I'm going to make doughnuts in his head."

"Tiny sharks in my belly eat all of my food before I can digest it," said Vincent. "That's why I'm always hungry. Always so very, very hungry."

The bakers returned to their stations and hurriedly began working on their final challenge.

"Fifteen minutes down," Edgar announced. "Forty-five minutes left."

"This is taking forever," Tiffany told the camera as she scraped away at her brother's severed head. "I needed more room in his mouth than was available, so I've been cutting stuff out, but I'm losing a lot of time. In the movies when they cut out somebody's tongue it just comes right off, lickety-split, but I had to hack away for almost five minutes to get Jacob's tongue out. I see that a couple of the other bakers opened up the skulls with the bone saws. That's probably what I should've done. I just wasn't sure how difficult it is to pull somebody's brain out. They're attached, right? You can't just tip over the skull and have it slide right out. I'm rethinking my strategy but it's too late now."

"I never thought I'd be nostalgic for the dog shit," said Cyrus. "This is genuinely awful. She's wearing the earrings that I got for her on our very first wedding anniversary, back when we were so poor that we couldn't afford to heat our apartment even in the middle of winter. We'd snuggle under the covers and keep each other warm. She was so proud of me for making it onto this show. I'm going to win it for her. If I'm not the Next Best Baker, I'm going to kill myself, right here on camera. It'll have to be in a way where the medical team won't have time to save me. If I slash my throat with a bread-cutting knife, that should do the trick. I hope I win."

"Anton's head won't fit in the deep fryer," said Helga. "I don't know what to do. I should have thought about that sooner. It's going to kill me to saw my beloved son's head in half, but what choice do I have?"

"I'm sorry," Vincent told the camera. "I thought I'd been talking for the past couple of minutes, but I guess it was just in my mind."

"You're halfway done," Edgar announced. "And now, everybody stop!"

The confused contestants stopped what they were doing.

"Yes, there's one more twist. Come on out, Gunther."

A hulking man in a bloody jumpsuit, wearing a mask of human flesh, walked out into the studio.

"This is Gunther. If you've been following the news, you know him as the Southwest Side Splatterer. The authorities were never able to apprehend him, but we were, and he'll be playing a key role in your final challenge. The Southwest Side Splatterer will be watching you as you bake, and if he doesn't like what he sees, he's been authorized to do what he does best, which is to mangle a human body beyond recognition."

"The twists never stop coming, do they?" asked Tiffany with a frustrated sigh.

"What might set him off? Nobody knows. That's part of the fun. And your time resumes...now!"

The bakers hurriedly got back to work.

"Though his mask is made of human flesh, I noticed that the stitching is very even," Cyrus told the camera. "My guess is that he likes dessert decorations to be very precise. I'll be sure to hold my hand extremely steady when I'm putting on the final touches."

"With a name like the Southwest Side Splatter...er— oh, that's hard to say, isn't it? —he probably likes chaos in his baked goods," said Helga. "So, I'll be sure to decorate the doughnuts in a haphazard fashion."

"I'm not even going to worry about the Southwest Side Splattererer," said Tiffany. "Did I say that right? Splatter-er. I think the other contestants will be distracted by him, so I'm just going to push him right out of my mind. I'm already worried that I'm going to run out of time, and... oh, fuck, why is he walking over—?"

Tiffany let out a shriek as Gunther plunged his machete deep into her belly. The other players watched in horror as he withdrew the weapon and then repeatedly hacked away at her, sending blood and scraps of flesh flying everywhere.

"Stay focused," said Edgar. "The clock hasn't stopped."

Ten minutes later, Gunther stepped away from the no longer recognizable body of Tiffany. Some crew members began to clean up the mess.

"I'm so embarrassed by how this is going," Cyrus told the camera. "I know I'm in mourning, but this is the final round of Next Best Baker, and I think I may have blown it. I'm really kicking myself."

"This is turning out better than I thought," said Helga. "I'm not suggesting that I'll start deep frying all of my doughnuts in the heads of my children, but I'm honestly pretty happy with this so far, and I hope the judges agree."

"All I see are spiders," said Vincent. "The blender is spiders. My hand is spiders. All are spiders."

"And... time's up, everybody!" Edgar announced.

Kevin and Meredith walked out into the studio and took their place at the judges' table.

"First things first," said Edgar. "We no longer need Gunther, so to make sure there isn't any further carnage, we'll put him down like a rabid dog."

A stagehand blew Gunther's head apart with a shotgun. Two interns dragged his corpse away, while a third intern followed them with a mop.

"Cyrus, bring your final bake up to the judges' table."

Cyrus placed it in front of Kevin and Meredith. Both of the judges frowned.

"What happened?" asked Kevin. "It's a complete mess."

"I tried to make a New York-style cheesecake. I didn't think about the batter going down Diane's throat and coming out of the hole in the bottom of her neck. It got all over everything. I'm sorry. I've never cooked in a human head before."

"We don't want to hear excuses," said Meredith. "This is the final round. If you can't use unfamiliar cooking techniques, how are you supposed to be the Next Best Baker?"

"Is there even anything for us to judge?" asked Kevin.

"I scraped some of it out of her mouth," said Cyrus. "It's the yellowish-brown stuff on the side."

Kevin scooped some up with his fork and popped it into his mouth. Meredith did the same.

"It's terrible," Kevin said. "Not completely inedible, but close."

"Quite frankly, it's insulting that this was presented to us," Meredith told him. "This is something that would get you eliminated from the auditions, and here you are serving it in the final round."

Cyrus nodded. "I'm ashamed of it. I have no excuse. I'm sorry."

"Your only hope is for somebody else to have done worse," said Meredith.

"Not to unduly influence your decision, but I did say that I will be slashing my throat with a bread knife if I lose."

"Noted," said Kevin. "You may return to your station."

Cyrus left; head hung.

"Your turn, Helga," said Edgar.

Helga brought a plate of doughnuts up to the judges' table.

"Those look delightful," said Kevin. "I like the anarchic tone to the decorations. It's fun."

"Yes, from their appearance, I'd proudly display these in one of my seventeen doughnut shops," said Meredith. "But of course, what's most important is the flavor."

Kevin and Meredith each took a bite.

"Mmmm," said Kevin. "That's really good. A bit overdone, but only barely. I get hints of your son's deep-fried flesh, but it's not overpowering. If I hadn't watched you pour the batter into his severed head, I might not have even known that's how it was prepared."

"Yes, I completely agree," said Meredith. "When I pop a doughnut into my mouth, I don't want it to taste like I'm chewing on somebody's head. That's disgusting. Like Kevin said, they're a bit overdone—I'd have taken them out maybe thirty seconds sooner. But, overall, a great effort. Congratulations."

"Vincent?" said Edgar. Vincent walked up to the judges' table, empty-handed.

Kevin cleared his throat. "I noticed that you spent the entire challenge gazing into Dylan's dead eyes."

Vincent nodded. "I was trying to see into his soul."

"I can respect that. But the rules are clear that if you don't actually bake anything for us, you've forfeited that round. You've given us nothing to judge except your mental state, and so I'm afraid to say that you will not be the Next Best Baker."

"That's okay, as long as I'm the Next Best Baker."

"You're not."

"I understand. Am I the Next Best Baker?"

"Moving on," said Edgar. "Tiffany, please bring your—obviously I'm kidding, but I can see that my joke is not being well received, so I'll abandon it halfway through. Who will be the Next Best Baker? Will it be Helga, whose doughnuts were slightly overcooked? Or will it be Cyrus, whose New York-style cheesecake oozed out all over his wife's severed head in a completely unappetizing manner? Time for the judges to deliberate."

Kevin and Meredith left the studio. Eighteen minutes later, they returned.

"There was a lot to discuss," said Meredith. "Before we announce the winner, I'd like to ask somebody on the crew to remove the bread knife from Cyrus' station. Thank you. The winner of this season of the Next Best Baker is..."

"Me?" asked Vincent.

"...Helga!"

Helga squealed in joy.

"Cyrus, though you came up short, you've greatly impressed us this season," said Kevin. "I know we can't stop you from committing suicide after you leave the kitchen, but I hope you won't."

"I probably won't," said Cyrus. "This experience has meant the world to me, and I wouldn't trade it for anything."

"Then congratulations to our Next Best Baker, Helga!" said Edgar.

"We did it, Anton! We did it," said Helga, hugging her son's deep-fried head to her bosom.

A MUFFIN IN THE OVEN

ARON BEAUREGARD

A Muffin in the Oven

By Aron Beauregard

Celine Spencer looked to her left at the spongy brunette treat sitting in the open but deactivated oven. Her gawdy grin screamed off her face as she took her eyes off the mini-cake and looked back at her close friends Joy Gaines and Lana Hart for a reaction.

"Maybe, I'm just a little slow this morning... but what are you saying?" Joy asked amused by Celine's charade-like gestures.

"Lana?" Celine asked, hoping she might understand.

"You're baking for us tonight?" Lana said.

"C'mon, it's obvious! Just think about it." Celine giggled, pointing back to the bready indulgence.

Joy and Lana looked at each other harboring an equal measure of confusion.

"It doesn't even make sense. You put a store-bought, already cooked muffin in the oven..." suddenly, she paused. As the words came out of her mouth, she realized that she'd cracked Celine's riddle.

"Oh my God! You're pregnant?!"

"Yes!"

Both Joy and Lana shot to their feet and wrapped their arms around Celine for a group hug. Their embrace was genuine and emotional.

"I'm *so* happy!" Joy squealed excitedly.

"This is incredible!" Lana added.

After the celebration squeeze concluded, the trio detached, and each plopped back down in front of their respective glass of red wine.

"I told you! I told you it would work out. Didn't I?" Joy continued.

"You did, yes you did!"

"I'm not going to lie, after that asshole Anthony cheated on you, both Lana and I were a little worried. You moved out here, in the middle of nowhere. We all know you're a city girl through-and-through. We thought you were having a mid-life crisis or something."

"You were so quiet and distant; we hardly even saw you. But now I see why, you were smitten by someone else! This is fucking amazing! But now you must tell us who, I'm dying to know! You didn't get back together with Bryan, did you?!" Lana prodded.

"That's a tough question to answer," she replied lifting the wine glass up to her lips and taking a generous gulp.

"Wait a minute... if you're pregnant, why are you drinking?" Lana interjected.

Joy hadn't even thought about the potentially harmful action until Lana mentioned it, but that kind of oversight was highly out of character for Celine. Both had grown increasingly more concerned about their friend's reclusiveness and anti-social behavior. Her heartbreak undoubtedly fostered her new hermit lifestyle; it had changed her. It had shattered her confidence. But drinking with child was a new level of egotistical recklessness that neither woman would have expected to see from Celine.

"Oh, it doesn't matter for me," Celine explained somberly.

"What do you mean?" Joy asked.

Celine's expression seemed to suddenly shift. A hard U-turn from giving gleeful news to the heavy daunting reality of her situation began to shine through.

"I don't... I'm not sure I can go through with it," she confessed, eyes glossing over.

Both Joy and Lana looked flabbergasted by the notion. Having a family had always been a goal for Celine. It was shocking to see the change in her trajectory.

"Listen, we support you in whatever decision you make, but this is something you've been talking about since... since high school. It's just not very like you to talk this way... is there something you want to tell us?"

Celine remained mum and swallowed another gulp from her glass as the salty reflective coat began to drizzle off her eyelids.

"Girl, we're here for you. No matter who it was with, even if it was a one-night stand, we'll help you through it. I know it's scary, but we can help you," Lana reaffirmed.

"You have no idea what scary is," Celine replied.

Her statement struck fear in each of them independently but for the same reason. There was something that she wasn't telling them, but she was keeping her secret close to the vest.

"I'm sorry, I'm sorry for bringing the two of you into this, but I'm just so frightened. I feel so alone. That's why I called you here for the weekend. I'm not sure what's gonna happen."

The heavy tone of the conversation was making Joy's heart pump furiously. "Celine... what are you saying? Did someone force this baby on you?" Joy dared to ask.

Celine slowly nodded her head up and down in response.

"Jesus, who? Who hurt you, Celine?" Lana demanded, anger now beginning to surge inside her ribcage.

Her hesitation was obvious, her emotional state was a rocky path of violent turbulence. She began to tremble and shake her head side to side.

"Who was it?!" Lana shouted, no longer able to control her boiling rage.

"They did," she whispered, pointing directly above her head.

Celine replenished her dwindling glass back to the top with a shaky hand. Then she chugged down the rosy fluid like water. In seconds the entire refill had disappeared.

"Whoa, slow down, *please*. You don't drink like this, you're gonna get wasted, and that's not going to help you," Lana said.

"Maybe... maybe it'll just help me forget," Celine reasoned.

Joy and Lana looked at each other both distressed and muddled. Neither had a clue what she was talking about. Neither had the guts to speculate any further. They needed to hear the explanation directly from Celine.

"Who are 'they,' Celine?" Lana persisted.

Celine's top row of teeth bit down hard on her lower lip. She looked at her friends another moment before finally mustering the courage.

"The people in the sky."

Joy and Lana's eyes widened. Has she gone mad? Was losing Anthony the straw that broke the camel's back? It was difficult to say, but they both truly started to fear for her mental well-being.

"Please, just tell me, he's a pilot. He's a pilot, and he travels a lot, so he probably won't be a good dad. That's what you're saying, right?" Joy rambled nervously.

Celine shook her head from side to side like a petrified child giving an answer to an abusive parent.

Lana couldn't believe the question she was about to ask but knew somebody had to ask it. "Are you talking about... about aliens?"

Drool began to slide out of Celine's sharp lips, and she sniffed the snot up as best she could. She tried to bottle her hysteria, but it wasn't possible. She broke down and laid her head in both of her hands.

Neither Joy nor Lana knew what to do next, but it was clear that Celine needed professional help. What they could offer wouldn't be sufficient for what she was going through. In that instant, they both knew they needed to calm her down.

Joy rose from her seat and walked over to Celine. She squatted down so she could wrap her arms around her.

"Shhhh, it's going to be okay, I promise," she whispered as soothingly as she could.

"No, it's not, no, it's not," Celine whined, slurring her words in drunken defeat.

Lana joined, making her way to the other side of her disturbed friend and placing her well-manicured nails on Celine's free shoulder.

"It will, that's why we're here for you. I think tonight you just need to get some rest. You've had a lot to drink. We're here for another two days, so first thing in the morning, we can figure out how to make this all better. Does that sound like an okay plan to you?" Lana asked gingerly.

"Well, I do feel really tired," Celine agreed through her sniffles.

"Okay, let's get you into bed. Don't worry, Celine, we're going to figure this out," Joy promised, helping her friend to her feet.

***

Lana gazed upon the Camel Crush with an eager eye. She'd been wanting to light one up ever since the strange talk started. She stuck it between her puckered lips and put flame to the tip. The ember end flared, and a deep drag entered her lungs, as she swatted a moth away before looking out into the rural field of shadowy nothingness.

"You still smoke those things?" Joy asked looking up from her cell phone. She nervously rocked on the porch chair she'd set herself down in while awaiting a response.

"Please, I'm in no mood for a lecture right now. We have bigger issues at hand than my vices," Lana said, pulling in another deep drag.

"True. I'm just glad she's finally asleep. That was... something else."

"It felt like putting a child to bed. What the hell happened to her? I hate to say it, but I really think she very well might've lost it. Maybe the wedding getting scrapped and being forced to leave Anthony just pushed her over the edge?"

"I don't know, but we need to find a way to reel her back in. Out of the three of us, I always thought for sure she was the strongest. I guess I was wrong."

"I guess so, life's a real mother fucker though. Just chews you up and spits you out," Lana said exhaling a massive cloud of gray.

"But Celine? I mean, seriously, did you ever imagine that she would suddenly move into the sticks like this? That girl was the life of the party, she practically lived at the bar. She was always the one dragging *us* out. Then, boom! Nothing. How does someone just detach from everything they know? How does someone just vanish like that?"

"Trauma contorts the soul into funny shapes. It's not supposed to make sense."

"I guess not."

"Hey, do me a favor. You have your phone out, look up what we were talking about earlier."

Joy wrinkled her brow, "Are you serious?"

"Why not? Maybe it's like some kind of known mental issue or something. Everyone's heard of abductions, but this is crazy. The internet has at least a little information on everything. Even if it's bullshit, I still wanna know."

Joy huffed and tapped the face of her phone a few dozen times, keying in words with sincere interest.

"Whoa," Joy said.

"What?" Lana begged.

"So, apparently Celine is not alone. Apparently, it's a thing."

"What does it say?"

"It says that thousands of women claim to have been impregnated by various alien species. The children are called hybrids. This one lady in Utah claims that they take her up every other weekend of the month so she can visit her son regularly still."

"Wow."

"Yeah, and get this, there's a group out in California called 'Sisters of the Sky.' Apparently, there's a community of thirty or so women who've banded together. They seem pretty open about it."

"So, it's a cult?"

"It definitely gives off that vibe."

"That's so fucked up. People just can't help themselves, they take advantage and manipulate, all for what?"

"I have no idea, but that still doesn't answer the primary question we're going to have to figure out tomorrow..."

"What's that?" Lana asked nearing the end of her smoke.

"How did that idea get into Celine's head?"

"I CAN'T! I CAN'T!" a voice from inside the house blared.

Both Joy and Lana jumped as the unexpected fright nipped them out of nowhere.

"Celine?!" Lana yelled flicking her filter into the dirt driveway.

Lana pushed through the front door back inside the house and Joy followed behind her. Upon entry, they saw Celine in her nightgown standing in front of the island in her kitchen. The dim lighting left an eerie feeling in the air, primarily because it was reflecting off the wide knife blade. Her arms shook as she clenched the handle tightly against the top of the island, leaving the point of the blade staring up at her.

"I DON'T THINK I CAN GO THROUGH WITH IT!" she screamed staring down at the unforgiving instrument.

"Oh my God, oh my fucking God," Joy whispered as the adrenaline blasted through her system.

"WHOA! CELINE! Relax, we're-we're gonna figure this out, just give me the knife, it'll all be okay," Lana said trying to comfort her, while descending in pitch.

"ALRIGHT?! IT'S GONNA BE ALRIGHT?! YOU WOULDN'T SAY THAT IF YOU HAD THIS FUCKING THING INSIDE YOU!" Celine screamed, insanity insulating her every word.

"We'll get it out, just believe me, we'll get it out," Lana pleaded, carefully stepping closer toward her.

For a split-second it seemed like Celine almost considered it. Then she shook her dribbly eyes side to side, brushing off the possibility.

"Perhaps... but even if you do, they'll just come back. They've been with me since I can remember. They'll come back and do it again! And again! I'm tired, I'm just so fucking tired... There's only one way out for me," Celine uttered oozing a sadness that said goodbye.

With the speed and ferocity of a headbanger in the grips of a death metal show, Celine whipped her head into the marble top of the island. Her throat aligned perfectly with the tip of the steel, the refined point pushed through her soft tissue, disappearing nearly up to the handle.

As Celine's thyroid parted profoundly, the harsh cutting edge crushed through her esophagus. An outburst of blood drenched her hands and the cold stone below her throat. She began to choke, making sickening and uncomfortable noises that entrenched the horror of the situation into both Joy and Lana's eardrums.

As their disturbed screams were unleashed, Celine gagged and raised away from the table continuing to choke and snort in a piggish fashion. The knife remained lodged inside her throat, leaving blood projecting like a powerful hot spring forward and drenching the kitchen. The hot spouting reached far enough to coat Lana's face and worm it's way into her eyes.

As Celine collapsed backwards, Joy and Lana continued screaming. They looked at each other for guidance while still trapped in the paralyzing palm that belonged to the hand of panic.

"What the fuck! Celine!" Lana bellowed, trying to wipe the blood out of her eye sockets.

"What do we do?! What do we do?!" Joy cried.

"I don't fucking know! Get a towel! No call-call 911! Call 911 now!"

Joy lifted up her phone and unlocked the screen. Just as it illuminated, suddenly, it went completely dead, along with all the other lights in the house.

Joy let out a shriek and asked, "What's happening?!"

"Did you call them?!" Lana said, gathering up a couple of dish cloths hanging from the stove handle.

"My-My phone is dead!"

"What do you mean dead!"

"I don't know, it just stopped working!"

Lana placed some of the cloths over Celine's shaking body. She covered her throat wounds as best she could and looked over to Joy.

"Hold these on here, try and stop the bleeding while I get my phone," Lana instructed.

Joy was crying uncontrollably. She wanted to help but was incredibly afraid.

"Listen to me, listen to me, Joy! Snap out of it, I know you're panicking, but if you don't put pressure on her neck, she's going to fucking die! Get down here, now!"

Lana's stern approach seemed to work. Joy found her will and crouched down beside her and held the cloth in place as best she could.

"I'm no fucking doctor, but I think if we take that knife out, she's gonna bleed to death for sure. But don't press down too hard, she's already having trouble breathing."

"Just go! Go get your phone, Lana!"

"Okay!"

Lana took off in a footrace to the living room. She found it beside her purse on the table where she'd left it to get away from the world for a bit. She'd gotten farther away than she ever hoped.

When she lifted up the device, she tapped the screen and pressed all the buttons. Nothing.

"What the hell is going on?" she mumbled, dread drilling through her insides.

She tried restarting the cell as she ran back into the kitchen to meet with Joy again. Still nothing.

"There something wrong with mine too!" Lana cried.

"Are you kidding me?! What-What are we gonna do?!" Joy moaned.

"We've gotta get her to the hospital, otherwise she's dead."

Without warning, all the windows in the kitchen and surrounding the house were bombarded by a white blinding light. The beams infesting every transparent barrier were so pure and powerful that it forced Joy and Lana to look away after the initial glance.

A hum that started out faint grew louder until it began to rattle their eardrums. Their fearful cries couldn't compete with the shrill noise as it left them both stunned, pressing their palms over their earholes.

After the initial shock, suddenly the audible anguish dissipated, and the blinding lights faded. It was hard to estimate how long they'd been frozen for, but it was long enough that when the darkness and silence resumed, all they could hear were the final gurgles escaping the gaping wound in Celine's gashed throat.

"This can't be real, this can't be real," Joy sniffled, rocking back in forth on the bloody tile floor like a child seeking comfort.

Lana was just as mentally blown away by the incident, but not so much that she hadn't noticed that Celine had just expired before them. Lana extended her hand and brushed it across the side of Celine's face.

"She's gone! She's gone!" Joy cried, drool dribbling down her chin.

Lana's turmoil remained bottled; she was also crying but tried to stay strong. She knew Joy didn't have it in her, and if they were going to get through the evening it was up to her. Putting her fear aside as best she could, she comprehended the urgency of the situation.

Lana put her hands on each side of Joy's face and forced her to lock eyes. "You're right, she's gone, but we can't think about her anymore. Something has gone horribly wrong, and we need to get the fuck out of here, do you understand?"

Joy nodded as the tears dripped off her cheeks.

Again, Lana checked her mobile to no avail. "It's dead," she said, as she stayed low like a soldier sticking to cover in a firefight and crawled over toward the kitchen window.

Carefully, she began to elevate upward to gaze out the window as discreetly as possible. Her pulse was thrashing relentlessly as her eyes caught an upward angle through the clear glass. When her brain finally accepted what she was seeing, the terror was like a Taser shot to her sternum.

The elongated platform blocked out most of the sky; a symmetrical black nothingness that seemed larger than life itself stretched on for miles. The blackout was silent, lying-in wait calmly, seemingly inviting reaction. The fear of the great unknown was pummeled into Lana's psyche. The anxiety behind what came next was the most difficult aspect.

Joy syphoned the dread from Lana's face and emulated it as best she could. They were both on equal ground. Joy knew Lana's reaction to whatever was waiting outside the walls of the country house was a rotten reality.

"What is it?" Joy finally managed.

Lana slid back down the side of the countertop and then onto the floor. Her arms thrashed wildly; her distress had reached a fever pitch. Suddenly, she knew what it felt like to be an ant dodging a magnifying glass.

When she finally resumed her slouching seat, she placed her hands on her forehead and responded, "I don't know, but it's fucking massive."

The utter devastation in Lana's tone pushed Joy past her terror. Joy couldn't help but take in whatever indescribable horror lay beyond the glass. She crawled through the crimson slick until she was hunkered down right beside Lana.

As she pulled herself up methodically, in the same fashion that her friend had, her eyes widened to saucer status. The reflective brackish gloss over her pupils was overtaken by the black, cancerous calamity snuffing out the sky.

"It's not how I imagined it... People always said they were discs. This-This is far more that I imagined," she whispered, shocked to the core. The tears seemed to have faded away. There was a grim aura of uncertainty in the air, like absolutely anything under the sun could happen next.

Joy quickly slid back down the counter and turned to Lana, "Wh-What do they want?"

"You think I know?" Lana replied shaking her head.

"What do we do?"

"What can we do?"

"Should we go outside?"

"Have you lost your mind?"

"Maybe they're friendly?"

"Friendly? I know you like to look on the bright side of things, but if they were so sweet, then why did Celine put a fucking steak-knife through her neck! Don't be stupid! I need your brain working right now, not spouting out nonsense! It's obvious that the safest place we can be right now, is inside this house—"

Lana's train of thought was interrupted by the sound of slimy flesh parting just a few yards away. Joy mimicked her gaze and aimed her eyes at their dead friend's corpse. The short-cut nightgown dropped just low enough to reach the top of her thighs, and the fabric covering her pubic region was beginning to flutter.

The girls remained silent and awe-struck. Neither had a desire to know what laid underneath, but instincts told them that they would soon find out.

The gray slick tissue was unveiled first. It displayed serpent-like dimensions and qualities as it wiggled its way out from Celine's nether-regions. The spiny points adorned on the dorsal side of the creature were reminiscent of a porcupine, and the numerous tiny legs that helped it move forward were a dark shade of seaweed.

Static, and in a stupor of trepidation, Joy and Lana watched the slimy thing wiggle its way from Celine's snatch and showcase even more of its horrific anatomy. The remainder was similar to the initial extremity but multiplied. Like a leafless tree branch comprised of flesh from origins unknown.

The legs were multiplied with a variety of duplication you might see depicted in age-old oil paintings of hell. They scratched chaotically against the slippery tile floor searching for traction. Eventually, the smokey moist skin that coated the limbs contorted until they were sharp and needle-like in appearance. The thing stabbed the tiny barbs feverishly into Celine's inner thighs, using her punctured limbs to pull itself from her feminine chamber.

The creature was just about large enough to fill the pit of a modest campfire. Joy and Lana would have given anything to drop it inside of one, but that was obviously not an option. As the countless oily limbs plopped down onto the slick floor, Lana looked over to Joy.

"GET UP!" she yelled, pulling her friend to her feet.

There was no longer any time for shock or morbid curiosity. The pair took off in the direction of Celine's bedroom. Lana figured putting a barrier between them and the dark entity in the kitchen would be the best they could hope for under the circumstances. But as the door closed behind them, they felt little relief.

"Get the—help me move the dresser!" Lana commanded.

Each of the ladies positioned themselves on the side of the bureau with a crushing grip. It was heavy, but the other-worldly adrenaline shot blasting through each of their cores turned a tricky task into a completed one.

They both slowly back away from the door listening intently, waiting to see what was going to happen next.

"What now! I told you we need to get the fuck out of here!" Joy sneered, her fear twisting into anger.

Lana remained silent and looked back toward the window at the far side of the room. The endless black craft continued to block out the glowing moonlight behind it. Escape didn't look promising.

"We've gotta fight it," Lana finally suggested.

"Fight it?! Fight it with what?!"

A thrashing of the slick boney limbs started against the door. The weak pounding was unnerving and multiplied the tension that was already thick enough to cut with a knife.

"Help me look around," Lana said, opening the closet door.

Joy remained were she stood, contemplating the concept, and shaking her head. Her eyes landed on the purse slung over the wooden chair in the corner of the room. She dove into Celine's bag, but she wasn't looking for a weapon.

"Fuck that, I'm not staying in here with that thing!" Joy replied, jingling the set of keys she'd just finished removing from the purse.

"Are you blind! You do see what's outside right now, don't you?"

"I'll take my chances. Celine's car is only about twenty yards away. If we just run, I think we can make it."

"I'm not going out there while that thing's outside!"

The knocking of the creature's vile legs increased in volume. Joy looked back at the door one last time as she lifted up the window.

"Suit yourself then," she said.

"Please, don't leave me here!" Lana cried.

Her protective cerebral walls were crumbling, along with the bravado and leadership abilities that were naturally entrenched in her DNA. She had suddenly been cut down; just another sheep in the flock, too frightened to make a choice that took guts.

Lana ran to the window just as Joy hopped out of it. She wanted to jump through and follow her friend, but another look up at the colossal hovering mass left her pulling the window to a close and cowering just beneath it.

As the mad pounding on the door rattled on behind her, she couldn't help but peek back every other moment to see if it was about to burst through. If it did, maybe she would be opening the window right back up again.

But until that nightmare came to fruition, she watched Joy pick herself off the ground and race toward the car. As Lana watched Joy get close to the vehicle, part of her was rooting for her friend's escape, but the other half, didn't want to be left behind. The internal battle was a guilty one.

Seconds later Joy was inserting the key into the car door and sitting in the driver's seat. Lana studied the expression on Joy's face as it transitioned from nervous and antsy, to pure terror. She watched her continue to move her arm like she was trying the key again.

"Phones don't work, lights don't work, of course, the cars don't work..." Lana mumbled to herself.

The banging on the door had quieted, she took a look behind her and saw the dresser still propped up against it without issue. She turned back to catch Joy's disturbed expression, just as the ray of blinding white light targeted her.

Inside the car, her body froze. Joy's mouth opened and her eyes eclipsed to a snow-white shade. Then, without warning, her head smacked face-first into the steering wheel. The seat that she filled curved back and Joy's body began to whiplash violently. From a laid-back position, she catapulted forward into the center of the hard plastic wheel.

Her pace was so swift that, to Lana, it looked like a movie being fast-forwarded through. The blurry chaos unfolding in the car had caused her face to resemble a cherry pie that a toddler had just finished playing with. Her facial bone structure had been blown up. The swelling, deep gashes upon her tissue, and bone fractures spelled doom.

Streams of blood painted the car's interior, splashing over the windows, and everywhere else that Lana's eyes touched. So much crimson had been unleashed that it only took a few seconds for Joy's dented and distorted face to disappear altogether behind a curtain of her own juicy essence.

The car went still, and the stomach-churning sound of Joy's bones bashing inside the vehicle had ceased. Lana, on the verge of sickness, held it in as she looked back at the door where the thing had been knocking.

Silence.

As she turned back to look for any sign of life on Joy's end, she immediately wished she hadn't. Lana watched as the lone barrier of red glass begin to crack, accompanied by a soundtrack of ghastly thuds. The front windshield spider-webbed first, then the driver's side door. The carnage rotated back and forth as Lana began to cry again. She could do little else but watch, until Joy's red skull and gory scalp blasted out the driver's window in its entirety.

The beaming light remained fixed upon Joy as her unnaturally rigid body levitated and was dragged through the now permanently opened window. Once outside the vehicle, the red rained down onto the short grass beneath from Joy's destroyed body. Her eyes remained open, but her language and emotional output had been turned off.

A patch that consisted of both rows and columns of ivory rays, layered over each other cubically like an enlarged screen door, descended directly in front of Joy's freshly tenderized floating vessel. Then abruptly, they reeled into her body, slicing through the carnal construct with ease. The blood dropped in buckets as her carcass was adapted into dozens of surgically sliced, odd-shaped hunks of humanity. Then, in the blink of an eye, the floating dilapidated squares were sucked up in vacuum-like fashion into the massive looming craft.

As soon as the traces of Joy vanished, Lana slumped down below the window. She looked back at the barricaded door as tears raced from her eyes and sweat beaded off her forehead. It was hard to think. She had no idea what came next.

"She's—She's gone," Lana mumbled to herself still in disbelief.

She felt exhausted thinking about the events that had unfolded. A murky sense of doom disturbed her soul. For a moment, she tried to push all the fear and negativity of the situation away. There was only one person that could help her now.

Lana was never religious by any means. She believed in a higher power but didn't pretend to know who or what it was. Had that higher power come to visit her? Or was the craft outside and the thing inside just another part of the massive creation that stretched further than she could've previously imagined.

She placed her bloody hands together and closed her eyes. She elevated her head upward, toward the heavens, past the dominant ship that blacked out the clouds. In her mind she traveled past it, further up, to a place that was safe. To a place where the creator slept with open ears, awaiting a worthy request.

I really, REALLY need you now. I'm not ready to go yet. I have more to offer. If you could just help me this once, just this once, I'll be better. I'll be better than you could imagine. I promise! Lana thought.

She felt the cool circulation of comfortable air contact her sweaty face. It was muggy as hell outside; she was thankful at least that Celine had sprung for a house with Central Air. In a moment that very well might be her last, she wanted to be grateful for the little things.

But as she opened her eyes, she realized that if Celine hadn't gone with that option, it might have afforded her more time. She was hoping the prayer to alleviate her horrors; for the craft to have left her behind, and all to be well again.

She tried to fight it, but much of her heart felt that slipping away was in her best interest.

***

The news of Celine's funeral and subsequent disappearance of Joy served to confirmed everything. What felt like initially bizarre and untrustworthy memories in Lana's mind had mutated; they were the reality. The weight of the news was so shocking and heavy that Lana found herself unable to even consider attending her dear friend's final services.

When Lana had awoken after that fateful night, things seemed as normal as ever. Somehow her clothing was clean; like she hadn't been present when blood erupted from Celine's body. Her car had returned to her parking space; like she had never driven it deep into the sticks to visit. The text chat in her phone that discussed her, Celine, and Joy meeting that weekend was nowhere to be found; like it never existed. Her instincts screamed that she was connected to the event, but in the real world, the police never even contacted her. In everyone else's eyes, she was somehow completely detached.

Despite the clues around her that argued she had nothing to do with the events, evidence of the disturbing evening still remained burned into her brain. The fogginess in her skull contained flashes of the frightening turn of events; the knife in Celine's throat, the platform that blocked out the sky, the thing that crawled inside her...

She didn't know what to think; was it all some horrific nightmare that just happened to align with a wicked tragedy? It all felt so real to her. As Lana's mind raced full speed, she couldn't help but question everything.

She questioned things so much that she had a doctor examine her after the pregnancy test came up negative. He assured her that she was not with child. But Lana knew her body. She knew that something felt different. The feeling of violation remained attached to her spirit like an uncurable fungus. She'd become not only disgusted with herself, but also her sticky imaginations of what foul foreign molecules were stewing inside her body.

The story isn't exactly one she could tell a friend or family member. It was taboo. It was embarrassing. It was utterly crazy. But what would she do? Just wait and see what happened? Just wait for the black platform to randomly visit her again?

The pressure was mounting. The paranoia was paramount. The stress was ruining her. She couldn't eat. She couldn't sleep. She couldn't think about anything else. How long could she keep pretending that everything was normal?

The answer was not another second. As Lana laid in her bed, tucked under the covers, the same position she'd returned to religiously and remained shaking in for weeks, she found the courage to reach for her phone. She opened up the Safari browser and typed in: Sisters of the Sky.

***

Maureen Morgan set the saucer and hot cup in front of Lana before taking a seat in the cushy chair across from the coffee table. The environment on the rural compound was one of peace, tranquility, and self-reliance. The farm was ostracized from society, and everything Lana had taken in seemed designed to deflate anxiety. As she inhaled the midnight mulberry incense burning in a dish a few feet away, she realized that it made perfect sense. If these women had experienced what she did, then the best way to disengage the trauma, would be calming distractions.

"I'm terribly sorry for your loss, and also for your gain... I just wish we knew. We might've been able to help Celine through it. There are many that have gone through what you've described, but the average person can't fathom it. They can't accept it. You're very brave to come here."

Lana sat in stunned silence. Maureen didn't seem like an extremist or tin-hat wearing whacko. Often times the people that Lana had seen who obsessed over alien life, UFOs, and abduction, didn't seem credible. Like snake oil salesmen trying to push an idea. Almost like the sporting aspect was to convince regular people of the utterly absurd. But she was different. She was just an average person.

Lana couldn't help but wonder, "I don't understand... how did I—how did I get home? How did the conversations on my phone just cease to exist?"

"It's a difficult question to answer. In my opinion it boils down to power. I don't know if they're gods, but at the very least, they've learned how to play the part. Everything we have on this planet is open to their manipulation. You saw firsthand what they're capable of, so, maybe everything we created wasn't really created. Maybe it was all just passed down..."

"It can't be real..."

"It is, but you mustn't let the insanity of it spread and infect you. Even if no one else believes you, we do."

"Why—Why won't people listen?"

"Well, why do you think we're sitting on a farm with just a few dozen women? Why isn't your story currently a global discussion? It's obvious, they cover their tracks very methodically. There's little to no proof of these fantastical encounters, all that's there is the person's merit, which, tends to sharply decline upon revealing their experience. I mean, think about it, would you believe your story before that night?"

Lana neither agreed nor disagreed with the notion, she just let out a huff of air in disgust.

"It's never the answer anyone wants to hear, but over time you'll come to accept it," Maureen said.

"I don't want to accept it! I want this fucking thing out of my body! If-If it's inside me, then how come the doctor didn't see it?!" Lana yelled, emotions flaring up.

"The best estimation we have is that the seed assimilates into the tissue, becoming one with it.

Essentially, it camouflages itself. All we know is that it remains as long as the host is alive."

"That's fucking bullshit! You're a liar! A god damn liar!"

"Lana, what do I have to gain by lying to you? All these emotions you're feeling are normal. You're going to experience the entire gamut. There will be ups and downs, highs and lows, but no matter what, the Sisters of the Sky will be here for you. We all know exactly what you're going through."

Lana tried to stabilize her sobbing, but it was difficult. Still, she continued through it, "What's going to happen to me?"

"You're eventually going to supply them with a hybrid child. A mix of their species and ours. Right now, is the hard part. But if you can just make it a few months, they will take the child when it's time, and you may be able to live a relatively normal life afterwards. Many of the women here have gone on to become sponsors and lend their support to other expecting mothers. We've built a solid community. While there is, and always will be some amount of stress, it gets much easier after giving birth."

Lana didn't know how to take in the information. The path that Maureen had outlined for her was madness. She pulled herself together and found the willpower to ask a question.

"When it's over they j—just leave you alone?"

"There may still be some visitations and check-ups... but we've never had the same girl give birth twice."

The thought of going through it felt hellish. As Lana continued to cry and imagine dark renditions of the horror that lay ahead, she could now understand exactly why Celine had taken her own life. It was either that, or a path of recurring torment and trepidation. It was, at the most granular level, a harrowing prison sentence with a petrifying blow-off at the conclusion.

Maureen rose to her feet and walked over to the loveseat that Lana sat crying madly on. She took to the space beside her and slid her arm around Lana's exhausted shoulders. They held not just the weight of the world but at least one other as well.

"You'll get through this. The problem with your friend's situation was she had no support system. No one to confide in. Everything was bottled up until her breakdown. It doesn't have to be that way for you. Join the Sisters of the Sky and you can find the light at the end of the tunnel."

Lana continued to sob incessantly, using her thumbs to wipe the tears from her eyelids. Her glossy pupils connected with Maureen's once again.

"So, is that a yes?" Maureen asked, flaunting a smidge of smile.

Lana, wholly traumatized, slowly nodded her head.

BLUEBERRY HILL

CARVER PIKE

Blueberry Hill

By Carver Pike

"You want a taste of Blueberry Hill? Get down on your knees and eat me."

It was right there, in my YouTube comments, staring back at me. Well, I was staring back me in all my naked glory. The quote accompanied a picture of me so drunk I could barely keep my eyes open. My naked tits were on full display, sagging to the sides, as gravity grabbed hold and pulled them into its embrace. It served to remind me I was a curvy girl and didn't look sexy on my back.

My fingers froze above my keyboard, as did my heart and soul, as I wondered how many people had seen the comment and photo. Then, my hand gripped my mouse as I frantically searched for the delete option even though I'd trashed spam comments a hundred times before. My head was a mess. My life was even worse. These bully fuckers had invaded my safe haven.

This wasn't right. Nobody deserved *this*.

My reputation at Mount Hope High was already obliterated. My channel, my baking show, was all I had. It was my private place where none of the sloppy teenage shit ever landed.

Each day was filled with phantom whispers, rumors spread along the halls about Blueberry Hill and how easy I was to climb, and how I allowed any boy to take a bite of my berry. Yes, those were my days.

At least my nights had remained mine. Once I reached home and the sun began to set, the sidewalks outside cooled off and inside my heart did the same, finally giving me a moment of rest. I closed my doors to the outside world, flipped my phone onto its camera feature, faced it at my stove, and taught other teenage girls how to whip up delectable concoctions.

The real world – the one I faced daily at school – seemed to know nothing of my online existence.

Yet, here I was.

Me.

Hillary Hightower – the host of Hightower Treats, a baking show where I cooked up confections for a viewing audience of exactly fifteen followers – flat on my back, in a photo everyone could see.

I knew I was a nobody in the social media world, but to that small batch of viewers, I was someone worthy of their time. They tried to duplicate my desserts each time I put up a new episode.

Now, I was a slut.

I should have never gone to that party. Before then, I was a loser, but I was an unknown loser. Now, I was on their radar.

How could they shatter me here? How did they even find me?

As far as I knew, my show was a secret. It wasn't like I was popular. Or... I wasn't before all the Blueberry Hill bullshit.

By the time morning rolled around, I'd had to delete fifteen comments calling me a slut, a whore, and mentioning all kinds of ways to eat or fuck Blueberry Hill.

I don't even like blueberries.

The bullying wasn't going to end, and I didn't understand why they'd chosen me to harass. All because I'd drunkenly given Justin Theon a blowjob?

I needed to go see my friend, Willow. She, too, had a YouTube show, but hers was all about reading tarot cards, casting spells, and other dark matters. Little was known about the woman draped in the dark cloak. Even I didn't know what she looked like. All I knew was she was friendly, kind, and had offered to help. We became friends when she commented on one of my Halloween-themed episodes.

We got to talking and it turned out she lived in the next town over. After that, we met a few times, always at her house, and she never took off her cloak. She claimed to have a rare illness that made her sensitive to light. I chose to believe her because that's what friends do, and who didn't like having a witch as a friend?

The first time I told Willow about the bullying, she offered to help, claiming she had a way to stop it forever. I turned her down. Now, after seeing these assholes weren't going to let up, I decided it was time to do something about it.

First, let me tell you how it all started.

I, Hillary Hightower, was a senior in high school and apparently an eighteen-year-old slut. I'd become known as Blueberry Hill, because as the rumors told it, *everyone* got a taste.

To think, I'd been a virgin until this year when a couple friends of mine thought it would be a cool idea to attend a party of our peers. While they were busy playing beer pong, I was busy getting hit on by Justin Theon, the school quarterback, who meandered up to me in the hallway and said, "Damn, Hillary, you look fuckin' hot."

After a quick look to my left and right to make sure he was actually talking to me, I replied, "Umm… what?" I really thought all the drinks I'd downed had gone straight to my brain.

"You have to have seen me checkin' you out," Justin continued flirting with me. "I've been wanting to talk to you for a while, but I thought you probably weren't interested."

Me? Not into you? Are you fucking serious? Everybody is into you! This isn't real. He's up to something.

The voice in my head was the intelligent one, because the devil on my shoulder said, *"Who cares if this is real? The most popular guy in school is hitting on you."*

Before I knew it, I was fighting back nausea as I gave my first awkward blowjob in an upstairs bedroom. His pre-cum was salty but kind of fruity at the same time.

Like salty strawberries. Who puts salt on strawberries? Salt on watermelon, maybe. Salt on apples... ok. But salt on strawberries?

My drunken thoughts were all over the place when Justin's thighs locked, his ass clenched, and he exploded in my mouth.

"Oh my..." I tried to say through the onslaught of semen hitting my tongue and cheeks with each twitch of his skinny cock.

I'd heard the question, "Do you spit or swallow?"

Guys always joked about that kind of shit, but you don't realize until someone is shooting warm spunk at your tonsils that it's a serious question and the time to contemplate isn't really now.

I couldn't swallow. If I did, I would have puked all over him, so instead, I kept him in my mouth until it seemed he was finished and then let it dribble out and onto the carpet. Sober me might have worried more about someone stepping in it later, but I wasn't sober, and I didn't care.

As I collapsed onto the mattress in a tired, drunken, frozen state, my eyes fell to the wedding photo of the party host's parents.

We're in their bedroom?

The dad stared straight-faced at the camera through big Coke-bottle glasses and sported a mullet while the mom smiled wide with braces and a bad perm. I could feel them judging me.

Justin was by my side, breathing heavily.

"You suck a mean dick," he whispered.

That's the most romantic thing anyone's ever said to me.

Then I passed out, and when I awoke, Justin was between my legs... fucking me.

Panic set in at first, but the deed was already being done, and the lusty side of me thought this might be the beginning of a sexual relationship with this hot jock. The super drunk part of me thought he might actually want to date me. Both of those bitches were wrong.

This was my first-time having sex. It hurt a little. Then it felt good, kind of, but it definitely wasn't lovemaking. Justin didn't even kiss me. He simply pumped a few times inside and then grunted through his second orgasm of the night.

It wasn't until he got up to leave that I realized it wasn't Justin at all. It was Mark Saunders, Justin's buddy. He, too, was a good-looking guy, but this wasn't what I'd agreed to.

But you didn't say no.

Then Mark was gone. I lay there for what seemed like forever, frozen, feeling like the world's biggest whore. My soul sank down deep in my gut. It was my lowest of lows, and I had to fight the urge to vomit. Nothing had changed yet it seemed everything had. My heart hurt and my insides felt like a bowl of mud, like mush, a fistful of yuck, like all my organs had rearranged themselves and now my body didn't make sense at all. I didn't want to leave the room because I knew, somehow, everyone would be able to tell just by looking at me that my virginity was gone forever.

When I finally descended the stairs, I knew both boys had already blabbed. Several of their buddies looked at me, pointed, and chuckled.

"You want a taste of Blueberry Hill? Get down on your knees and eat me."

According to Justin Theon, that was how I'd convinced him to go into the bedroom with me. Because, of course, he hadn't wanted to. He wasn't into big girls like me, but who wouldn't want to taste a blueberry? He'd only wanted to try a serving, and I wasn't worth seconds.

Mark backed up his story by claiming he'd stumbled into the room by accident and saw me lying there on the bed. Again, this plus-sized senior looked at him through lust-filled eyes and said, "You want a taste of Blueberry Hill? Come and get it."

He told them I even leaked a little bit of blueberry syrup when he fucked me.

I hadn't thought about the homeowners finding my blood on their bedsheets until then. The thought haunted me after. I imagined this adult couple cursing the girl they call "Blueberry Hill", as they bunched up the sheets and threw them into the garbage before rushing off to buy new ones. Nobody would want blueberry syrup on their sheets.

After the night of the party, I tried to ignore the gossip and the bullies for as long as possible, but now they'd found my YouTube show. They'd intruded on my private life. Something needed to be done.

Willow wasn't called the Wicked Witch of Wailing Way for nothing. She'd shown her many dark talents on her YouTube channel, and she was willing to help.

***

"Yes?" Willow asked through the heavy iron door at her home's entrance.

"It's me, Hillary," I replied.

Silence. Then, "I'm sorry, Hillary, I'm busy at the moment."

"I really need your help. That help you promised me before. About the bullies at my school."

A sigh and then Willow replied, "Go to the window on the right side of my house."

This was odd as Willow had let me in the last time I'd visited. When the young witch met me at the window, she had her cloak hood pulled over her head as she always did.

She wiped the back of her hand across her mouth, and in the dim light, I could swear I saw blood on her hand.

Her cloak was pulled tight around her body, but it fell open slightly and I thought I saw bare skin. She was naked under her robe.

"Are you sure you want to do this?" Willow asked. "I have to warn you to be careful what you wish for."

"I don't know what this is, but I want to put an end to the bullying."

"And punish them."

"Yes."

"Good. You told me once that one of them took your virginity."

"He did," I admitted.

"Okay, go fuck him again."

"What?"

"Fuck him again," Willow hissed. "Make him wear a condom and keep the used condom. Do this with each man you want to punish. Here." She handed me a wooden box. "Keep them in this pine box. Make sure each condom has semen in it. And always make sure you use a condom. Do you understand? Always."

"Yes. I understand. Can… can I ask what we're going to do?"

Willow laughed, and it was a weird, strange, phlegm-filled laugh. Cold chills ran through my body.

"We are going to punish," she replied. "Now, go. Do as I told you and only what I told you. Then, come back to me when you have collected the seed of all you wish to punish."

That night, I looked over at the pine box sitting on my bedroom desk. In the darkness, I couldn't see the strange symbols on the lid, but I'd run my fingers over them the entire way home. So many times, I could still feel the snakes beneath my fingers. I could sense how they wrapped around the woman's legs and stretched out to take a mouthful of the man's dick while his head fell back in agony. Other snakes were watching the couple and fire danced all around them.

Snakes, fire, and wild animalistic sex between couples I didn't know haunted my dreams. I woke wet between my legs and wondered if this was the female version of a wet dream. As far as I knew, I hadn't experienced an orgasm, but I was horny, and I was full of energy. I was ready to start collecting semen for my pine box.

It was a Tuesday afternoon, a couple of hours after school ended, when I ran into Justin as he was leaving football practice. I was struggling with a bag full of supplies from my baking club meeting.

"Hey, you need help?" he asked as he raced over to me and caught a muffin pan before it clattered against the floor.

"From you?" I replied. "No."

"Fair enough," he said, with a solemn look on his face. "Look, I didn't mean for things to go down like they did. You know teenagers. I told one friend that, you know, you did what you did."

"Let me guess. Mark?"

He nodded and stared down at his feet, ashamed.

"So, Mark figured he'd go fuck the fat slut," I said.

Justin breathed deep. "I don't know what was going through his mind."

Remembering the pine box and what Willow requested, I decided this could be the start I needed. Boys weren't so complicated. Their minds weren't all that mysterious. Suck them, fuck them, and avoid them. That was how things were supposed to go. Well, I was done avoiding them. I was going to fuck them, and I was going to punish them.

"You know," I said, "You didn't have to be mean to me. I like you. I could have been your secret, you know. Just a fuck whenever you wanted it. Your... Blueberry Hill."

He chuckled, "That's a horrible name. I'm sorry."

"No, it's grown on me. I like it."

"Blueberry Hill it is," he said.

"Blueberry Hill it is," I agreed. "You know, it was you I wanted. Not Mark. I was a virgin, and I wanted to give it up to you."

Justin smiled. "Yeah?"

"Yeah."

Getting him into the girls' bathroom stall was easy. Riding his cock was even easier. I fucked him good. This time, I was in control.

As expected, he rushed out as soon as we were done, and I was left looking at the used, filled condom he'd ripped off and thrown on the bathroom floor. The old me might have cried at that moment. Once again, used. Once again, ditched and left in a dirty bathroom stall. But I had a collection to start in a pine box.

So, I wrapped that spent rubber in some toilet paper and tucked it into my purse.

"For later," I said with a smile as I hummed a tune on my way out the bathroom.

***

On the other side of town, Willow was busy, too. She had a man bent over on all fours on a mattress. He was completely naked, hairy ass and all. This customer had come to her for entirely different reasons than the young high school friend of hers. This was his second time visiting. The last time, young Hillary had shown up in the middle of their meeting and had ruined everything.

Michael Lansing wanted children. He came to Willow with complaints that his wife wasn't ready to start a family. She was too focused on work. Michael desperately wanted sons. So, Willow was going to give him some.

With Michael bent over on the bed, she held a stone cup under the tip of his cock while she put two gloved, lubed, fingers inside his anus. She started rubbing gently while the man moaned in sexual satisfaction. Of course, like most men, he'd been opposed to the idea at first.

But this was the way.

Milking the prostate was an important part of the process. In fact, it was the key.

Michael groaned in complaint at first, but then his tight hole eased around her fingers, and he began to back into her, forcing her to fuck his asshole faster.

This had been the moment Hillary arrived last time. Now, she would be uninterrupted.

Michael was loving it.

With her left hand, Willow reached around and tugged on his hard member while continuing to stroke the inside of his ass. He would come soon. This never took long.

As expected, Michael began to huff and moan, and then he whined, "Mistress Willow, I'm gonna come. Now..."

She let go of his cock and stuck it inside the stone cup while her fingers continued to thrust inside him. Michael's body shuddered, his cock jerked, and he came.

This wasn't about pleasure. It was about the product. She had what he came for, so she pulled her fingers out of his ass and walked away with the cup.

"That was incredible," he said.

"Yes," she replied with a straight face. "Now, get dressed."

He did as he was told while Willow walked to her table of ingredients. She put a pinch of this, a flick of that, and a drop of the other. Then she mixed it with a wooden spoon and handed it to the now-dressed businessman. "Give your wife her morning coffee with *one* drop of this mixed in with the cream. It must be in the coffee, the first cup she drinks. Do you understand?"

He nodded.

"Good," she replied, "because if even one part of my rules are ignored, there will be dire consequences."

"But won't she notice the taste?"

"It won't matter if she does. Once a drop of this is on her tongue, she'll produce a child. Don't you worry."

Michael paid her and left. She snickered as she poured herself a glass of wine. Michael was overzealous. She could already see what would happen. She had instructed him to put *one* drop in his wife's coffee. He would put *eight*. Each drop would bring a child. He was not only going to get *one* child, he was going to get *eight*. All Willow's spells came with consequences. It was the reason she always started conversations with new clients with the warning, "Be careful what you wish for."

Young Hillary wished for punishment. She was going to get it.

Willow wasn't an evil woman, but she'd made a deal the day she received her power. Every pact came with satisfaction. She was to give strict instructions. If followed, satisfaction would come for the client. If not, it would come for her and her dark father. It was that simple.

***

With Justin's condom folded nicely in the pine box, I turned my attention to the young man who took my virginity.

Mark had already had me once, so when I showed up at his work, he didn't pay me much attention - just as I'd expected.

I had to admit, he looked cute in that ice cream parlor hat with his messy brown hair wisping out of the sides, curling up at his ears.

"Oh, it's you," he'd said as he met me at the cash register to take my order.

My jaw dropped. "Jeez, is that any way to talk to a lady?"

"A lady?"

"Well, it wasn't a dude you put your cock in."

Mark smirked. "What can I get for you?"

"I haven't been able to stop thinking about you," I said, and it wasn't a lie. In fact, he was probably my troll since he was the only person ever to be alone with me when I was naked and on my back. If nothing else, he'd taken the nude picture and passed it around.

He gulped. "Really?"

"I was so fucking drunk that night. I wish I could say I remember it clearly, but I was pretty wasted. It's kind of sad, really. I've always had a crush on you."

"Well, we can meet up tonight if you want," he said, easily falling into my trap. "I was supposed to hang out with the guys, but you know…"

"Pussy matters more?" I asked.

He laughed and nodded. "Pussy definitely matters more."

"Well, you know what they say," I replied with a devilish grin. "If you want a taste of Blueberry Hill…"

And, boy, did he get a taste of Blueberry Hill. He took me home to his house that night. His parents were out on a date night together. Of course, I didn't have a bathing suit, so I swam in my bra and panties. Then, on the side of the pool, he pushed my head back, so I was lying on the concrete with my feet dangling in the water. He pulled my panties to the side, and he ate all the Blueberry Hill his mouth could handle.

When I led him out of the water and over to one of the lounge chairs, he excitedly dropped his shorts, but he wasn't too thrilled when I pulled a condom out of my purse and ripped open the wrapper.

"You want me to wear that thing?" he asked, standing there with his erection on full display.

After that drunken night at the party, I'd asked myself a hundred times if he'd used protection. I was pretty sure he hadn't, and I'd been terrified until my next period came. I wasn't going to take that chance again, plus Willow's instructions required a condom.

"Of course, I want you to wear this," I replied, giving his dick a tight stroke.

"But I can pull out," he said, "I mean... that's what I did the last time."

"No, you don't get to pull out tonight, stud," I told him in the sexiest voice I could pull off. "Tonight, I'm gonna make you come hard... that's why you have to wear this."

I rolled the condom down on the tip of his cock. He bit his bottom lip, and I knew he couldn't wait to plow into me.

"Lie on your back," I ordered.

He did as he was told, I sat down on him, and I rode him poolside with my fingernails digging into his chest. He wasn't taking it, I was. I was the one doing the fucking. Alcohol didn't have me in a numb state, flat on my back, catching his cum. No, I was in control.

But then, just like with Justin, as soon as Mark released himself into that rubber, he gave a few strong thrusts and then collapsed. He spent a few seconds catching his breath while I tried to get a little more use out of him. Then, when he decided he was finished, he lifted me off his lap and suggested he take me home.

He pulled off the condom, but I offered to throw it away for him, snatching it out of his hand a little too eagerly. Then, I made my way to the bathroom to "clean up" where I wrapped the spent rubber in toilet paper and tucked it away inside my purse.

The trap was set. Victory would be mine.

And I didn't stop there.

Buddy Taylor was the typical school redneck. He drove a pickup truck, blasted country music, and sported a rebel flag in his ride's back window. The kid was an asshole to most of the people around him, but he was always sweet to me, so when he asked me out during our chemistry class, I accepted. For the first time, in a long time, this wasn't a date I dreaded or one I expected to spend seeking revenge.

This was an honest to God, real date. At least it started that way.

Having always been a fan of horror movies, I was ecstatic when he said he wanted to go see a scary film. It took him about half the movie before he finally leaned over and made a move. When he kissed me, I felt warm inside, like this might be the guy I'd one day call my high school sweetheart.

We made out through the rest of the movie, and he coaxed me into giving him a hand job before it was over. Later that evening, I let him climb through my bedroom window. I wasn't planning on sleeping with him, but I'd already had sex three times, so it wasn't like I was losing anything. Plus, by this time I'd started to enjoy sex. Buddy hadn't mentioned anything about Blueberry Hill, and he seemed trustworthy, so I let him make love to me.

Another spent condom later, and Buddy was climbing out my bedroom window only to join all the others in telling meanspirited stories about me. This one, I heard, was about how we'd been watching a movie together when I leaned over and whispered to him, "You want a taste of Blueberry Hill? Come to my house later, spread my legs, and eat me."

I cried. I mean, how could he do this to me? Not Buddy. He was supposed to genuinely like me. My heart was shattered. I fucking sobbed over him. Depression was real. At eighteen years old, I had the worst reputation at my high school.

All my used condoms were still folded nicely and kept in the pine box. Willow would reveal the endgame soon enough. For now, all I knew was I needed to keep collecting them from the people I intended to punish. Buddy was added to that list.

Later, I recorded a new episode of Hightower Treats. Much to my surprise, I'd gained a hundred new subscribers. My comments had blown up. Trolls had taken to harassing me and in turn, some of my viewers - old and new - were defending me. It was something like this:

Argyle1786: Whores belong in the kitchen. Keep baking and spreading your legs.

QBSneek11: Smells like blueberries. Tastes like chicken.

DrewBBad88: You mean smells like fishy blueberries.

FMAlchemist911: It's easy to see who the small-dicked boys are. Real men know how to treat a beautiful woman. Your fathers should be ashamed.

Angie9Akers: FMAl exactly! Thank you! She's gorgeous and doing what she loves. Please ignore these assholes, sweetie.

I cried when I read the comments. First, as usual, the negative ones crushed me, but then seeing how people defended me really brought me back to life, and I decided to record a new show.

In the episode, I thanked everyone for defending me, laughed about how lame the offenders were and talked about how I kind of liked the nickname Blueberry Hill and decided I was going to change the name of the show from Hightower Treats to Baking with Blueberry Hill. From there, the show ran the same as it always did, and I taught my viewers how to make my grandmother's famous peach cobbler.

I uploaded it and not long after it went live, Willow called me.

"It seems you're taking things well," she said.

"I'm not, but what was I supposed to do? People were defending me, and I wanted to honor them by being strong—"

"I like it," she said, interrupting my near breakdown. "It seems like you're about ready to end this. Have you collected from everyone you need?"

I had to think about it. I wasn't sure who all was involved. Justin and Mark were the ringleaders, but their merry band of morons had other members, and I wasn't sure which were spreading the rumors, and which were trolling me online.

"I need a little more time," I told her.

She sighed. "Fine. But hurry this up. I think next Friday is a great deadline. It's a Friday the 13th... kind of fitting really, being bad luck and all. Do a short video announcing to your fans that you will be doing a special live episode on Friday the 13th that is dedicated to all the bullies who have been trolling you."

Butterflies went wild in my stomach and chest. If I did this, everyone would watch. All the bullies and their girlfriends and their friends. They'd all want to see what I have to say.

"That's the point," Willow's voice came through the phone.

Did she hear me? Had I said that out loud?

"Do as I said," she ordered.

The next day, I took to all my social media outlets informing my followers and viewers about my special Friday the 13th live episode dedicated to the bad luck of all my bullies.

I had a little less than two weeks before the episode would air. If ever there was a time to be a slut, it was now. None of the pieces of shit at my school were being held accountable for the mean things they said or the evil acts they performed. Young adults these days weren't punished for their wrongdoings. That was about to change.

And if the assholes at school wanted Blueberry Hill, I was about to give them Blueberry Hill.

My wardrobe, hair, and makeup were about to change. Everything needed to be navy, sky, or royal. I was going blue. When I was finished, my lips looked like I sucked off a *Smurf* and my nails could have peeled the blue skin off the back of *He-Man's* Skeletor. I was goth if goth girls were the pale of the moon instead of black of the night.

I'd never thought of myself as a flirt, but I made myself easier than ever to access.

If guys wanted to taste Blueberry Hill, they could. Anyone and everyone.

I'd become a blueberry buffet.

A fucking feast for all who wanted me.

Why? Because the good guys wouldn't, and the bad guys deserved what was coming to them... whatever that was. Willow still hadn't exactly explained it yet.

With only about two weeks to go, I thought I'd play with the baking theme. I wanted to be able to say I'd fucked a full dozen. Since I'd already had sex with three guys, that meant I had a lot of sex to make up for. I needed nine guys in less than two weeks.

What are you, a fucking porn star?

That's what they wanted me to be. That's what the world thinks I am, so why the hell not?

I remembered who'd been waiting at the bottom of the stairs when I came down the night, I lost my virginity. Nick Brower had been there whispering and laughing with the others.

He was easy. I bumped into him at school, excused myself as I gently rubbed his forearm, and that was all it took. Later that afternoon, he took me from behind as he bent me over his dresser. He had the fucking audacity to tell me my blueberry was nice and moist. I collected his condom and left.

At Benji Watson's party, I fucked him and his buddy Colson after everybody else went home. I collected two used condoms from that. When I left, I heard them snickering and saying something about double teaming that blueberry.

In the sauna at Rex Reed's condominium recreation room, I spread my legs and dug my fingernails into his shoulders. That time I came along with him. He whispered into my ear that he could feel my blueberry syrup running down his balls. Yes, I collected that bastard's condom too.

Clifton Scholl fucked me in a hotel room after taking me to IHOP. The fucker ordered blueberry waffles and had the nerve to ask if I wanted to take a selfie with him. I agreed. I even held up the blueberry syrup just to show I had a sense of humor. I definitely took his condom.

A boy named Scott McCall asked me out on a date and took me to a lake to have some drinks. I didn't know his buddy Ryan would be there. Ryan was older. He'd graduated from our school the year before. If I hadn't gone willingly, it would have been a forced situation, but they both asked about my blueberry pie and I told them it was a buffet, all they could eat, but they both had to wear condoms.

I might have made it to my dozen if one boy didn't derail my plan.

A guy named Evan approached me on the 10th, just three days shy of my live event, and told me he'd heard the rumors and couldn't believe guys would be such douchebags. I vowed to myself that I wouldn't sleep with him. We went out on a date and enjoyed ourselves. There was no sex involved.

On the 11th, Evan went down on me. I didn't even have to do any of the work. He made me come, and I was sure this time everything would be different. The next date, Evan made love to me, with him on top. It was romantic, it was great, and it happened so naturally I forgot to ask him to wear a condom.

Then he came inside me, and when he pulled out, he stared down at me with the most disgusted face I'd ever seen on a boy. He said, "Things could have been great, but you had to pull that Blueberry Hill shit and give it up so easy. Fucking gross." Then he tucked his dick in his pants and walked away.

I lay there frozen. I trembled. I cried. And I realized I'd fucked up. I didn't use a condom, but I thought it might not be too late. I had one in my dresser. Evan climbed out the window and I scurried to recover from my mistake.

Ripping open a condom package, I reached down and dug two fingers into my pussy, scooping up as much of Evan's cum as I could and slathering it all over the rubber. I shoveled more of his ejaculate out of myself and wiped it into the condom. He'd poured so much of himself into me that digging out his seed was easy, and soon, I had the latex Trojan at least an inch deep with his semen. It would have to be enough to satisfy Willow's plan.

Then, I collapsed on the floor and cried myself to sleep.

Later, on social media, Evan made a post with him making a disgusted face. The caption read: Tried Blueberry Hill. Who knew blueberries were so sour?

I was mortified, I was fucking fuming, and I wanted revenge.

Finally, it was Friday the 13th, and I was ready. I called Willow.

"Hi, love," she said, "are you ready?"

"I am. What do I do?"

"You bake."

"That's all?"

"Yes, make blueberry muffins to celebrate the name you've been given. Only… add that special specimen you've been collecting to each muffin and once you've got all the muffins in the oven, read the spell I'm going to send you through to your phone."

"That's all?"

"Yes, you did follow my directions, right? All of them came inside the condom?"

I had to think about it for a second. Surely, Evan counted. I'd scooped his cum out and wiped it into the condom.

"Yes," I said.

"Good. Then, yes, that's all. They should all be watching, and they will all get the surprise of their life."

"Wait, can you tell me what's going to happen?" I asked.

"That would ruin the surprise," Willow said. "Believe me, they'll be bubbling over with joy."

Later that evening, with the pine box by my side and my camera pointed at my kitchen island, I started the show with the ingredients all well underway.

Of course, I wasn't going to pull condoms out and show myself pouring jizz into the muffin pan, so I did it beforehand. I scraped some of Justin, Mark, Buddy, Nick, Benji, Colson, Rex, Clifton, Scott, Ryan, and Evan into the pans. That made eleven. Just short of a dozen. The twelfth would have to be just the regular ingredients.

I was suddenly nervous. I was set to go live in less than a minute and I was considering backing out. A million thoughts ran through my mind.

What if I put the muffins in the oven and all these men suddenly show up and profess their undying love for me?

What if they each drop to one knee while I'm live and propose?

What if they're each hit with the sudden urge to go online and admit who has been trolling me?

What if they each start unwittingly sending nudes to my comments section?

What if they each start vomiting blueberry muffins?

That thought made me laugh and laughing helped calm my nerves.

It was time to go live. So, I pressed record on the camera, and I got things started.

"Hey, you sexy snackers, it's time to get baking with Blueberry Hill, and tonight is a very special episode since

I'm live and it is Friday the 13th. I've got quite the delectable dessert on the menu. It's simple but it's sweet and it matches my new nickname. Yes, queens and kings, I'm talking blueberry muffins."

The words flew from my mouth naturally, as did the ingredients going into the mixing bowl.

I almost forgot there was an end act of revenge in this. My smile was genuine. I enjoyed the time spent with my followers. I was good at what I was doing, and I'd even picked up another hundred viewers since the last time I'd uploaded a video. I was on the rise. Things were looking up. I'd been bullied into giving my sex away like a cheap whore, but tonight the spotlight was on me, and I was shining bright like a diamond.

The batter was ready, and I spooned it into the muffin pan, on top of each boy's special ingredient.

Somewhere out there, all eleven of the boys who'd fucked me and made fun of me, were watching. At least, Willow claimed they would be. Maybe they weren't. It didn't matter. According to her, the plan would still work. All the effort I'd put into this revenge scheme was about to pay off. I'd followed her directions, I'd paid attention to her instructions, and it was about to happen.

"And into the oven they go," I said as I slid the muffin pan in and closed the door, pretending to tinker with the oven dials as I glanced at my phone screen and silently recited the words to the spell Willow had sent me.

My heart raced as I read her words. Each syllable slammed in my chest. My knees wobbled and I nearly fell over as flashbacks hit me – one violent sexual thrust – from each boy:

Mark going rigid on top of me at the party.

Justin gripping my thighs as I rode him in the bathroom stall.

Buddy's ass clenching as he came.

Nick pumping into me from behind.

My mouth around Benji's cock while Colson gripped my hips and pounded me.

Rex driving into me in the sauna as I dug my nails into his back.

Clifton bending me over the hotel bed.

Scott and Ryan at the lake.

And Evan... the boy I thought truly liked me. "Tried Blueberry Hill. Who knew blueberries were so sour?"

Gripping the countertop, I fought to keep my balance and maintain my composure.

Get ahold of yourself. Your audience is watching.

For the first time since all this started, it occurred to me that these boys were only boys, all in my senior class or beyond, but they were just sex-crazed assholes, and I'd enjoyed my time with *some* of them. I'd gone after the sex they'd provided.

Because you, too, are a horn ball. And aside from a few of them, you kind of led them on. You went after them.

A short laugh escaped my lips, and it wasn't a happy one. It was more like, "Oops, what have I done?" The plan had already been set in motion. I was sure whatever was going to happen was something silly. Willow would embarrass them, play some harmless trick, and it would all be over soon.

I'd already let the show linger on dead silence for too long. This was the reason I didn't like doing live feeds. When it came to baking, it was much easier to upload later. That way I could edit. I could record myself mixing ingredients and putting the muffins or pie or whatever into the oven. Then I could cut to the point it was time to take it out. No boring dead space.

Fill the time. Talk about movies you've seen or the kind of music you listen to. Typical teenage stuff.

So, I babbled. I spoke about anything and everything that came to mind. This episode would either be a hit or a complete disaster.

I thought it only a coincidence that at about the five-minute mark, when I was talking about how warm it had been outside, I began to sweat. Snatching a paper towel off the roll, I dabbed at my forehead and said to my viewers, "Whew, speaking of heat, I'm beginning to sweat. Something must be going on with my air conditioner tonight."

A professional never lets her environment slow her down, so I continued to find things to speak about until the heat became unbearable and beads of sweat rolled down my face and dampened my neckline.

My breathing became labored.

"It really is starting to boil in here," I said, checking the time on the oven, "and these have only been in just under ten minutes."

Something else odd was happening. I was hot down there as well. And by down there I mean my vagina. My pussy was absolutely smoldering. I was dripping sweat. It was like someone had sprayed Bio Freeze or Icy Hot on me.

I tried to talk my way through it but as it got worse, I couldn't control my facial expressions, and I even started sucking air through clenched teeth and wincing. "I'm not feeling so great, guys."

It now felt like I'd sat on a fire ant hill and the pissed off bugs had run up my thighs and into my pussy where they were tearing into my insides. Invisible pinchers squeezed my flesh, bringing up welts and making my flesh swell.

I fell to the floor on the other side of the island, out of camera view, and hoisted up my sundress, pulled down my panties, and stared at the swollen, red, bubbling and blistering mass between my legs. It looked like I was about to give birth.

***

Willow had given specific instructions to Hillary and honestly had no negative intentions, but as she always told her clients, she needed to be careful what she wished for, and she needed to follow every direction down to the letter.

As the young woman running the live baking show was flat on her back, writhing in pain and wondering what was happening to her, eleven young men who'd made the mistake of crossing her were experiencing the same kind of agony. Each was someplace different and only watching because he'd heard the show was dedicated to boys like him.

Of course, none of them could see the muffins inside the oven. Each boy couldn't watch the special ingredient, his own semen, bubble and blend with the rest of the batter as the cake rose from the center and exploded outward, but each would experience it for himself. His own muffin. His own Blueberry Hill eruption.

Justin was shopping for shoes in a sporting goods store when he dropped his phone and fell to the floor, yanked down his shorts, and watched in horror as his bloody cock seemed to be folding outward around itself like socks being paired.

Mark was about to have sex. His new girlfriend, Avery, was in the shower and he was in her bed waiting for her, already naked under the blanket. He turned on her laptop and found Baking with Blueberry Hill. When the pain started, it felt like he'd been kicked in the balls. It was a dull ache that ran up his shaft and turned to blazing heat. Like hot lava had started sizzling at the base, ran up the length, and burst forth from the tip, turning his cock inside out. Avery stepped out of the bathroom just in time to see his dick split at the top and curl outward and into itself on both sides, like a hot dog that had been boiled for too long.

Buddy was fishing when it happened. His phone was open to the baking show. He was laughing his ass off as Hillary stumbled over her words. *The dumb, fat bitch.* "Ah, what the fuck?" His dick suddenly hurt so bad he didn't care if his buddies saw. When he threw down his jeans, everyone jumped back. His cock looked like the top of a muffin that was in the middle of baking. Liquid ingredients were bubbling up from the center and expanding outward. His cock was exploding. He dropped to his knees and screamed.

Nick Brower was driving to the store with his buddy Jeff when it happened. Jeff thought Nick had dropped his cigarette into his lap when he started slapping at his own crotch. It was funny at first. But then blood soaked through his shorts, Nick wouldn't stop screaming, and neither of the boys saw the tree coming at seventy miles per hour until it was too late.

Benji and Colson, the two Hillary had a threesome with after their party, weren't together when it happened. Benji was swimming and took a break to watch her by the side of his pool. He was later found floating, the entire pool soiled with his blood. Colson, who'd been asleep and missed the show, woke up screaming in agony. His parents rushed him to the hospital where his dick had to be amputated.

Rex Reed, the guy from the sauna, was in the greeting card aisle at Walmart when he collapsed on the floor. Paramedics arrived to find his dick had exploded outward like a baked muffin.

Clifton Scholl was masturbating when it happened. He thought it would be funny to beat off to Baking with Blueberry Hill. It turned out to be no laughing matter.

Scott and Ryan, the two who'd taken Hillary out by the lake, were bi-sexual. More gay than bi, really, and had used Hillary to help them ease into their first time together. She didn't know it. Neither did they really. First, they tried it with a woman between them. Then they simply removed her. It worked out really well for them until the night they watched Baking with Blueberry Hill. This night, their cocks turned inside out at the same time, while in bed together, and that was their coming out party. *Surprise!*

Then, of course, there was Evan. He who'd pretended to do no wrong. He who acted so perfect. Evan was in church when it happened. His self-righteous ass was asking for forgiveness for sins he hadn't yet committed, knowing full well he was about to fuck another young woman and treat her like shit after. Well, he got his when he fell to his knees in front of the entire congregation and bled out on the floor with his cock erupting like a volcano of blueberry muffin proportions.

If only Hillary would have listened to Willow and followed her directions. She'd been so hellbent on making sure Evan got his punishment. The day she'd allowed Evan to come inside her, and she'd scooped his semen out and wiped it into the condom, sure, she'd gotten enough of his seed into the rubber, but in doing so, she'd also succeeded in scraping some of her own enzymes in along with it.

So, while all across town the men who'd done her wrong suffered agonizing muffin-eruption torture, she too, was hit with this odd, excruciating ailment. There, between her legs emerged a growth that resembled a blueberry baked treat. She watched in horror and spread herself wide to make room for the widening mass that seemed to keep growing and growing with the crusty, crumbly texture one might find on the outside of a Dutch apple pie. It rose and rose until... finally... it... popped.

Blue, pink, yellow, and red puss and blood ran out of her body like multicolored rivers that met the grout lines on the tile floor and obeyed the texture as they ran in straight lines, only branching to the right or left with each new tile, forming perfect squares of disgusting, mucusy mess that drained her of all the life left in her body.

Yes, you could say Hillary died there on the cold kitchen floor, giving birth to Blueberry Hill.

THEY'RE ALWAYS WATCHING

PATRICK C. HARRISON III

They're Always Watching
by Patrick C. Harrison, III

"Who is always watching, Mom?" I say. This is the third time she's said that today and the first time I've inquired as to what the fuck she is talking about. It's blatantly obvious her dementia is progressing. Dementia *progressing*, everything else *regressing*.

"Oh," she says with a chuckle, a disgusted kind of laugh that suggests whoever *they* are, are individuals of unmatched ill repute, "you know. You know."

I sigh. She repeats everything she says and probably has no idea who or what she is talking about from one moment to the next. The kitchen smells wonderful, though. Apparently, dementia hasn't destroyed her ability to cook yet. It's like the doctor said, the long-term memories and tasks she's done for decades will be the last to go.

"Oh, where's that wooden spoon, Jill? The wooden spoon."

So much for that long-term memory idea.

"It's Mia, Mom," I say, "Jill is in Akron, remember? And you left the spoon over here." I grab it from the counter in front of the coffeemaker (which probably hasn't been used in the six years since Dad died) and hand it to her.

187

"Oh, that's right, Mia. I know Jill is in Akron. I know that. Must be cold up there this time of year." She bends over the large mixing bowl and starts stirring.

"Must be," I agree. But I'm not thinking about Akron. I am not thinking about the chicken pot pie, despite how wonderful it smells from the oven. Nor am I thinking about the carrot cake she's currently working on, even though I know it will be divine. I'm thinking about what I have to tell her. I'm wondering how she will react when I tell her it's time, that it's no longer safe for her to live here alone. Lord, hopefully she won't react like Aunt Wanda; she called the police on Jim and Harlan for trying to put her in a home.

"Grab the carrot shavings from the fridge would you, dear?" Mom says, smiling, her head rocking back and forth as she stirs, as if she's humming some song silently to herself.

"Sure," I say setting my purse on the counter and turning to the fridge. It's an old green refrigerator that's nearly as old as I am, and it's decorated from top to bottom with old photographs of me and Jill and Dad and Mom, and other family members. The magnet letters I played with as a child, and my son played with years later, are still there. Someone has spelled out "I see you" with the magnets. I open the fridge, half expecting to find there to be no carrot shaving to retrieve. But there they are, sitting on the top shelf in a glass bowl covered in plastic wrap. I get the bowl and set it on the counter before Mom.

"Thank you, dear," she says, dumping the carrot shaving in the batter then resuming stirring.

I wonder if she's calling me dear because she can't remember if I'm Mia or Jill or someone else. She may think I'm some random chick who wandered in off the street to help her cook, for all I know. She's gotten much worse. It's been two months since last I saw her, and she was bad then, spending the better part of the two hours I was over searching for her purse, which ended up being in the dirty clothes hamper. But at least she remembered who I was, and there was none of this business of people watching her. That's new and worrisome. And that has made up my mind—the time has come for her to go to a home. As much as I hate it, the time has come.

"Did you hear Francine died last week?" she says, still stirring. Francine died years ago. Longer ago than Dad.

"Francine George?" I ask, just to be sure we're talking about the same person.

"Francine George," she says. Then, "She was murdered."

"Murdered?" I say, almost shouting at the absurdity. "Mom, Francine died of pneumonia."

"It's appalling what they did to her body, butchering her that way."

My mouth hangs open. I have no idea what to say to this. Butchering her that way? What the hell? She must have read something awful from the paper or watched some tv show, then somehow associated it with Francine George.

Mom is way worse than I thought. I lean against the counter across from her and rub my face with my palms. I'm no drinker but I could use a drink right now. Mom starts whistling, still stirring. The song she's whistling rings familiar, but I can't place it. She seems pretty chipper for someone that thinks her best friend was hacked to pieces, or whatever, in the last week. From behind, I look at Mom's hair—the curly, blue-gray hair synonymous with women over seventy—and see there is something caught in her thin strands. Is that yellow paint flakes?

"Mom, have you been in the attic?" I ask.

"Oh, dear, would you get the nutmeg from the spice cabinet?" Mom says, ignoring my question. "I almost forgot the nutmeg."

There is only one place in this house that has paint like that, and that's the attic. Jill and I painted the attic yellow when we were kids, thinking it would make a cool clubhouse. It was an endeavor we undertook while Dad was at work and Mom was volunteering at the church. Needless to say, the yellow attic never became our clubhouse. Mom was none too pleased about us rummaging around in the attic unsupervised and Dad was downright mad we'd gotten into his paint. (He painted houses for a living, and I shudder to think how much of his inventory we rendered useless as we searched for the color we wanted.) Yellow from the attic is in Mom's hair. Why?

I go to the spice cabinet and search for the nutmeg and finally find it and hand it to Mom. She opens the lid and gently taps in whatever amount she needs. I've never understood how she can eyeball everything. I'd be lost without measuring cups.

She goes back to whistling.

I wish Jill was here. She was always better at talking to Mom about things, especially important things. But I guess when you marry a surgeon and move eleven-hundred miles away, you get to relinquish your talking with Mom responsibilities. What in God's name was she doing in the attic? Going through Dad's old camping gear? There isn't a single thing up there she could have needed. I'm about to ask her about it again when she speaks.

"Oh, could you get me the cake pan, dear?"

"Sure," I say, feeling somewhat relieved that she stopped me from asking her about the attic. I almost don't want to know why she was up there. No reason she could give would matter. It would most likely be a ridiculous reason and would further upset me and further prove that it's time for the nursing home. If she even remembers going up there.

"The round one, right?" I ask as I open the cupboard with all the pots and pans.

"The round one," she sings rather than says.

I find the round cake pan and grab it. I freeze, my hand still holding the pan inside the cupboard. There is a gun—

a blue steel revolver—in the pan. It's one of Dad's old guns, I think. I'm not positive, though. Fuck. Fuck, fuck, fuck!

"Mom," I say sternly, bringing the pan out of the cupboard and turning to face her. She is still stirring and whistling, rocking her head to the beat. "Mom!" I say again, forcefully.

"What, dear?" she says. She stops stirring the carrot cake mix and turns toward me. She has an oddly pleasant smile on her face.

"Mom, there is a gun in the cake pan. Why the hell is there a gun in the cake pan?" This comes out more scornful than I should probably say it, but the thought of Mom walking around the house with a gun and storing in it odd places has me beyond terrified.

"Well, Jill, just take it out of the pan. I don't plan on baking the gun."

She's lost her damn mind. She's fucking bonkers. She's mistaken me for Jill again, which I choose to ignore. Next, she'll be mistaking me for Francine or Dad or fucking Gomer Pyle.

"I've never heard of gun cake, have you?" she says joyfully, then goes back to mixing. "That doesn't sound very yummy."

"Mom, why is there a gun in the cupboard, in a pan? This isn't a joke."

"I'm not a child, dear. I can have a gun."

I want to tell her that she may not look like a child but mentally speaking, she may as well be one. I should tell her that. I should tell her she's going nuts. Dementia has its fingers so deeply imbedded in her brain that she's hardly the same person. Sticking the gun inside the back seam of my jeans, feeling absurdly like I'm doing this in a crime movie with undercover cops and drug dealers, I place the pan next to Mom on the counter.

"Mom, look at me," I say, putting my hand on her shoulder.

She stops stirring and looks at me. There is concern in her eyes. She knows I'm being serious.

"Mom, I don't think you should have guns in the house. I know you and Dad had them for years and years, but..." My mind stalls. How can I say this without hurting Mom? *Mom, you're going blow your fucking toes off or worse!* is what I want to say.

"Take them if you want," Mom says, turning back to the bowl and stirring. "Guns don't scare them, anyway."

Them? Who the fuck is them?

"Who is *them*, Mom?" I can't help raising my voice a little. Was she waving Dad's gun at someone? The mailman, maybe? That young couple that moved in next door?

"The thieves," she says. She taps the spoon on the lip of the bowl and sets it aside, then picks up the bowl to pour its contents into the pan.

"Thieves? Mom, let me help you with that."

"I got it, dear. I got it. And yes, thieves. Of course, thieves."

Mom's neighborhood isn't as great as it once was, that's true, but I haven't heard of any burglaries or break-ins. Still seems like a pretty quiet neighborhood. Surely Mom knows to call the police if she thinks someone is trying to get in the house. Surely nothing. I can't assume such things. I just found a revolver in a cake pan, after all.

"What thieves?" I ask, knowing whatever she says will be absurd.

"Will you check and see if the pot pie is ready?" she says, smoothing out the carrot cake mixture in the pan.

I sigh and decide to let it go for now. I seriously doubt there are people trying to break into the house but trying to tell her otherwise would be pointless. Maybe I can use her claims of thieves to help convince her to move into a home. For some reason this seems like a mean tactic. I don't want to use her ridiculous claims against her, but...I may not have a choice. I open the oven, the hot air hitting me, and peer in and see the pot pie has that perfect golden-brown color. In one spot, the crust has split and the contents within are bubbling up. I love it when it does that. It smells like my childhood.

"Looks done," I say. "Want me to take it out."

"Sure, dear, that would be delightful. You pull that out and I'll put the pound cake in."

"Carrot cake," I remind her, grabbing oven mitts from the drawer and taking out the pot pie and setting it on the oven.

"Right, carrot cake," she says, leaning over and sliding it into place on the rack before closing the oven.

"I'll go set the table," I say. What I really want to do is get this gun out of the back of my jeans. It's very uncomfortable. I don't see how Bruce Willis does it.

Mom smiles and nods and for a split second I see that look in her eye that she's completely lost. No idea who I am or where I came from or how I got in the house. If she had the revolver in her hand this very second, she would raise it, point it at my skull, and call me a thief before blowing my brains out. Then her eyes clear and I see vague understanding.

"That's fine, dear," she says.

Grabbing plates and silverware, I head into the dining room. I put them down on the dining table, and before setting the places, pull the gun out. I look at it closely. A Smith & Wesson something or other. I'm pretty sure it was Dad's. At least she didn't steal it, I guess. I swing out the revolver's cylinder and dump the five rounds of .38 Special into my hand. To my utter shock, one of them is just an empty casing. It was fired. Mom—because who else could have done it? —fired this gun. I'm about to yell for her when she screams.

Quickly, I open the glass door to the China cabinet, placing the revolver and ammunition inside then close it and rush into the kitchen. Mom is standing there by the oven looking at her hands. She's crying.

"Mom, what's wrong? What happened?" Running to her, I put my hands on her shoulders and try to look into her eyes but she's still looking down at her hands. I look at them and see the red line across her fingers and see where the skin is broken and peeling away on her right index finger. She burned herself.

"I was just trying to move the pan off the oven," she says, sniffling.

"It's okay, Mom. It happens sometimes. The oven mitts are right there on the counter. I can move the pan. But first, let's get your fingers doctored up, okay?"

She nods. She really does look like a child now, the way her bottom lip is stuck out and tears are rolling down her face. Like an upset child. I feel horrible for thinking this but it's true. I lead her over to the medicine cabinet at the rear of the kitchen by the laundry room. I open the cabinet and begin rummaging through.

"Do you have Silvadene or Neosporin?" I ask. There is more crap in here than I ever remember. I doubt she's thrown away any medicine in decades. It's mostly expired, guaranteed. Her hoarding of medicine, expired or not, is nothing new. Not dementia related.

"I don't know what silver-deen is," she says from behind me.

"It's for burns." I notice a lot of this medicine has Dad's name on it. Metformin, Ultram, Prilosec. Even a full bottle of 20mg Norco. Mom could deal in prescription medications if she felt like, along with shooting up the neighborhood. Finally, I find a half empty tube of Neosporin. Getting a roll of gauze from the top shelf, I turn to face Mom.

"Are you mad at me, Mia?" she says.

"Of course not," I say. I'm actually kind of thrilled she remembered my name. Not that that changes anything. "Let's rinse your hands off first."

Going over to the tap, I turn on the water and Mom holds her hands beneath it. Her flesh looks so soft and fragile. Her fingers are odd, twisted memories of their former selves. She used to do so much with them.

"Okay," I say, pulling her hands from beneath the water and drying them with paper towels. "Did the water make it feel better?" I feel stupid for asking this, like something I would ask a baby.

Mom nods, then says, "I burned a cat when I was twelve. Set it right on fire."

"Oh," I say, my eyes wide with shock from this revelation. I squeeze dabs of the ointment on each finger and rub it gently in. "Why—uh—why would you burn a cat?"

She shakes her head, looking confused. "Maybe that was a story I heard."

"Let's hope so." I bandage her fingers without saying anymore, applying tape to keep them from unraveling. Seeing each of her fingers bandaged reminds me of that guy in that movie that cut off the tips of his fingers so he wouldn't leave fingerprints. He was crazy. Mom is too, I suppose.

"The pound cake will be ready soon," she says.

There are still tears in her eyes, so I refrain from correcting her about the cake. Instead, I nod and give her a hug. Poor Mom. I lead her into the dining room, telling her I'll worry about getting the cake out. She can relax while I set the table and bring everything in. So, I do this, setting up the two dinner plates and silverware, one set in front of Mom and the other set across from her. I add a smaller plate for the carrot cake. Using oven mitts, I bring in the pot pie with a dipping spoon and place it on a trivet at the center of the table, telling Mom not to touch it, that I'll dip it out when I return. I go to the oven and turn it off and remove the carrot cake, which smells absolutely divine. Steam plumes up when I slide a cake knife into it. Taking it into the dining room, I place it on a trivet next to the pot pie.

This whole time, all I'm thinking about is how I'm going to say this to Mom. Now is the time to tell her. Over dinner is the time to do it, and after she's burned herself and claimed thieves are coming around and said other crazy stuff. Not to mention the gun. What the hell did she shoot at?

"What were you doing in the attic, Mom?" I ask, scooping pot pie onto her plate.

She looks up at me. She's been quiet the whole time I've set the table. "What?" she says.

"You must have been in the attic earlier. You have yellow paint in your hair."

Reaching up, she runs her hand through her permed gray hair, then looks at her hand, seeming confused by the bandages on her fingers. Then she looks at me. "Oh, they hide up there sometimes. In the attic. They hide up there."

I had a feeling it would be something like that. Scooping pot pie onto my plate, I say, "Who is that, Mom?"

"The thieves," she says without hesitation. "They're always watching. Waiting for me to go to sleep."

I sigh, shaking my head, then take a bite of the pot pie. It's wonderful. I knew it would be. She hasn't lost her touch in the kitchen. "Mom, there is no one watching you, unless you count me. And there is absolutely no reason to go in the attic."

"That's not true. That's just not true, Jill."

"It's Mia, Mom. And it is true. No one is watching you. And why had one of the bullets in the gun been fired? Did you shoot at..." I almost ask if she shot at *someone* but, for some reason, that's too terrifying a question to ask. "Did you shoot it?" I know the answer is yes. It has to be.

"The gun does no good—already told you that," Mom says, taking a bite of pot pie. Some of it dribbles down her lip and chin and she does nothing about it. Again, like a child. A toddler, really.

"Did-you-shoot-the-gun?"

"Well, naturally!" she yells, dropping her fork on the plate and staring at me with an anger I haven't seen since my high school days, when I could act like a little shit. "How else do you think I know it does no good against the thieves?"

Placing my elbows on the table, I put my head in my hands and groan. I'm no longer hungry. "Mom," I say, dropping my hands and glaring at her, "there are no *thieves* trying to get in here! If there were, they would have gotten in. They would have stolen something. No one is watching you or trying to steal anything from the house. You need to get that out of your head!" I might have hurt her feelings by raising my voice, but it's come to that. I don't feel bad for it.

"No," Mom says, shaking her head, then picking up her fork and taking another bite of pot pie.

"No what?"

"No, not that kind of thieves. Not trying to steal from the house. They're…" she pauses, looking at the ceiling, mulling it over as she swallows a bite of dinner, "memory thieves. They're memory thieves."

"Memory thieves?" I say, utterly perplexed. As if this evening couldn't get any stranger and concerning. Is she suggesting that some hoodlum off the street is prying open the window, then sneaking up behind her and sucking some memories from her head with a Dirt Devil? Because that's what it sounds like she's saying. Sadly, I realize, this is probably her way of coping with her memory loss. Creating a fantastical—and possibly preventable—reason for losing her memory is preferable to admitting she has dementia.

"Memory thieves," she says again and takes a big bite of pot pie. Her plate is almost clean. "They take away all kinds of memories." She's talking with her mouth full now and much of what's in her mouth isn't staying in her mouth. "And they replace memories with awful things. Such awful things."

I get up and walk around to her side of the table and clean her face off. I take her plate into the kitchen and place it in the sink, then I cut her a piece of carrot cake and put it on the smaller plate and set it in front of her. She's the child, I'm the mother. I sit back down at my spot and tentatively take another bite of pot pie, even though my hunger has long since fled.

"Mom," I say calmly, when the bite is swallowed, "I think it's time we look into placing you in a home. You know, a home for older folks. I think it might be good for you."

She's staring at the carrot cake. Hasn't picked up her fork yet.

"I mean, if you feel like there's…thieves trying to come in here and get you, maybe you'll feel safer in a home. You know?"

She slowly looks up at me. "You mean a nursing home. A *nurs-ing home.* Not a home."

"They're not that bad, Mom. They have this new facility over in Waxahachie that's actually quite nice. Spacious and lots of stuff to do. They even have a little pool, for water therapy or something. And lots of, you know, games." I feel ridiculous. It's like trying to talk a kid into going to daycare for the first time when they're perfectly happy at home. I'll have to force her to go, I know I will.

"It won't matter," Mom says, finally picking up her fork and cutting into the cake. "The memory thieves will find me there. Always do. They found me at Dr. Hanson's office. Right after the nurse took my blood pressure and left the room. They're always watching."

I don't know what to say to this. She's completely delusional. I can't have one normal conversation with her. I'll have to get power of attorney if she won't go willingly. I should probably look into that anyway. She's not of sound mind, clearly. She could hurt someone or herself. It's amazing she hasn't already. Except for maybe a cat when she was twelve. Good lord.

I cut myself a piece of carrot cake and put it on my plate. It's soft and fluffy and smells just right. I take a bite and let it melt away in my mouth. It's just like I remember. It's been years since she made carrot cake. I'll take her to look at the home in Waxahachie tomorrow. Maybe she'll like it and I won't have to get power of attorney yet. But I'm not going to tell her this tonight; she's upset enough. She's fragile, inside and out. I can see that.

"The carrot cake is great, Mom," I say, smiling at her.

"Of course, it is," she says, smiling back at me. She takes a bite then looks oddly at her bandages.

After consuming more carrot cake than I thought I would, I lead Mom into the living room and tell her to relax in her favorite chair while I clear the table and warm up some tea. I fill the kettle with water and put it on the burner on medium-high, then I put the dirty dishes in the dishwasher and put the leftovers, of which there is very little, in the fridge. As I wait for the water to boil, I scroll through my phone, checking the news and social media just to pass the time. I send Nathan a text telling him I'll be home later than I thought, and that mom is much worse than last time and that I'll explain in horrifying detail when I get home. While I'm typing up this text, Jill sends me a photo of her and her surgeon husband holding up champagne glasses, toasting the picture-taker at some fancy cocktail lounge. *Missing you!* is the message she's sent with the photo. I don't respond.

The kettle whistles. I turn off the burner and retrieve two mugs from the cabinet, the one depicting ducks flying over a picturesque lake for Mom. It's always been her favorite. I pull open the drawer beside the stove—the tea drawer. There are a variety of teas here. Green, black, chai, herbal, sleepy time, and several others. I pick two Earl Greys out of the bunch, opening them and putting one in each of our mugs. I pour the water in and steam billows up. After allowing it to steep for a few moments, I add a little tap water to Mom's, so she doesn't burn herself.

Grabbing the two mugs from the counter, I walk out of the kitchen and through the dining room, thinking of how I sat at that same table when I was five or six years old, when we moved here. It's held up well. Dad refinished it twenty years ago or so and Mom knew how to take care of things. The table still shines. I turn into the living room and freeze, my mouth and eyes both opening with wonderous terror, the two mugs of hot tea falling from my hands as I step back. In the time it takes for the mugs to leave my grip and shatter on the floor, I take in all of it.

It's tall—nearly reaching to the ceiling—and milky white, with long, whip-like arms and legs that appear free of bone, the arms sagging like a U where an elbow should be, the legs appearing to melt onto the floor like French vanilla ice cream, puddling there but not causing the thing to grow any shorter. Its head is oval-shaped and turned away from me; smooth, almost like porcelain, except with a strange liquidy reflectiveness. At the ends of its arms, where hands should be, are hundreds of thin white tentacles. Though, *tentacles* are not the right word. They're like angel hair pasta, long and flowing; some of them waving in the air like plant life on the ocean floor, most of them hovering around Mom's head, and some of them— lots of them—feed into Mom's ears and nostrils. Mom appears to be dead or sleeping—surely dead—as this thing hulks over her with its appendages slithering into her head.

The mugs of tea shatter and I realize I'm screaming. Without moving its body, the thing's head whips around— all the way around—staring at me with hollow holes that must house eyes somewhere in the depths of their darkness. There is no mouth, nose, or ears, only milky blankness. But now a new hole is appearing in the middle of its horrible head—a deep, cavernous, gawking hole—and it begins emitting a sound like wet static, and its whole body ripples with the sound.

Tears are streaming down my face, and I can't stop screaming. I stumble backward and fall on my ass, my right hand landing on one of the shards of broken mug. I barely notice. I want to get up and run; run and never stop running until I awaken from this nightmare, for that's surely what this is.

The hundreds of slithering pasta-like fingers are retracting, softening and disappearing into the arms, and the gaping, static-screaming mouth shrinks and disappears, as does the sound it was making. The strands of pasta emerge from Mom's ears and nostrils—several of them at once—and they're curled at the end, wrapped around what appear to be tiny stars, some of them twinkling like Christmas lights. These lights—*memories*, I realize—blink out and dissolve into a black pepper-like substance as they join the thing's milky body.

Now it's pulling apart and some of it is falling in clumps to the floor and some of it is rising to the ceiling, like it's lighter than air. On both the floor and ceiling, it breaks apart into even smaller pieces, becoming worm-like and slithering into cracks and crevices and beneath furniture and into the carpeted rug. On the ceiling, they slither and vanish into the AC vent and even seem to spread out, stretching themselves thin, becoming one with the ceiling. And several of the milky worms fill a hole directly above Mom's chair. It looks like a bullet hole, until it's filled.

My eyes drift back down, red and wet with tears. Mom is awake. She's looking at me.

"Jill?" she says. "Jill, what are you doing on the floor? What spilled?"

I look at the space beneath Mom's chair and at the cracks along the walls and the vents in the ceiling. I look at the bullet hole where there *is* no hole. I don't see them, but the memory thieves are watching. They're always watching.

MY LIL' CUPCAKE

LEE FRANKLIN

My Lil' Cupcake
By Lee Franklin

The headlights bounced over the road as Dave Pearson steered his 4wd with one hand, whilst he licked thick dollops of chocolate icing off his fingers. The best thing he did was quit his job as a Driving Instructor, he thought as his stomach gurgled. Well, ok he didn't quit, but who cares about technicalities. If he was still driving them uppity, cock-teasing teenage bitches, Lindsey wouldn't have taken up baking to pay the bills. And then her dreams of a cupcake empire would never be realized. With lemon butter sitting on his lips, he knew it was a win-win scenario.

His stomach rippled and gurgled. Lifting his leg up on the vinyl seat, he cranked out a screaming trumpet fart and sighed. He reached back into the sample box, with the DO NOT EAT on a fluorescent? post-it-note. Well, if she wasn't going to get up to cook him breakfast before he went fishing, he wasn't going to go hungry. His fingers crawled over the icing as he counted the remaining cupcakes. It was a thing, his thing. Everything had to be done in numerical order. You don't jump from first gear into fourth. Even Lindsey agreed and had taken to numbering her cupcakes in the sample boxes she sent out to clients.

His fingers wrapped around number three, and he rammed it into his mouth. The coffee cream icing oozing around his mouth as his teeth crunched on the gritty chunks of walnut. He shoved it down his throat, barely chewing. Oh, hell yeah! Cupcakes and fishing, this was the life.

**

The morning sun was a yellow slash across the lake that stretched to the horizon. His private fishing paradise. Well, not his technically, it was some rich bastard's holiday home, so Dave borrowed it from time to time. If you own a lake as big as a public reservoir, you should share it… right? Dave jerked his 4wd drive to a halt. He looked at the box and weighed up his options. Should he eat them now, or risk ruining them with bait fingers.

Cupcake number five was a tart, berry flavour with pink-purple icing shaped into a ribbon over its crown. Dave's stomach gurgled as he backed his boat into the water. Even though the sun had just risen, the heat clung to his skin with a damp sweat and the day promised to be a scorcher. As he climbed out of the truck, a smile crept across his lips as another howling fart tore from his ass. He'd be back before midday, just a few hours of peace.

Dave pushed the eight-foot tin dinghy into the water, slapping at the insects that honed in on the sugary sweetness on his fingers. He cursed when the insect repellent can rattled empty. Oh well, sun will be up soon and should send these blood suckers packing, he rationalized as he chucked the can back in the cab of his 4wd. He grabbed his thermos of coffee, an aluminum bottle of water and the last cupcake in the box. He considered his phone, but there was no reception anyway, so he tossed it back into the cab.

The rich perfume of apple cinnamon tickled Dave's nose.

"An apple a day keeps the Doctor away," he muttered to himself.

Covered in thick green icing, it even looked like an apple. A stick of cinnamon stuck out the top like a stalk. Yeah, '*she was a clever one, that Lindsey*' he thought, as he crammed it into his mouth. Spent too much time making them look pretty, not just making more. What was it she called herself these days, an artisan? It was that stupid new friend of hers, Robin, from the café she sold them to. That woman was a bad influence. He would have to meet her one day soon. *Maybe Lindsey was dyking up?* They spent far too much time together, if you asked Dave.

Dave climbed into the boat. Everything had been packed and refueled last night. Don't want to get the smell of gas on your hands when dealing with bait. No siree. The little outboard engine spluttered and then roared into life, churning up the water as Dave cut through across the lake toward his favourite fishing spot.

The anchor plopped into the water, sliding down into the stillness like a cotton thread. Dave sucked in a deep breath as a sharp pain twisted in his gut. He tensed and pushed to pass wind to ease the pain. The air gurgled out of his ass, wet and watery. Must have been last night's curry, certainly reeked of it. Thoughts of calling it a day crossed his mind. But the bright blue sky and quiet of the lake was like a balm to his soul. A rush of peacefulness buzzed through his body. Why let a little gas send him back to the nagging and whining?

The lake shimmered and rippled as if in agreement, the sun stretched out towards him, embracing him. His heart fluttered in his chest. A little caged bird, much like himself. He wiped at the sweat that beaded along his forehead as he pulled out his bait box. Insects buzzed around him almost lazily. Iridescent flashes of blues, greens, and reds flashed before his eyes. He gasped as the insects came into sharp focus. Wow, they were so beautiful, little armoured bodies glimmering in the sunlight. Large eyes, searching for… searching for a connection with him.

A flash of wonder spilled through Dave's body, quelling the gurgling of his stomach. The sky wasn't just blue, it was thousands of blues, violets and silvery puffs of cloud. He passed wind, and a hot squirt of liquid followed. Like he was overfilling with warmth.

Dave giggled and reached into his bait box for a worm. Its purple body squirmed between his fingers. It looked at him and smiled. Thin lips over a toothy mouth. Dave dropped the worm in shock. Its squeal of terror as it fell into the bottom of the boat clawed at Dave's eardrums. Guilt tugged at him as he scrambled around the tin deck to find it. *Poor worm*. There, he found him. He picked up the worm with care and nursed him against his chest, whispering sweet nothings to it. The worm looked at him with accusation, then with forgiveness as it snuggled into his wrist like a kitten on a pillow.

An urgent clenching in Dave's bowel snapped him out of his reverie. As he held the worm, he unbuttoned his pants and balanced his ass cheeks over the side of the boat. The exodus tore through his ring like hot lava. Gasping in agony, the boat rocked and rolled as he attempted to brace himself and not drop the worm. Dave slipped, cracking his head on the side of the dinghy, his ass leaving a smear of shit as he slid down the side of the boat, slumping in between the two bench seats.

The worm was lost and forgotten as Dave buckled over with stomach cramps, chewing on his intestines. Struggling to stand, to clear the boat of his foulness, he perched his buttocks on the lip of the boat. It was as if his bowel was firing shot gun pellets from within his lower intestine as it sprayed into the lake with a chug, chug, chug motion, shredding his anus. The boat tipped, dipping into the water. *What had he eaten?*

Sweat stung his eyes, salty rivers splashing onto his lips. He rested his head between his knees as a wave of nausea crested in his throat. In the sludge at his feet was Worm. Relief quietened his heart, for a moment. Dave blinked the sweat out of his eyes. No, not just Worm. Hundreds of worms squirming and crawling in a contortion of pink-purple bodies, reminding Dave of intestines he had once seen spill out of a pig at an abattoir.

The pink purple of a tart flavoured cupcake. Smiles wide, teeth sharp, they slithered towards him. Jagged, dagger-like fangs gleaming in the daylight as they sank into his sandaled toes. Dave's scream came in a rush of hot, sticky bile that poured like steaming acid onto the clump of fleshy worms.

The worms shrunk and shriveled, melting together like a giant wad of discarded bubblegum.

'*Poor Worm*', Dave thought as he sunk to his knees into the sludge of his shit and vomit. Another tug of his guts and unable to find the strength or will to stand, Dave squatted, waiting for the torrent of vile liquid. Instead, a wet meaty fart belched from his nether region. The stinging pain bringing tears to his eyes, his hand clutched at the sensitive piece of anatomy.

He winced as his fingers touched the flayed pieces of flesh that dangled from his body. Blood, bright red on his fingers, shimmered against the bright blue sky. Something grainy glistened amongst the shit and blood. Like sand, but coarser. Dave grunted. He needed to go… his mind couldn't wrangle with the rest of the sentence, and it floated off into the sky above him before he could grasp it. Then the image of his outboard motor singing 'Take me home, country road', played over in his mind like a bad GIF on repeat. Home. He needed to go home.

Slipping and sliding, he crawled to the rear of the boat. He gagged on the stench of his own refuse. Vomit spilling from his mouth, its acidic burn strangling his throat. Dave launched himself over the rear bench where the engine sat in silence, not singing. He had to make it sing, to take him home. Dave stared, trying to focus on the rip cord as it swam in and out of focus. He grasped it between his fingers, he tugged. Nothing. He climbed higher onto the bench, the cord slipping between his fingers. Again, a spasm rocked his body and Dave braced himself as a giant beast of fecal matter clawed its way, screaming, from his body.

He collapsed into the sludge between the benches, his cries for help lost in the gentle breeze across the water. As he had wanted, he was utterly alone. His hand fell against the aluminum water bottle. Water! The concept flickered in his mind and disappeared as a cupcake shaped silver eye appeared on the dark blue metal. It blinked before turning its attention to Dave. A red slash for a smile appeared. Silver teeth, like little axes, pushed through the slash, grinding together in excitement.

Dave screamed, and jerked himself upright, away from the beast. The chocolate coffee icing that he lay in yanked on his long golden locks. Out of the sludge came delicate frosted flowers in a mix of pastels, each gripped onto the end of his hair like bait on a line with sharp little teeth. They wriggled and squirmed, climbing up his hair by swallowing mouthfuls of it.

Dave's hands tore at the flowers, tearing them and his hair free by the handful, flinging them into the lake. The beast, just a bottle, once again. He was losing his fucking mind. Grunting and sobbing, Dave wedged himself between the benches in a sitting position, his ass burning like it had given birth to a branding iron. He gagged on the stench, his chest heaving as reflux scratched against an empty stomach. His eyes closed as he sunk into the darkness.

Slivers of blue sky peeked down at Dave as swollen, puffy eyes peeled open as wide as they could. Sunburnt skin pinched and pulled across his aching body. Blisters erupted with his movement, suppurating a yellow pus. A choking wheeze rattled over split, bleeding lips, the copper tang of blood, a slick layer on the bitter bile that coated his throat and tongue. His head throbbed like a John Bonham drum kit. One arm dragged itself out of the concrete that had half entombed him. The heat clung to his skin in a mockery of a mud bath. The stench of shit that ripped fresh through the air with his movement reminded him it was anything but.

Water! He always stashed emergency water under the rear seat. With a massive groan, he pushed himself back off the bench, his body flopping into the sludge. The aluminum water bottle dazzled like gold in the shadows. He could see it smiling at him, beckoning him. The beast was long gone and forgotten, the desperate desire for water overwhelming any residual fear.

Dave's shit-slicked hands jerked and trembled as he reached for the bottle. He fumbled it between uncoordinated fists and unscrewed the cap. Water, and he'll feel better, he reasoned. He leant his head back as he poured the life-saving elixir down his throat.

Dave gagged after the first mouthful, his hands not responding when his mind screamed at them to stop. He coughed and spluttered on the salt water as it spilled over his face. *What in the holy fuck?* Dave slipped back onto the undulating tin floor, the beautiful flashing insects swooping in closer and closer as Dave struggled to frame a coherent thought. A thought, an idea, a suspicion that sat like a prickle in the silky slipperiness of his mind. *Why was his water salted?*

He grabbed onto the question for a whole moment until a paroxysm of agony wracked his body again. He waited for the torrent of liquid, when instead, several lumps of bloodied tissue slid between his thighs in a stream of thick red blood. The world spun in a blur from bright blue sky into black.

Dave's hand slapped back into the sludge of shit and vomit, the sudden movement rocking his dinghy underneath him. Flies and insects, no longer flashing a myriad of colours, rose around him like a black veil and then settled back to their work. Their work? Dave fumbled this idea around in his mind. What work do insects do? They eat, breed, and die. Such a clear parallel to his own life. They eat! The idea jarred a spasm of energy into his wasted body. He lifted his arm again to swat them away, the thought of their hairy legs tickling his skin as they nipped and supped on his flesh. The swarm scattered and then descended with the fall of his hand.

His hand knocked against the tin sides of the dinghy. A flash of burning pain snapped his mind away from the panic. Despite being in water, the little tin boat was like a baking tray in the heat. His tongue filled his mouth like a hairy sponge as he fought back the comfort of sleep.

His skin pulled tight against his body with sunburn and dehydration. How long had he been out here? Surely, Lindsey would sound the alarm soon. He was due back after lunch. His watch was coated thick with crap. But the sun sat lower to the West. It was then he noticed several large red welts on his arm with scratch marks gouged through them. Hives? But he had eaten no shellfish. That is the only thing that caused him to break out in hives. Inspecting the shit-smeared skin, he realized how badly he had scratched himself. Something moved at the edge of one cut. Dave shivered as he poked a finger at it.

It squirmed and flicked under his touch. Insects, breeding. David's heart punched into his chest, as he struggled to draw in enough air to breathe. A feverish shiver raked up his body. Maybe he was just seeing things, like smiling worms? He peered at his arm again. A black shape stretched and pulsed under his skin. Dave pushed it back towards the opening, hoping it was like a splinter. His fingers closed on the shiny carapace as it twitched between his fingers. Dave wailed in terror and flung it out into the water.

His skin quivered as he imagined a nest of insects crawling, fornicating and laying eggs inside of him. His hands scratched down his arms as he spun around to start the motor. The world kept on swinging past him.

In his left eye, a black blot appeared. Dave's heart pounded against his chest as it grew larger and larger, blotting out the blue sky above. All weakness forgotten, he grabbed at his eye with a fecal smeared hand. The other lurched forward and tore at the ripcord with a strength he thought long gone. The engine spluttered into life and Dave's heart sung with joy.

Still blinded in one eye by a fat pulsing body, Dave revved the throttle and started steering the boat for home. The boat lunged forward and jerked to a stop, the outboard screaming in protest. The fucking anchor! Hot with frustration, Dave leant over and started tugging up the rope. He dropped it, cursing in pain as red slashes appeared on his palms and fingers. Shards of glass glimmered like diamonds as they were wedged into and encrusted onto the rope. Small, gritted grains shone in the blood, reminding Dave of his bleeding ass earlier.

Dave gaped at it in disbelief, his heart sinking in horror as he started connecting the dots. Violent diarrhea, hallucinations, salted water, and now this? This was not a coincidence; this was a plan.

Dave reached over the side of the boat and washed the blood from his hands. He splashed water on his face, trying to wash away the fatigue and fuzziness that twanged on his nerves. The water was ice compared to his body heat and too brackish to consider drinking without severe repercussions. Dave's tender ass protested at the thought. He couldn't endure anymore of that. Still, the water called to him like a siren. So, tempting to drop over the side, cool and refresh his burning body.

Dave stood on the boat, reprieve just a short dive away into the restorative waters of the lake. His hands trembled and legs buckled in weariness. There is no way he could climb back into the boat by himself. His fishing lines snagged often enough on branches and debris close to the surface. Dave was a dickhead, but he wasn't a complete fool. He shook his head. He needed to focus.

Tearing off his t-shirt, he tried to ignore the festering sores on his bulging chest and belly and the insects that swarmed around the new buffet. He tore his favourite fishing t-shirt in two and wrapped it around his hands before proceeding to pull the anchor up, avoiding the larger, jagged cuts of glass. His hands were a bloody mess, when a light bulb idea sparked in his foggy mind, he dropped the rope back into the water. *Stupid idiot!* Grabbing his fishing knife, he hacked through the rope with grim determination, sweat stinging his eyes. The normally sharpened blade, blunt. After excessive effort, the rope slipped away into the water and Dave panted in relief.

The motor fired to life again. Dave laughed in triumph as the little boat ripped across the lake.

"Daddy is coming home!" he rasped, pumping a fist in the air.

The boat ramp came into view as Dave swung the dinghy around a culvert. The engine whined in excitement. Dave's heart soared. A smile split the cracks in his lips when he saw the sun reflecting off the windscreen of his truck. The motor belched and stopped, realization not sinking in until they had glided several meters through the water in silence.

"No, no, no!" Dave pleaded with the Gods, the whine of a lone mosquito the only answer. He checked the fuel. Empty! Impossible. He refueled it the night before, like he always does. He should have hours of fuel remaining. The cupcakes, the water, the illness.

"That fucking bitch! Why?" Dave raged tears of frustration as the boat bobbed on the water some two hundred yards from the boat ramp.

Paddles! Exhausted, Dave fat-fingered the wing nuts to the brackets that secured them to the side of the boat. He raised them one at a time only to see the head of the paddle slide from the handle into the depths below. Despair overwhelmed Dave, the weight bearing down like the coming dusk. His skin felt too hot and tight. The tickle of insects sent shivers down his spine. Mosquitos droned, bombing his uncovered torso like Pearl Harbor with a savage appetite.

Dave looked at the water as it changed from shades of dark blue to an inky black as the sun sat low in the sky. He looked at the distance. His muscles weighed him down like concrete. There was no way he could swim that far, not even on a good day. Dave was dehydrated, exhausted, and his ass was bleeding fire. All he wanted to do was curl up and go to sleep.

Dave allowed his eyes to close and willed sleep to consume him.

"Just a little rest, that's all I need," he mumbled to himself. But the assault from the mosquitos and midges was relentless and his reflexive slaps on sunburnt skin, a constant flash of pain that dragged him out of sleep before he could get there. Dave curled up in the fetal position; his hot skin twitching, sheer exhaustion, and limbs that felt like melted wax, tugged on his sanity.

In the dying light, Dave again re-evaluated his situation. The breeze was pushing his boat further away from the ramp, but closer to a jutting out peak of land. Fifty yards of swimming and another two hundred on land through the scrub, he guessed. With his life jacket, he could make that. Or be stuck on his tin island of shit until it became his coffin.

Dave reached under the middle bench for the self-inflating life jacket. He tugged it on over his raw skin, his fingers trembling as he buckled it on. With limbs like dough, Dave rolled over the side of the boat and into the water with a splash. The chill of the water stole his breath, yet he was almost delirious with joy as it soothed his ravaged body.

Dave waited for the hiss of the lifejacket as the gas canisters activated by water would fill the lungs of the jacket. Nothing but the splutter of his own rasping breath. Instead, the jacket dragged him down. That fucking heartless cow! He should've known. She probably put concrete powder in it or something he raged, fumbling with the clips to release its grip on him.

Pulled under the inky void of the lake, panic and adrenalin shot through Dave's body as he tore the lifejacket free from his body and pawed his way back up to the surface. His arm flailed for the boat, but already it had drifted a few meters away. Dave tread the water, the moon dull despite the expanse of stars above him. Enough light to show him the shadow of where the land lay, and off, he swam.

The initial soothing of the water turned into an aching cold as he paddled along towards the promise of land. Terror nibbled at his mind, as flickers of movement brushed against him in the water and what he hoped was land never seemed to come closer. Pausing several times as his muscles cramped and spasmed, pure anger and hate drove him on. His feet snagged on branches, a burst of pain flared in his calf as he pushed off something solid, and doggy paddled until the mud sucked at his belly, scratching his knees and hands on the jagged rocks and twisted roots that skirted the shoreline.

Dave dragged himself shivering out of the water into the scratchy foliage of the bush. He clung to the trunk of a tree as exhaustion dragged him into the void.

Consciousness came back to Dave with the stinging bite of a mosquito, followed by a reflexive slap to the cheek. It was not yet morning, the sky a bruised purple overhead. Dave's body jerked and trembled as his eyes closed again. He shook himself and slapped himself hard again. He had to keep moving.

He crawled and stumbled through the woodlands, trusting his sense of direction because he had nothing else.

The sky lightened as the sun broke across the lake. A twenty-four-hour nightmare and it wasn't over yet as he staggered to his truck. Tears and sobs of relief racked Dave's battered body as he reached underneath the wheel arch of his tire and retrieved his key. Lindsey had dropped the ball. Or, thought he wouldn't have gotten this far.

Dave cackled with delight as he slid his weary body into the cab. He looked at the sandwiches she had made for him.

"Fuck that bitch. I know what you did to those cupcakes," he said as he dropped them out of the window. He picked up the half empty bottle of coke that had been rolling around under the seats for the last month and gulped the sickly syrup down.

He rifled through the glove box. There in a little paper packet. He smiled as he dabbed the powder onto his withered gums and licked his cracked lips. Checking his phone, he noticed the messages laced with concern from Lindsey, the anger burning in his gut.

"I'm coming home, my Lil' Cupcake, I'm coming home," he grinned, tearing up the dirt behind him as he raced down the track, the empty trailer swinging behind him.

***

Lindsey's hands gripped tight on the cloth as she wiped down the stainless-steel counter tops. The pleasant fragrance of flour and cinnamon spun in the air. She loved this place, her place, her sanctuary. No man was going to take it away from her. As she had planned with Robin, she sent a few more anxious text messages to Dave, begging him to contact her. It was almost twenty-four hours, and she would have to report him missing to the cops soon.

She swept the crumbs into her hand and dropped them into the bin. All previous ingredients, the walnuts, apple, cherry, dehydrocholic acid, peyote, ground glass, castor oil, crab oil, Ipecac, flour, butter and sugar had been incinerated two days ago. Even her favourite mortar pestle, chipped with a hammer to justify throwing it out in case of trace elements. She shouldn't have used her favourite, but it felt important to do so at the time.

Robin assured her their plan was fool proof, Lindsey wondered if she had underestimated Dave's sheer bloody mindedness. Dave was a lazy bastard, but he didn't like to lose. Neither did Robin, as he liked to remind her of that. Lindsey sighed and leaned against the workbench, surveying the tray of cupcakes in front of her. Coconut, Key Lime, Cherry, Cinnamon, Apple Pie with the Chocolate Raspberry just waiting to be iced.

All of Robin's favourites and made to his precise instructions. He would be blind to her artistic flair, as usual. Lindsey checked the clock and picked up her piping bag full of her special raspberry icing. Their apprentice Maggie would be in soon and then Lindsey would make the call to the police. An hour or so later, she will be delivering her order to Robin. Business as usual, he had explained.

The police call was non-eventful. No, she didn't know where he had gone fishing, no, he didn't normally tell her. Yes, it was unusual for him to be out of contact for this long. Yes, she would keep her phone on her and inform them immediately of any developments. The complete lack of interest and concern by the officer that took the report, was just as Robin suggested it would be. Lindsey picked up her tray and waved good-bye to Maggie who was working hard on a new flavour of icing. The sweet sugary smell was rich in the air, along with citrus tang of lemon mini cheesecakes. Yes, this was her home. She was grateful to Dave's indiscretions for pushing her to find her passion, but she wouldn't let him run it into the ground.

Despite the knot of fear in Lindsey's stomach, Robin greeted her with his exuberant personality. It was what had attracted her to him in the first place. Never able to make the time to meet him, Dave had always assumed that Robin was a woman, and that was fine with Lindsey. His blue eyes shone, as he took the tray from her. He glanced at the tray, his smile breaking into a grimace.

"I thought we agreed the chocolate raspberry was going to have chocolate icing," he threw over his shoulder and sat it in the kitchen behind. He snapped some orders at the cook and came smiling toothily into the dining room. A sliver of unease crawled down Lindsey's spine; she recognized the smile too well.

"Coffee, dear? You look awful. Problems with Dave again?" he winked.

"Actually, yes. Dave didn't come home yesterday. I had to report him missing to the police this morning," she responded on cue.

"Oh dear. How truly awful for you.," he crooned. "Breakfast is on the house this morning, my lil' Cupcake."

He continued not noticing her flinch at the pet name.

"Jonah," he barked, "Breakfast for Ms. Lindsey, her usual please. Actually, hold the butter."

He looked at Lindsey, "You've got to watch your figure you know. Don't want to end up all... doughy."

He poured her coffee and moved the sugar bowl out of her reach. "Sugar or cream, you can't have both if you are my girl, and with your secrets, you are my girl," he whispered.

Hot tears spilled down Lindsey's face.

'What was I thinking, getting involved with another asshole?'
Robin glared at her.

"You don't need to act that distraught. There is only the worthless Jonah here. Or... are you already regretting? I hate it when women cry, it is ugly and unrefined. Go to the bathroom and clean yourself up."

Ice settled into Lindsey's heart as she stood up, dabbing her nose with the napkin as she entered the toilets of the service entrance. After washing her face, Lindsey went to push back through the door, when a familiar voice froze her in her tracks.

"So, where is that murderous bitch?" Dave shouted.

"I have no idea what you mean, good man. By golly, you look a wreck. Do you need an ambulance?"

Waves of sewage filled Lindsey's nose, making her gag. She peered through the gap in the door, transfixed by the filthy, bloated wretch that stood in the cafe. Dave was bouncing on his toes and nursing a crowbar between his man boobs. He swung his head around, his long blond hair, now patches of brown, black clumps clinging to his face.

"Where's that scheming bitch, Robin? This is Robin's Cafe, isn't it? Lindsey left a message saying that I would find her here this morning." he growled.

"I am Robin," he huffed in indignation, his nose crinkled in disgust at the sight before him.

"But you're a bloke. Robin is a girl's name." Dave answered, subconsciously gouging his nails into his skin, tearing at the weeping wounds.

"I assure you; it is used for both genders. Remember Batman and Robin?"

"I don't give a fuck. I thought it was bad Lindsey was leaving me for a woman. But you? That is just depressing," Dave's face crumpled into a grimace as he released a trumpet of wind. He grabbed at his ass, blood seeping through his shorts.

"How dare you? Now, unless you want an ambulance you must leave this establishment" Robin shouted, followed by the sound of broken glass.

Lindsey snuck quietly out of the service hall and into the adjoining kitchen, grabbing the fire axe in a tea-towel on her way. She put her fingers to her lips to hush Jonah and waved him over.

"Light a candle in the cupcake" she whispered and swung the axe at the main gas pipe. It split open with a hiss. Plates, glasses and insults continued to fly across the dining room as the two men raged at each other. Jonah nodded; curiosity pasted across his face. She took his hand and dragged him out the back of the cafe into the parking lot as she called the police on her phone.

"Dave did this, he slipped in the entrance, threatened you with the axe. I slipped out of the toilet behind you. You tried to warn Robin, but he wouldn't listen. Then they started fighting. We slipped out the back." Jonah nodded mutely. The blast shook the cafe and blew Lindsey and Jonah off their feet into the dirt.

"What did you do, Lindsey?" Jonah asked, his face twisted in terror.

"I took my life back. I have a job for you, and I'll treat you much better than Robin ever did. Both of them are parasites. No one better call me 'Their lil' Cupcake' ever again," she said, enjoying the searing heat from the raspberry jelly gelatin.

JUST A LOCAL THING

KENZIE JENNINGS

Just A Local Thing

By Kenzie Jennings

It was the smell they noticed first. The owners, the Davidsons, had attempted a beachy ambience, even though the nearest beach was a good seventy miles away. There were coconut and suntan lotion-scented candles meticulously placed around all of the rooms, even in the master bathroom on the windowsill by the jetted tub. However, the pleasant tang of the better smells of the beach couldn't really mask the sour-smoky stench of mold and cigarettes that pervaded the condo.

Odie—short for Odette, also known as Lady Odetta Prinssetta for reasons obvious only to the Raney family—crinkled her nose as she flitted about the common spaces, opening, and closing cabinets and drawers.

"It stinks bad here," she said from the open kitchen, just before she slammed the refrigerator door shut.

"Lady Odie P., we don't slam doors. There are other guests in the building." Kat was having none of the attitude while on vacation. "Help me with these. We'll be making supper in a little while," she said. She put the groceries away, setting out everything needed for the spaghetti dinner they'd all agreed on during the long car ride over.

But Odie was already off somewhere down the hall, exploring the other rooms. It was supposed to be a two bedroom, two-bathroom place, as they'd wanted her to have her own bathroom for a change, the big part of the tween-growing-into-a-teen life of a girl who needed her privacy. They never normally had separate bathrooms while on vacation, so Kat knew it would be a welcome change for the royal one.

Del had finally made it in, plonking down their suitcases with a giant huff. The thunk echoed throughout the condo, startling Kat. She peeked around the corner of the kitchen only to catch her husband bent over, his hands braced on his knees, his broad back heaving with each gasp of air. She took a couple of steps towards him, but he held out a finger, signaling her to wait. Del made a show of stretching and bending his back, then twisting his torso this way and that.

"You okay there?"

"I tell you I am so goddamned out of shape. Wasn't there supposed to be a *working* elevator?" he said, as he dragged in the suitcases. "Odie! Come get your suitcase! I'm not your porter!" He then made a face in Kat's direction. "Smells funky in here."

"I think they were going for upscale beach resort, but it's more like local yokel motor lodge."

Del chuckled, picking up the heaviest of the suitcases and heading in the direction of the hall. "Coconut, check. Cigarettes, check. Mold, yup. What's that other smell? Is that—?" He turned back around to look at Kat, his face pinched in disgust.

Kat nodded. "Eau de Booty Call."

"Now that's just nasty," he said over his shoulder as he made his way down the hall, peeking into each room as he did. He stopped in front of a doorway and snapped his fingers, working to get his daughter's attention. "No, ma'am. No earbuds when we're talking to you. Go get your bag like I said."

Odie grumbled something Kat couldn't quite catch, but if her daughter was following her usual script, it would go something like "I shouldn't have to do *anything*. We're on *vacation*!"

And like the reliable preteen drama queen she was, she came tromping out of her room to get her suitcase, passing her mother as she did. "You know, I heard you, Mom," she said as she made a show out of pulling the handle out so she could wheel her suitcase to her room. "Eau de Booty Call. You mean sex!" Odie said with a smirk, as she flounced by her mother, rolling her suitcase behind her as she did.

Before Kat could retort, Odie had already slammed her bedroom door shut behind her. Kat rolled her eyes in exasperation at her husband, who shook his head at her, chortling, before he brought the suitcases into the master bedroom, leaving Kat to put the rest of the groceries away.

But not before she sprayed the entire living room and kitchen in a cloud of Lysol and then opened the balcony sliding door to let the muggy air in. After all, they couldn't possibly enjoy a spaghetti dinner with the lingering odor of stale smoke and funk in the air.

***

After dinner and a round of Scrabble, they took an evening stroll downtown to check out the immediate area, or "get a sense of the locals," as Del put it. He was the kind of guy who preferred to shop and eat at local places rather than at any of the chains. Kat didn't care one way or the other. Sometimes, in fact, she preferred the reliability of the chain restaurants and stores. There were no surprises with chains, and she liked that. If you had an issue, you'd call corporate, and that was that. With local places, you were dealing with people who knew people who knew people, and everyone around seemed *too* aware of you while you were visiting.

Their condo complex was only a couple of blocks from the town center, one of the reasons why Kat picked the place (the second reason, arguably the most important to Odie, was that the rental website promised a twice-daily shuttle to most of the theme parks). If she had to shop locally, she'd much prefer the easygoing busyness of an old-fashioned town center than some pit in the middle of Hicksville.

And the downtown there was adorable, and bustling somewhat with other tourists, just enough of them to keep Kat from feeling uncomfortably out of place. The shops were open, and the restaurants all boasted sidewalk seating to give the place that not-quite-indoors-not-quite-outdoors vibe that the area boasted, and Kat enjoyed. They were barely on the Main Street sidewalk when Odie had already found "her" place; the Sunny Day Baking Company, with its green and pink striped awning and display of deliciousness in the windows, everything from buttery loaves of Brioche to alligator-shaped sugar cookies decorated in the bakery's signature pink and green colored icing.

Before Kat could say anything, Odie had promptly ditched her parents, disappearing into the bakery. Kat turned to her husband, who had a dreamy look on his face as he ogled the display in the window.

"We should get breakfast for tomorrow," Del said to no one in particular, even though it was more than likely he was addressing Kat. "Smells like grandma's place up in Ashland."

Kat let out a deep sigh, one that was supposed to signal her husband of fifteen years that she didn't like the idea, but she'd tolerate it only because she was outnumbered. They'd agreed weeks ago to limit the sweets during the trip because the detoxing from the last vacation had been a hard stomachache of a lesson learned.

"We're gonna be here for the next four days. Couldn't hurt to have a routine." Del shrugged in Kat's direction. "Just sayin'."

"We'll be working it off when we get back, you know." Kat returned the shrug with a sly smirk. "Just sayin'."

Del ushered Kat inside, and they joined their daughter at the bakery counter. Odie already had the teenaged girl, 'Haylee' according to the nametag, at the counter filling a box with goodies. Haylee looked like she hadn't even indulged once in the goods she was selling; she was so gaunt and grey. The only spark of life about her was in her eyes that seemed to do all the emotive work for her.

"This your mom an' dad?" Haylee offered what Kat supposed was a half-attempt at a friendly smile, but it came out all wrong as if the corners of her mouth had been tugged with invisible wires.

"We are, but she won't admit it to strangers. It's like we're not even here half the time," said Kat, who had joined Odie in perusing the sweets on display.

It was an odd assortment there behind the glass, almost everything locally themed. There were chocolate covered key lime pie slices on popsicle sticks ("Local key lime pops!" shouted the pink and green sign), alligator shaped cookies, summer fruit tarts, croissants, cupcakes topped in pink and green frosting and gummy alligators, cream-filled pastries, and perhaps the strangest item acting as a centerpiece—a giant alligator shaped loaf of glossy sweet bread complete with a doughy, little naked man caught in its jaws.

Odie suddenly shrieked with laughter, the ring of it echoing throughout the little bakery. "Oh, my God, Mom, look! He's got balls and a dick!"

Unfortunately, there was nowhere in the little bakery for Kat to hide from the kind of embarrassment reserved for parents who knew perfectly well where their kids learned such cutesy slang terms like "dick" and "balls." While Del and Haylee exchanged a snicker, Kat nudged her daughter who was still loudly chortling over the sight of the Brioche shaped into a naked Florida man.

"Can we *not* say things like that in public?" Kat said.

Either Kat's tight-lipped expression worked, or Odie had simply lost interest, her focus on the pastel-colored cupcakes on display.

"You want him? You get Poincy, he comes free. We make a local thing like that every mornin'," Haylee said in Kat's direction. She was still leering at Del though, which was starting to unnerve Kat. She knew her husband was a handsome man, and she usually accepted it and all the guaranteed baggage it came with, stares and everything else. However, there was a time limit to the staring until it reached the point it became full of obvious intent.

"Poincy?" Del asked. Luckily, he seemed oblivious, but he often did.

"The gator. He's named after one of our locals here. Can't miss 'im. You'll know what I mean when you see 'im. Everyone says we get the details just right. Even put us in the paper a few times." Haylee nodded in the direction of the framed news clippings beside the door.

At last, Odie had another distraction. "Do you guys have lots of alligators here?"

But Haylee ignored the question, instead, focusing all of her attention on Del because that's just how it was with any woman of any age encountering the Raney family man. "You want anything else? I got room here for a couple more items, an' I'll throw in a gator roll free."

"Yeah, how about one of those cupcakes for the lady of the house," Del said with a shrug in Kat's direction.

"Only if she apologizes for her language." Kat wasn't about to let it go. Before Del could protest, Kat shook her head at him. "She can't get the idea that that's okay, Del. It's not, and I mean it."

Odie was instantly at her mother's side, her eyes glued to the rainbow-frosted prize. "I'm sorry! I'm so sorry I said 'dick' and 'balls.' I will never say that again, ever. I promise!"

"You just did," said Del, trying hard not to chuckle.

"Wait, that didn't count though!" She turned to Kat. "Mom! That didn't count, right?"

That sort of thing was going to carry on all evening. It was just inevitable. And of course, it did.

***

Sitting around the wicker table on the balcony, they'd dug into the sweets just after dinner. Del had made the decaf with a touch of cinnamon cream just the way Kat liked it. It was his way of smoothing over any of the residual jealous edge she had left after the innocent, idle flirtation Del had known was going on but had pretended to ignore. He couldn't help it, and if she'd not been around, he probably would've flirted right back. It never hurt anyone, really, anyway, and it wasn't as if his wife hadn't had her share of young men checking her out. She was a damned fine woman who'd grow into old age looking eternally in her 40s at most.

Del had barely settled back into his chair beside Kat when Odie suddenly bolted up from her seat, gooey remnants of unicorn cupcake in hand, and gawked at the flurry of action and sound happening over by the complex's pool several stories below. "Ohmygod! What is THAT?" The last of Odie's cupcake fell from her hand over the balcony, landing with a pastel-coated slap to the sidewalk below.

The noise coming from the pool was enough to startle some of other residents of the complex as well who'd come out of their air-conditioned vacation sanctuaries to see what was happening. Del and Kat joined Odie at the railing to see what the commotion was.

An enormous alligator, at least 12 feet long and looking much like a damned dinosaur out of a movie, held a chubby, fish belly-pale naked guy in its powerful jaws. It had dragged the flailing, howling man into the pool, causing everyone who had been using the pool, or had been sunbathing in chairs nearby, to scatter, scooping up their towels and pool gear, screaming and hollering as they did.

Before Kat could say a word, Del had his cell out and was already dialing. He put the phone up to his ear and held a finger up at Kat and Odie who'd turned in his direction, panic in their eyes. Kat held her daughter tightly to her, as if several floors up, they were still in peril, even if logic showed otherwise. As it turned out, there had been no need to call 911 whatsoever. The police, EMTs, and wildlife control were already on their way. Every other person who'd been watching the horrifying scene unfold had done exactly the same thing.

Meanwhile, the alligator had the poor guy in a death roll, flipping his body around and around in the pool, splashing pool water every which way. The man had finally stopped screaming at least.

"I think it's safe to say we've just met Poincy," Kat said, her voice barely a squeak of sound.

Del slowly nodded. "Those details down to a T."

"Right down to the dick and balls," murmured Kat.

"MOM!" Odie spun to gape at her mother. "We don't say things like that in public!"

***

Kat didn't sleep much that night. Her heart pounded loudly in her ears, and her mouth had gone chalk dry. She couldn't understand how her husband could just sleep so soundly there beside her, snoring away, like what they'd actually seen hadn't happened at all. She could still hear the man's gurgles and frantic splashing coming from the pool.

She could still see the blood spreading, blanketing the pool water.

Kat and Del had their first vacation argument that night right before they'd gone to bed, which was another reason why Kat wasn't sleeping. During their last session, their couple's therapist had warned them about fighting before bedtime, and they'd been doing so well since then, talking through their issues rather than blaming the other on them.

This time though, Kat thought she'd been reasonable enough in her demands for them to leave. Del, on the other hand, wasn't having any of it.

"We got a good deal on this place," he'd said around a mouth filled with a pasty mixture of water and toothpaste. He'd spat the contents into the sink, wiped his

247

mouth with a hand towel and faced his wife, who was in the process of slathering on her night cream. "We can't let something like…*that*…keep us from having a good time. And where are we gonna stay at the same price? Places are booked solid now."

"It was an *alligator attack*," she reminded him. "We just watched a giant alligator kill a man…right there…in real time. Right there, Del."

"And wildlife rescue and the EMTs took care of it. That guy was probably messin' around with the nest."

"Listen to you! You and everyone else, all acting like it's just a thing that happens around here, like it was nothing. We can't let Odie see something like that again, Del. That was fucking terrifying."

"Let's just sleep on it, baby. I dunno. Maybe we can call the Davidsons tomorrow if we're still on the fence here."

"*I* am not 'on the fence.' This wasn't part of the agreement we signed."

"What, you think they're gonna advertise a giant alligator roaming the place on the website?"

"When there's a bakery downtown that makes a bread version of what we saw, it should be on the goddamn website. Like it's a cute, local thing that just… *happens*."

Del had laughed at that, but Kat had started to boil. "It's not funny, Del. We're calling them tomorrow to see about a refund."

"Okay, baby, we'll do that, and we'll see if they know of another place around. We're still going to the waterpark tomorrow though, right?" he said as he tried to pull her into an embrace, but she pried herself away and padded back into the bedroom, cold shoulder more than a little evident. "We can't disappoint Lady Odie. This was all about keeping her happy, remember."

"We'll talk more tomorrow," Kat muttered over her shoulder. "We are *not* done here."

And no matter how many times Kat replayed the scene in her head and heard their argument in her thoughts, she still couldn't shake the creeping dread that a giant alligator eating people there was simply a cute, local thing that just...*happens.*

***

Haylee, seeming paler and thinner than the day before, confirmed what the Raneys had witnessed as she filled another box with goodies for them the following evening. "Yeah, normally Poincy doesn't take his food to any of the pools around here. Too many folks around. He's a lakeside kinda guy that likes his privacy."

"What are they gonna do with him?" Del asked. He looked over at Kat, to see if she had pulled her attention away from the strange display behind the glass, but she hadn't yet.

"Oh, he's protected by the feds. American gators are classified as a 'threatened' species, so our boy's gonna be just fine. Can't say anything about his food though."

"What, they normally eat *people*?"

"Oh, no-no," she said, shaking her head with a chuckle. Then she lowered her voice. "That's just Poincy. Only a local thing. You know what I mean."

"No, we really don't. We have shootings, car accidents, things like that. Never an alligator attack. We don't have alligators where we're from."

Haylee grinned at him, a skull's leer that chilled Del to the bone. "There ain't anywhere that has somethin' quite like our boy Poincy."

Del turned to Kat who had rested her head against the glass, her gaze still homed in on the display. There wasn't much of a selection in the evening at any good bakery, but the Sunny Day Bakery seemed to at least keep some of the popular items baked fresh…

…and that included the huge, glossy brioche centerpiece. Instead of a doughy rendition of the local monster alligator-and-dinner, however, it was of a wild-haired, bug-eyed man with an unhinged jaw tearing off the face of another man covered in red-dyed icing splatter. The details were uncanny if one were looking at the centerpiece from a distance. Up close though, Del could see the cracks in the shiny, buttery crust and the fluffy white of the bread.

"It looks like he's eating a guy's face off," Odie pointedly remarked, as if it needed to be said aloud. "That's SO gross!"

"That's just local lore," said Haylee. "We had a student here awhile back, out doing spring break with his friends on the lakes. Got all crazy on bath salts. Had hisself a snack." She embellished the last word with a wet, lip-smacking noise that had Odie tittering.

But Del wasn't paying much attention to anything in the moment other than his wife who was still leaning against the glass and staring at the centerpiece there, breathing heavily as she did.

"Hey, baby, you okay?" He gave her a slight nudge, hoping to break her from the bizarre trance she was in.

It worked. Kat shook her head, blinking as if she'd just woken up from a deep sleep and was unsure as to where she was and how she got there. She turned to Del, a frown twisted there on her face.

"Did you pick anything?" she asked.

"You already ordered," he said, returning her frown with a confused one of his own. "Remember?"

Kat looked down at her daughter who was staring at her with wide eyes. "Did you get anything, Lady Odie P? You pick out something?"

"Yeah, Mom. I got a cupcake and a sticky bun. You *said* I could!"

"Are you alright?" Del couldn't shake the worry out of his tone, and that was worrisome in itself.

"Yeah, why?"

Del exchanged a look with Odie. "It was like you were in a daze there for a moment, like you were spacing out."

She managed a smile. "No, I'm fine." Kat turned back to Haylee who was still holding the box of goodies in one hand and the tongs in the other. "I think that'll be it. Thank you."

Haylee's grin had widened again, her eyes glinting. "You got room for one more item, if ya wanna."

Kat froze up when she met Haylee's gaze. Something shifted there between them. Del wasn't sure what it was, but it was certainly unsettling and chilly.

"No, thanks, that will be all," Kat said curtly.

"Oh, come on. I'll put one in on the house." Haylee's expression had softened. "Somethin' with sprinkles." She aimed that directly at Odie who nodded in agreement. Something *definitely* with sprinkles.

Before Kat could protest, Haylee had opened the case's sliding door and was making a show of selecting and taking out a unicorn bun that had been set directly beside the grotesque centerpiece. She beamed at Odie as she placed it in the space in the box and then taped up the box with the shop's signature sticker.

"What do you say, Lady O?" Del nudged Odie to the side.

"Thanks a lot!" Odie grinned at Haylee. "It looks scrump-delicious!"

Haylee winked at Odie. "Save it for after supper. Gotta eat everything on your plate first. Ain't that right, Mama?" She aimed that one specifically at Kat, the light in her eyes shutting off.

Only Kat seemed to have caught it. She felt as if her breath had lodged in her throat. It wasn't just the blatant defiance on Haylee's part. It was the flat expression in Haylee's eyes combined with the girl's crooked smile...

...that leer filled with two rows of sharp, yellow teeth. Lots of teeth.

Much like an alligator.

"You have yourselves a good evenin', folks. Hope to see ya again tomorrow!" Haylee said, with a wink at Kat.

But Kat would do her damnedest not to return.

***

It was Odie who first met their new roommate when they got back to the condo.

She'd bounded straight to the hall bathroom—*her* bathroom—as soon as they'd entered, and then she'd promptly screamed, an earsplitting sound that shook the walls of their little haven.

Both Del and Kat ran down the hall to the bathroom just as Odie turned right into them. The girl buried her head against her mother's shoulder. Her body trembled in Kat's embrace.

The young man who was sitting cross-legged there in the bathtub couldn't have been more than twenty. His wild eyes might have been grey once but were no longer any discernable color but red due to the broken capillaries worming throughout. His short brown hair had formed sticky peaks, creating a slapdash faux hawk.

And he was completely naked, his tanned skin splattered in gore. A meaty mass of flesh and bones, what once might have been a man, was congealing in his lap.

Apparently, the Raneys had interrupted his meal when they showed up. He'd been chewing on a large, oval slice of skin in his hands.

The slice of skin had eyeholes… and a nose…and a pair of full lips still attached.

Once Kat had joined her daughter in screaming, the young man in the tub had resumed chewing on that delicious slice of meaty goodness.

***

"I've given them both a sedative to take tonight, so that should help some." The EMT was young but experienced enough that the sight of the horror show in the bathtub didn't seem to faze her. She had sat down beside Del on the living room sofa, once she'd worked with the police and her colleagues to pull the writhing, wiggling, gore-streaked man from the tub, and get him into the ambulance.

In the course of an evening, Del had become a hollow husk of man, sitting there on the sofa, elbows on his knees, his head in his hands. He rubbed at his eyes and then slumped against the cushioned back of the sofa.

"We gotta stay here," he muttered. "There's no place else. I've checked every goddamned hotel, every Airbnb. Every single place around is booked for the entire month."

"Yeah, that's summer here. I'm so sorry. Were you able to get a flight out tomorrow at least?"

"Got a 1pm flight. There's some hope in that, I suppose. Would've had one earlier, but it's limited seating everywhere."

"Well, that's something. I advise you to stay put. Don't go anywhere if you don't have to, between now and a couple of hours before your flight."

"Wasn't planning on it. We're all sleeping in the master bedroom for the night. Gonna use the bathroom in there, too." He shuddered at just the very thought of the bathroom.

"That's a solid plan. I asked the officer on duty if they could spare someone to keep an eye on the place just for peace of mind. He said there'll be a patrol car in the area."

"What, they can't send someone to guard the place? Just someone to sit outside?"

"No, they're stretched pretty thin right now. Everyone's on vacation here, and that means lots of drinking and partying. You know how it goes."

Del turned to face the EMT, worry lining his haggard face. "Tell me again how it goes when some crazy motherfucker breaks into your condo and eats a guy in your tub. Think that's normal? Think *that* deserves some police assistance?"

"I know. I wish there was something else they can do, but, Mr. Raney, you need to keep something in mind about all this…"

"Keep what in mind?"

When the EMT smiled sheepishly at him, there was something so creepy…something so damned *familiar*…about her grin.

"When stuff like that happens around here, it's just a local thing," she said.

***

"So, what brings you here at this hour, Mrs. Raney?"

Kat blinked in the direction of the question. The formality behind it was strange, its speaker's voice so calm and gentle, soothing even.

The figure came into focus. It was Haylee, or at least an attractive facsimile of Haylee. She had filled out, her fresh curves stretching the pink pinstriped shirtdress she wore as a uniform in all the right places. Her skin glowed, rosy-ripe with health. Even her hair had grown lustrous and thick curling over her shoulders and framing her sunny face.

"It's early, Mrs. Raney. You should probably go back to bed," Haylee said softly. She had stopped filling the display case long enough to catch Kat's befuddled expression.

Kat glanced up at the retro cat clock over the door to the bakery. Its mechanical eyes clicked back and forth, back and forth, and then rolled downwards to stare directly at Kat.

It was 4:35 in the morning. Quite early. The world outside seemed dark and endless.

And Kat had absolutely no idea what she was doing there... or how she even got there.

Had she *sleepwalked*?

"Well, since you're here," Haylee said, returning to the display case, "you may as well take a look at this one. I think it's my best, but I know I shouldn't get cocky about it. I know I can always make it pop with icing and candy, but only after some customer feedback." She switched on the backlight of the display case. "Ta-da! What do you think?"

But Kat couldn't form any words, her voice caught in a web in her throat. She had already been sucked right into the stark void, the whirling, shifting black centerpiece behind the glass. The cupcakes, pie pops, and pastries that surrounded it merely acted as a cartoonishly colorful frame against the spinning nothingness there. Kat felt the void's pull deep within her, the brittle coldness there threatening to rip her insides apart.

There was a sudden, loud cracking sound coming from somewhere in town, like a forest had been struck by lightning, the trees snapping one by one. The noise jolted Kat, causing her to look back around and glance out the windows overlooking the darkness outside.

Haylee chuckled into her palm. "You need to go back, Mrs. Raney," she said in between giggles. "You don't want to miss it."

Kat turned, facing Haylee. "Miss what?"

"Oh, you know.... just a local thing."

***

She returned only to discover the condo building where her family had been staying was just...no longer there. It had been sucked into the yawning mouth of a sinkhole that had formed directly underneath it. Firefighters, police personnel, and a search and rescue brigade had already congregated around the gaping hole.

Some of the neighboring vacationers had formed little clusters, whispering their concern amongst themselves, shaking their heads at the latest disaster, the very thought of it.

A local thing.

Kat wandered away from the scene, having shrugged off the emergency workers who'd reached out and had tried to get her to talk to them. What was the point?

"Fucking local bullshit," Kat muttered.

She found herself in the complex's parking lot that was teeming with fire trucks and police cars. She fumbled around in her pajama pants pocket, realizing then she wasn't carrying the rental car keys. Just the realization alone was enough to snap her awake from what had felt like the drugged coma-haze of a deep sleep.

A dirty, hairy hand clamped on her shoulder, squeezing it tightly.

Kat spun around, her eyes wide, right as the naked, laughing man with a mouth filled with jagged alligator teeth yanked her in close to tear out a big chunk of her face.

Meaty goodness, after all, was just another local thing.

OF DOUGH AND CINNAMON

DANIEL VOLPE

Of Dough and Cinnamon
By Daniel Volpe

Friedman's bakery smelled like heaven on earth. Fresh bread, and pastries, the rugelach was Sarah's specialty, steamed in their respective bins. It was still early, just after 4 am, but the store would be opening soon, letting the bustling Brooklyn crowds in for their breakfast.

Dov Friedman carried a tray of fresh bagels in his arms. The display case was closed on his side, and he couldn't seem to nudge it open with his knee.

"Sarah," Dov said, calling for his daughter.

Sarah came out from the small kitchen. Her curly, black hair was tied back in a red bandana, and there was a dusting of flour on her apron.

Dov nodded towards the display door, which was shut.

Sarah slid in front of her father and opened the door, holding it so he could slide the bagels into the basket. He set the tray on the counter.

"Thank you," Dov said, pulling a handkerchief from his back pocket to wipe his head. Even though it was early in the morning, the temperature was nearing 80 degrees already. The addition of the ovens running at full blast didn't help. When it was 5 am, Dov would open the front door and keep it propped, hoping to get a slight cross breeze in his little bakery.

Sarah closed the door on the case. "Anything else? I need to finish the cinnamon rugelach and get them in the oven."

Dov took a seat at the stool behind the counter. It was a family heirloom, a piece of furniture used by his father and grandfather when they'd first opened the bakery. Long dead, the patriarchs of the Friedman family created a well-known and respected establishment. Dov did everything he could to keep it open.

"No, I have a few more trays of bagels, but I'll wait for a few minutes before finishing them up." He checked his watch. "I'll finish them soon so they're hot when the doors open."

"Ok," Sarah said, walking back into the kitchen.

Dov watched her go, the door swinging shut behind her. Every day she got a little older, just turning 21 the week before. And every day, she looked more and more like her mother. Dov took a deep breath, willing the tears away that seemed to arrive every time he thought of his late wife.

6 years prior, Chana, his wife of 32 years, was diagnosed with breast cancer. She was a strong woman, salt of the earth, but the vile disease gave her no quarter. Within 8 months of diagnosis, Chana was dead. It rained on the day of her funeral. Even the skies wept when she passed

from the realm of the living and into the arms of her God. Dov crumbled, like old bread. His world had been crippled and if it weren't for Sarah, he would have withered away to nothing.

Sarah.

She was the reason he was still breathing. She was the reason *Friedman's* was still open and producing some of the best baked goods in all of the city. Sarah was the glue that held him together. Now, she was the last thing he had left in the world. His parents were both many years dead and his only brother was killed in a car accident as a teenager. It was only Dov, Sarah, and the bakery.

Dov looked at the city streets, which were starting to glow with the rising of the early morning sun. He checked his watch again, realizing nearly a half-hour had passed since he'd sat down. His reverie had robbed him of precious time, but filled his mind with happier ones, followed by sad ones. He stood, listening to the many creaks and pops his body made. One hand went to his aching back and other to the counter, providing him with balance. He was only 56, but he felt like a man in his 80s.

Sarah came out of the door with a tray of assorted pastries, fresh and steaming. She was just in time because the clock above the door was minutes away from 5 am.

"I took care of the last trays of bagels, Dad," Sarah said, loading the pastries into the case.

Dov watched, admiring her. She finished and turned, shocked to find her father standing inches away.

"You know, Sarah, without you I don't know what I would've done." He rubbed her arms. The tears he'd chased away prior were returning, a whirlwind of emotion settling on him.

Sarah could see the mist forming in her father's tired eyes. She held the tray in one hand and wrapped him in a tight embrace. Every time she hugged him; she was shocked at how thin he'd become. He felt more and more brittle every day, a shadow of the strong, stout man he once was.

Dov held his daughter, breathing the scent of her. It was all her, but in the recess of his brain, he could smell the ghost of Chana.

Tapping on the front window broke their teary-eyed hug.

Dov turned and looked at the door, noticing the clock above showed it was 5:05.

"Damn," he said, walking around the counter to unlock the door. Dov pulled it open and saw his first customer of the day.

"Oy, I thought you forgot about me," Ezra Rywski said as he walked into the bakery, his cane supporting him.

Dov smiled at his old friend and long-time customer.

"Forget about you? My best customer and family friend? Never," Dov laughed, patting the old man on the back. If Dov was brittle than Ezra was downright frail.

Ezra was 90 years old, but still did it all. He lived alone, was widowed for nearly 40 years, and never had children. During World War 2 (he always called it 'the war' as if there were never any other ones) his family had been killed or lost. After he'd fled to America, he'd received a letter from his brother, Josef, but that was it. No follow-up and no more contact.

Sarah came from around the counter wiping her hands on her already stained apron.

"Mr. Rywski," she said, kissing the old man on his smooth cheek. "How nice to see you."

Ezra smiled. Every day they played this game and every day he looked forward to it.

"Please, Sarah, I've known you since you were a pink, little thing. Call me Ezra." Again, he'd tell her this every morning, but still she never listened.

"Sure thing, Mr. Rywski," she smirked, walking behind the counter and plucking a couple of rugelach out. She put them on a plate and brought them out to him.

"Thank you," Ezra pulled out a chair at one of the small tables as Sarah set the plate down.

"Coffee this morning?" Sarah asked. A stray curl of hair had sprung free and sat just above her brown eyes.

Ezra rubbed his stomach. "No, I'll have a very light tea."

Sarah grabbed his drink and just in time; the morning rush had arrived.

***

Summertime in New York City saw a massive influx of tourists, but that was mainly reserved for Manhattan. The small corner of Brooklyn where *Friedman's* was, wasn't much of a tourist locale. It was old school, full of families that fled the Nazis or left the old countries before Adolf's reign of terror. Either way, the people of the neighborhood were always on the quest for something better, to help the next generation. Some even left for good, but most would come back.

A trio of those who made their way home walked through the door of the bakery as Sarah was wiping down the coffee station. It was almost noon, closing time.

"Sarah Friedman," a voice said from behind.

Sarah noticed customers enter, but paid them no mind, figuring they would go to the counter and wait. She stopped cleaning and turned.

Ari Kohn, Lieb Blau, and David Taub stood behind Sarah.

It was Ari who spoke, but his eyes were doing the talking now. He looked Sarah up and down, lingering on her breasts, which were tight against her apron.

Reflexively, she crossed her arms and looked away.

"Oh, hi Ari," she said, still not wanting to look at the young man.

"What are we, chopped liver?" David said, in a joking, yet serious tone. He smacked Lieb, getting his attention.

"Yeah, we just wanted to drop in and grab a few loaves, if you have any left," Ari said, looking towards the display cases. "My mother is having a little get-together, you know, to welcome us all home from college."

Sarah smiled, the most forced smile of her life. The bakery was her legacy, but she always yearned for more. College, maybe, but to leave her small section of the city, to see the world, to learn, to love, to experience life. No, that was being wasted on the three miscreants in front of her.

"Sure, we have a few left," she turned and began walking towards the counter. A hand grabbed her ass, squeezing it. "Hey!" she said, turning around. It was David who was pulling his hand back, a wry grin on his face. "Don't touch me."

David put his hands up in mock surrender. "Sorry, you had something on your pants. I was just trying to help." His lie was so thinly veiled, a blind man could see through it, but they were there to buy, and their money was green. "Jeez, next time I'll let you walk around with it."

Sarah stilled her temper, taking a deep breath.

"Is there a problem out here?" Dov asked as he walked out of the kitchen. He was drying his hands on a towel, but his eyes were locked on the three young men.

"No, Mr. Friedman. We were just picking up a few loaves of bread for dinner." Ari looked at Sarah, "and catching up with Sarah. That's all." He had the glare of a viper and a tongue of poison.

Dov watched them as Sarah walked back behind the counter. He shuffled up to the display case and grabbed a few loaves of bread. His hands were shaking, and Sarah moved close to him.

"It's ok," she said, touching his back. "I'm fine."

Dov licked his lips, took a deep breath, and bagged the bread.

"That'll be $6, boys." Dov set the bag on the counter and rang them up.

"Six bucks for day-old bread?" Ari complained but still pulled out his wallet. "I thought day old was half price?"

He was right, of course, but their attitude and downright disrespect for Sarah warranted a full-price transaction.

"Sorry boys, bills to pay," Dov said, laughing inside. These 'kids' had more money in their trust funds than 3 generations of his family had combined. They were the last ones who should be complaining about money. Dov took the money and dropped it into the register.

Ari grabbed the bag and looked at Sarah. "There's a party tonight," he smiled, showing off his expensive dental work. "It's in the backroom over at *Rush*, but I can put you on the list if you're interested.

Sarah looked at him and did little to hide her disdain and disgust. "No, thanks, I already have plans," she said, taking out her towel and wiping down the already clean doors of the display case. That was it, conversation over.

Ari sneered. "Fine. We'll see you around." He turned and walked out the door, David and Lieb in tow.

***

Within an hour the bakery was clean and the next day's prep work was finished. Sarah tied the laundry bag tight and left it by the back door for the late-night linen service.

"So, what are your plans tonight?" Dov asked, flipping off the lights in the kitchen as they walked out.

Sarah shouldered her purse, checking her cell phone.

"Well, Denise and Carol wanted to go to the village to see a comedy show. I was thinking about catching the bus and heading there."

Sarah watched her father deflate. It was her curse; stay home and be miserable, watching game shows with her father until he fell asleep in front of the TV, or upset him by leaving for the night. She wasn't his wife; she was his 21-year-old daughter with a life of her own.

Dov forced a smile. "That sounds like a great time," he said, pulling his wallet out.

"Dad, no," Sarah stopped and reached for her father's hand, but he already had a stack of bills clenched in his fist.

"Take it," he said, holding out the money, "take it and have fun." He pushed the money into her hands. "Just not too much fun, I need you baking bright and early," he smiled as she took the cash from him.

Sarah held it in a messy wad as she leaned in and kissed her father on the cheek.

"Thank you. I won't be late," she smiled, "well, I'll be at work. That's a fact." She laughed.

Dov joined and for a second all was right with the world.

By the next morning, Dov's world would be destroyed.

***

The city streets were never truly dark, even though it was 10 pm. The streetlights bathed the sidewalks in yellow and Sarah stayed away from the alleys as she walked.

Her bus, the one that had a stop only a block from her building, broke down. The replacement was coming from Mid-Town, and she didn't want to wait the hour for it to arrive. Besides, she was only 10 blocks from home. It was better to walk than to wait.

The night was warm, and Sarah's skin was sticky with sweat. The comedy club was small, an intimate and cozy setting, but also a damn furnace. The ancient air conditioner did next to nothing, and she doubted the owners even had it on.

Cars whizzed by and she thought about hailing a taxi. Her fiscally responsible self thought better, and she kept walking. She was almost always aware of her surroundings, but somehow, she didn't notice the Mercedes SUV slowing down.

***

Ari was behind the wheel of his father's Mercedes Benz GLS450. He had a bottle of vodka in one hand and the other on the wheel.

"Here, hold this," he said, passing the bottle to David, who was in the front seat.

David grabbed it, just before it fell into his lap.

"Pass that up," Ari said to Lieb, who was smoking a joint in the backseat.

Lieb pinched the joint and handed it up to Ari, careful not to burn him, or even worse, the seats.

Ari smoked the potent weed, taking it deep into his lungs. His head swam as a cloud of smoke rose before his eyes. He coughed, hit it again, and passed it back to Lieb.

"Gimme the bottle," Ari demanded, looking over at David. "Hey," he swatted his friend in the arm, "Gimme that shit."

David wasn't paying attention. His drug-addled brain was focused on something outside. Not something, but someone.

"There's the fucking bitch," David slurred. They had intended to pre-game before going to *Rush* but whatever pills Lieb had scored were a bit stronger than the Xanax they were used to.

"Huh?" Ari asked, slowing the car down, so he could see what his friend was looking at.

"Fucking Sarah," David said, as if in disbelief.

Ari saw her walking and slowed down. "Let's see if she needs a ride," he grinned, pulling the car to the curb.

"Oh, I'll give that stuck-up cunt a ride, alright." Lieb chimed in from the backseat.

"Hey Sarah," David said, rolling down the tinted window.

She looked up, recognizing the young men in the car and began walking even faster.

Ari kept up with her alongside the road.

"Do you want a ride?" David asked, gesturing to the inside of the car. "There's plenty of room."

Lieb but the back window down, "Yeah, you can sit back here with me." He sneered but tried to sound charming.

"No, thanks, but I appreciate it," she picked up her pace, moving just under a light jog.

"Oh, come on, Sarah," Ari yelled across David. "Just get in the car." He felt the rim of the wheel grind the curb.

Sarah didn't respond, just kept walking.

"Sarah!" Ari screamed, making her jump. "Get in the fucking car!"

Sarah broke into a full sprint, running down the street. The few people on the block didn't even look; worse things were happening in the city that doesn't sleep. Her flats came off and the rough sidewalks chewed up the soles of her feet. She left bloody footprints as she ran. Shards of glass stabbed her, and cigarette butts clung to the blood.

"Help!" she screamed, running from the pursuing SUV. The one thing about New Yorkers; they didn't give a fuck unless it was happening to them. Sarah reached an intersection, the SUV bearing down on her. If she didn't stop, she'd be run over. She stopped, her feet sliding in her slick blood.

"Fucking grab her!" Ari yelled. "Fucking cunt made me curb my rims."

Lieb threw open the back door and grabbed her.

Sarah punched and kicked, but she was tired from running.

Lieb began swinging, his fist hitting her stomach, taking the fight out of her. "Go, go, go," Lieb said.

Ari peeled out, sending the big SUV into the night. He flew down a few dark streets, a rarity in the city. He knew exactly where he was going.

The old school stood dark, like an ancient monolith. It was closed after 9/11 and hadn't been reopened.

Ari drove around back and killed the lights. "Ok, Sarah, let's see what you're made of." He climbed over the seat, unbuckling his pants as he did.

Sarah screamed again and kicked out at him.

"Fuck! Lieb, hold her down would you." Lieb hit her again as Ari pulled her dress up.

"Ah, so that's what you're working with." He ripped her underwear off, staring at a thatch of black pubic hair, leading to a bald slit. "Boys, this is going to be a hell of a night," he laughed.

Sarah screamed.

***

Sarah was battered, broken, and bloody, but she was alive. She lay in a stupor on the plush backseat of the Mercedes. Her throat was raw from screaming and felt like she'd inhaled glass.

"What the fuck are we going to do?" David asked, a fresh bottle of booze hovered under his lips. He took a sip, grimaced and handed it to Lieb.

"Get rid of her," Ari said, his dark eyes staring at nothing.

"What the fuck do you mean *get rid of her*?" Lieb asked, drinking from the bottle. He had an unlit joint behind his ear.

"Kill her, dump her, go to *Rush* like nothing fucking happened. That's what I mean." Ari ripped the bottle from Lieb's mouth, a stream of alcohol landed on his shirt.

"Hey, what the fuck?" Lieb wiped at the wetness, but it was in vain.

"What else are we going to do? Let her go? We'll go to fucking prison." Ari stated, as if it were a matter of fact. "Even my dad couldn't get us out of that, not with her testimony and —" he paused, a realization hitting him. "Fuck! We didn't use rubbers. Our fucking jizz is in her." He rubbed his head in frustration, spitting in disgust. How could he have been so stupid? The fucking drugs and booze, that's how. In college, if he was a little *forceful,* he always wore a rubber. This was different. He was careless.

"Fuck, man," Lieb said, the realization of what they'd done set in. He looked at David. "We have no choice. She needs to go."

David stared into space and nodded. "I agree, but what are we going to say?"

Ari took a deep breath, willing his brain to clear. "Fire. We have to torch her. Kill her and set her ass on fire." It could work and hopefully destroy the evidence. Ari licked his lips. "I'll fucking do it. I'll kill her." The other two stared at him, a silent weight of relief was lifted from them.

"You sure?" David asked, hoping his friend didn't go back on his work. Even drunk and high, he didn't think he could kill her.

Ari nodded, "Yeah. Get her out of the car." The other two stood frozen. "Now!" he yelled, his voice echoing off the buildings.

Lieb and David moved, opening the back door of the car.

"Hey, Ari, we have a problem here," David called to his friend.

"What?" Ari asked, walking over. The overhead lights showed a mess.

Sarah lay in a stupor, coagulated blood and semen seeped into the seats and floor mats.

"There's no way we'll be able to clean that, and if the cops come looking, we're fucked," David said, as if they didn't know that.

"My dad loves this car, but I'm not going to fucking prison," Ari said as he walked to the back of the car. He opened the back liftgate and opened a box. Bottles of liquor stood in there, each separated by pieces of cardboard. He searched through them, pulling two out. They were special edition and 80% alcohol. He was saving them for the club, hoping to get a few girls beyond their limit. Well, they'd be used for a different girl. "Here," he said, handing a bottle to David, who'd walked back with him. "Dump this on the front seats." He shut the hatch. "I'll take the back.

David dumped the bottle on the seats, not wanting to see Ari in the back.

"Ari," Sarah gasped. Her face was battered and bloody. Her left eye was swollen shut and her teeth were shattered. "Please," she reached with broken fingers, begging him to stop.

Ari pulled the cork from the bottle and dumped it on Sarah.

She screamed; the potent alcohol burned her open wounds. Writhing in pain, Sarah began squirming towards the exit.

Ari watched her crawl. *'Pathetic,'* he thought. He grabbed the lighter from his pocket, heart racing. He touched it to Sarah's bloody foot. There was no turning back. Ari spun the wheel of the lighter.

Flame, the bluest flame he'd ever seen, engulfed Sarah. He slammed the door, sealing her in.

She screamed, but the roar of the fire drowned out her cry.

Ari, Lieb, and David stepped back and watched black smoke pour from the seam in the car. A black hand, charred, and bloody pressed against the glass and was gone.

The fire roiled, engulfing the luxury car and the girl inside of it.

Ari looked at David and punched him in the face.

"Ow, what the fuck?" David asked, holding his swelling eye.

"Hit me," Ari said, standing in front of the inferno. He slapped himself in the face.

"What?" David asked, confused. His mind racing and the dull ache from the punch had him seeing double.

"Those fucking mutts carjacked us, right?" Ari asked, stepping closer to David. "They sucker punched you and when we got out, they attacked us," he pointed to his chest and Lieb's. "Beat us up and stole the car."

David and Lieb were starting to catch on. Before he could react, Ari punched Lieb in the face, breaking his nose.

"You motherfucker!" Lieb yelled, cradling his nose, which was gushing blood. He lowered his head and tackled his friend.

Ari's head hit the pavement, splitting his scalp.

Lieb punched him a few times, cutting his lip.

"Ok, ok, fuck," Ari said, raising his hands in defense. Lieb helped him up with a bloody hand.

They watched the car smolder, flames still alive.

"Come on, let's get the fuck out of here and call the cops."

***

Dov woke to a loud banging on his apartment door. His alarm clock, which sat next to his picture of him, Chana, and Sarah, said it was only 2:50 am. He was supposed to be up in 10 minutes and couldn't believe he was losing sleep.

The banging rattled the doorframe and it finally registered in his sleep-deprived brain. It had to be Sarah. She must've forgotten her keys and was locked out.

"I'm coming," he said, putting slippers on. "Sarah, do you know what time it is?" He unlocked the door and opened it. "We need to leave in —" Two NYPD detectives stood solemnly...Rabbi Kirsh behind them.

"Dov, we need to talk about Sarah," Rabbi Kirsh said.

Dov's head began to spin. It was all a blur. The visions of Chana in bed, the doctor telling him she was gone. It was that again, but worse. Blackness closed in around him, sucking him down, pulling him to the ground. He couldn't fight it; he wanted the earth to open and swallow him.

The detectives caught Dov before he hit the ground.

***

"I'm sorry, Mr. Friedman, there's no evidence those boys had anything to do with the murder of your daughter," Detective Barca said, dismissing the grieving father for the third time that week. "Now, if we get any leads on the individuals who stole the car, we'll be sure to reach out to you, but for now, that's all we have."

Dov shook, the phone vibrating against his ear.

"Again, I'm sorry for your loss and I'll be in touch."

The line went dead. Dov held the receiver against his ear, waiting for the shrill wail of the 'off the hook' sound. He dropped the phone into the cradle and put his face in his hands.

Tears, hot and full of rage, grief, and anguish poured from his eyes. He screamed, willing Sarah back to life, praying for her salvation, and promising his eternal soul for just another hug from her. Another smile from her; anything.

Dov sat in his chair, wiping the snot across his stubbly cheeks, not caring about it. He hadn't showered since Sarah's funeral a week prior. He didn't eat and only drank the most minimal amounts of water. His frame, thin before her death, was gaunt and sickly. The bakery, his realm, his workshop, remained closed. He would never open the doors again. He would die in his room, melting into the chair, only to be discovered when a neighbor noticed the rancid smell of his decomposing corpse.

There was a knock at the door, but it didn't sound like a fist, but a solid object.

"Dov, open the door," a voice said from the hallway.

Dov turned, willing his visitor away. The knock sounded again; this time followed up by a hacking cough.

"It's Ezra, Ezra Rywski, your favorite customer." There was a pause, a cough, and another knock.

Dov rose, his clothes felt grimy and stuck to his body. He unlocked the door and opened it.

Ezra stood there, his horseshoe baldness and white hair stuck up at every angle. He hobbled forward, his cane in one hand and a bottle of bourbon in the other.

"Thanks," Ezra pushed into the apartment. He looked around and moved towards the couch. He collapsed and set the bottle down. "Get some cups."

Dov was in a fog. Moments earlier he was thinking about death and now he was about to have a drink with an old customer. As if on autopilot, he went into the kitchen and grabbed two glasses.

"Ah, thanks," Ezra said, taking the cups and setting them down. He opened the bottle and poured a generous amount into each one. He raised his glass in a silent toast, waiting for Dov to do the same.

Dov raised his cup as well.

"HaShem yikom dama," Ezra said, throwing back his drink in one gulp.

Dov put his head back and swallowed the hard liquor. He winced and put the cup down, motioning Ezra to fill it again. Dov put back another one, the alcohol hitting his depleted bloodstream.

Ezra put his cup down and stared at Dov.

"Have I ever told you about the pure evil of man?" Ezra asked, rolling up his sleeve. A faded tattoo of numbers was inked on his forearm. "Bah, I don't have to tell you." Ezra took another small drink and pushed the bottle away. What he was about to tell his friend needed a little liquid courage, but too much and he'd be sleeping.

"I know about evil, Ezra. Oh, I fucking know."

"When they, the Nazis, came for us, I was terrified. I was only a boy, but I wanted to fight back, wanted to rally the men and kill them. Fight those," his head was swooning from the alcohol, "fuckers off. Kill them all. We had a grand Rabbi, Lipshitz, who told the men to fight, repel the invaders. To protect our way of life, our women and children, our homes." He was getting drunk but didn't care. He poured more in both cups. The men drank, their grimaces even less.

"The Rabbi was old, as old as I am now, but he had the heart of a warrior. But his body was far from a fighter. He needed a champion, but our men were scared. The Nazis had guns, tanks, and trained soldiers. What could a few scared Jews do against that? Well, Rabbi Lipshitz had a way. A dreadful, cursed way, but a way. The Nazis took up residence in the village, occupying a home. It wasn't many of them, but a small unit of men. In the night, they were slaughtered, ripped apart in a brutal, violent way. A way that was obscene to God and man, torn limb from limb. It was blamed on rebels and many men paid for the attack with their lives, not willing to give up any names. They would've if they knew who attacked the unit, but they didn't." He was glassy-eyed and slurring worse. "I know who it was," Ezra spat.

Dov was listening intently, for a moment his woes were almost forgotten. "Who was it? The Rabbi?"

Ezra nodded. "Yes and no. It was a golem, a monster of earth and clay, summoned by the Rabbi."

"A golem? Like from the Torah."

Ezra nodded again. "Exactly, but this beast was different. The Torah tells us the golem is uncontrollable, given a task and set to it. They have no thought, just perform their tasks and go back to the earth. The Rabbi found a different way. A way to make the monster into his champion, but at a cost." He took another sip of booze. "The Rabbi was found dead the next morning, his heart stopped, and a pile of dirt was at his front door. He was part of the golem, and the golem was part of him and together they died."

"Why are you telling me this?" Dov asked. He was seeing double, the alcohol dulling his mind.

Ezra had a drunken glint in his eyes. "Because, we're going to fucking get them," he filled the glasses again. "HaShem yikom dama," he said. "May HaShem avenge her blood."

It had been almost two weeks since the murder of Sarah, and finally, the cops had left David alone.

The first couple of days had been touch and go, with the questions coming rapid-fire, but they all stuck to the story of the carjacking. The corroboration and the fact Ari's father was a powerful, well-known attorney helped.

Which was good; they were home on break and didn't want anything hampering their good time. Speaking of good times, David was on a mission; buy drugs for the party that night. The last time they tried to have fun, they encountered Sarah and the night went to shit. At least they got to fuck but ended up in a tricky situation for a while.

David parked his car in a less than desirable part of Brooklyn. He wasn't worried, his dealer, Grimy, ran the block. Anyone fucking with a customer of his would pay and pay dearly. Now that was the way to do business. Grimy was just that, grimy, but David had been buying drugs from him since middle school. His prices were better than that of the Jewish kids in his community, who would always jack them up. No, David went to the source.

The streets were busy, and David ended up having to park on the opposite side of Grimy's building. He looked at his BMW, hoping it would be okay. His wellbeing was accounted for, but his car was another story. He was able to park in a space behind a closed Chinese restaurant, which was behind Grimy's building. David eyed up the dark alley, which would take him straight to the front of the building. He hated alleys and avoided them at all costs, but time was of the essence. He spent too long circling the block looking for parking and was going to be late. Ari was already in a bad mood and David didn't want to feel his wrath for some stupid shit.

David took out his cell phone and turned on the flashlight feature. The small LED gave him a little light, but not nearly enough to dispel all the shadows. He entered the alley, watching his footing around piles of garbage.

A smell hit him, the smell of fresh bread and cinnamon. He was pleasantly surprised, most alleys smelled like human waste and garbage.

"Huh, must be a bakery on the other side," he said aloud, thinking of when a bakery had opened in the area. He saw a massive pile of garbage ahead and moved as close to the wall as possible, but without touching it. As he closed in, he realized the smell of baked goods was coming from the garbage pile. David shined his light at the trash.

The garbage pile, which looked like a blob of semi-baked dough, began to move.

David stood frozen with fear, only his hand moving, using the light to follow the monster's ascent, which never seemed to stop. In front of him, standing 8 feet tall, was a demon, a monster, a golem.

It looked soft and squishy, like it was proofed dough because that's what it was. Its shape was humanoid, but it was devoid of any human features, save for its eyes. Where a human's eyes should be sat two perfect swirls of cinnamon rugelach.

David watched, frozen with fear, only a squeak coming from his throat, as the creature began to reach towards its stomach. Knives stuck out of the golem's belly. Knives of every shape and form. There was even a rolling pin.

The golem grabbed a butcher knife, old and well used, and slid it from its body.

David finally found his senses and turned to run...but the golem was too fast.

A doughy paw wrapped around his neck, stopping him and pulling him close to the baked beast.

The golem raised the knife, relishing the fear in the eyes of the young man. It plunged the blade in the crook of David's neck, right where his collar bone was. The hardened steel made short work of flesh and bone. Blood flew and David's world began to fade to black, but the golem kept stabbing. Each pull of the knife was wetter, throwing more gore onto its tan 'flesh'.

David fell dead, his lifeblood flowing onto the dirty alley floor. He was nearly decapitated, with severed tendons and blood vessels exposed.

The golem plunged the knife back into its belly; its work was far from over.

***

"This motherfucker is late again," Ari said, looking at his phone for the tenth time in the last 2 minutes. "He probably tested the shit and passed out." He put his phone back in his pocket and walked over to his dresser.

"Next time," Lieb, who was sitting at Ari's computer desk, playing an online game, "I'll get the drugs. I like them as much as the next guy, but I know better."

"Yeah, sure," Ari ignored him, rifling through his socks until he found the small box. "I hope this is still full." He pulled the box out and set it on the dresser. Luckily for him, it was full. Pills, ranging in color, size, and make-up looked back at him. There was a small bag of weed, but it was dry. They'd still smoke it, but it probably wasn't the best. "Perfect," Ari said, filling his pockets with the narcotics. He took his phone out and checked it again, this time not thinking about his friend. "The car should be here any minute. Let's go wait."

Lieb's character in the game died in a blast of gunfire and a red screen. "Sounds good." He shut down the computer and followed his friend out to the street.

It wasn't unlike David to flake on them. In college, if he hooked up with a girl, he'd go missing for a day or two, only to resurface as if nothing had happened.

They didn't have to wait long before their ride pulled up. A brand-new Cadillac, sleek and black, stopped in front of the building. It had a rental car barcode on the window, but Ari and Lieb didn't seem to care.

"That was fast," Ari said, sliding into the backseat.

"Yeah, we just walked out," Lieb followed his friend in through the same door, making him slide over.

"I'm always on time," the old man behind the wheel said.

Ari and Lieb looked at each other when they heard the old man talk. He sounded ancient and it was dark.

"Hey, grandfather, are you ok to drive in the dark?" Ari asked, partially as a joke and partially as serious.

The old man laughed, "Young man, I'm perfectly fine and my vision is sharp. Now, please buckle up. My name is Ezra and I'll get you right where you need to be."

Ezra pulled away from the curb and began driving. He had a mission; a destination and he was getting there one way or another. He turned, the wrong way of where the boys wanted to go, but neither said anything. Another wrong turn and finally one spoke up.

"Do you know a shortcut or something?"

"Yeah, I've been in this city longer than most of the buildings. You'll be fine."

A couple more turns and another complaint.

"I think you're lost, gramps. Pull over and I'll drive," Ari said from the backseat.

Ezra ignored him. They were almost there. He pressed the accelerator, throwing them into the seats.

"Hey, what the fuck are you doing? Are you trying to fucking kill us?" Lieb yelled, thankful he listened and buckled his seatbelt.

Ezra drove, seeing his destination in the distance, the old school.

"What the fuck!" yelled Ari, realizing where they were.

Ezra pulled in; a massive man stood waiting in the distance. He turned off the lights and stopped the car.

The night smelled of dough and cinnamon as Ezra jumped out of the car. He locked the doors on his way out.

Ari pulled at the door handle, realizing the child locks were engaged.

Lieb figured it out too and climbed over the seats to the front doors. He flung open the passenger side door and started to run.

In the moonlight, Ari watched the giant move. It didn't look human. Besides the fact it was 8 feet tall, it looked like a man in a wrinkled fat suit. The monstrosity pulled something from its stomach, it was a cleaver. It wound up like a baseball player and hurled the blade.

Silvery light glinted off the sides as it flew true, landing in Lieb's lower back.

"Ah, fuck!" he screamed, falling face first in the parking lot. The golem lurched over to the injured boy. The beast grabbed and twisted the handle, cracking the pelvic bone in which it was embedded.

Ari watched in fear as the monster raised the blade and began hacking away at his friend.

Blood, bone, grey matter, it all flew into the night air. Lieb was dead, but the monster hacked and hacked, until the cleaver was stuck in the asphalt.

Ari needed to make a break for it and seized his opportunity. He scrambled out of the car, forgetting about Ezra.

The old man had fought evil, knew evil, and wanted to kill evil. With every bit of strength he could muster, he swung his cane into the back of Ari's skull.

Ari thought he'd been shot and fell face first, just catching himself from breaking his nose. The smell of bread was almost nauseating as he rolled over and looked at the golem above him.

The golem grabbed him with an unnaturally strong hand and dragged him to the trunk, which Ezra had popped open.

Ari saw what was in the car and pissed his pants. A gas can, full and sloshing, sat waiting.

"No, please God, no," Ari begged, punching into the soft dough of the golem with the cinnamon rugelach eyes.

The golem grabbed the can and pushed Ari to the ground.

Ari fought and kicked, but another arm of dough formed from the golem's body. Two fat hands of dough grabbed his upper and lower jaw and pried his mouth open. He tried to fight it, but his jaw unhinged; the bone resting on his chest. The golem used its third arm and jammed the nozzle of the gas can down Ari's throat.

Cold gasoline flooded his mouth, some spraying from his nose as he coughed it up. His jaw sat slack as he began to choke on the gas. Ari's throat and sinuses burned from the chemical, but he had no idea what burning was.

The golem reached into its doughy body and pulled out a Zippo lighter. Fine fingers made of dough formed, snapping open the lighter with a ting sound.

Ari tried to scream, but without his jaw connected it was just a guttural roar of primal fear. His eyes widened as the orange flame licked at the wick in the lighter.

The golem paused, holding the flame in its hand. Slowly, it turned its head, its rugelach eyes looking at the pathetic, scared man on the floor. It threw the lighter at Ari's face.

He tried to scurry away, but the flame touched his gas-soaked shirt. A snake of fire, red and orange, slithered up his chest, seeking his mouth. The fire moved almost instantly, but to Ari, it was in slow motion. The chemical burning of the gas was replaced with the fires of Hell. His tongue seared, sticking to his teeth. Flames ate his perfect hair, consuming the product he'd used before his night on the town.

In moments, he was dead. The flames continued to feed, casting a shadow of the golem on the side of the school. Finally, Ari was nothing more than a charred husk of red and black flesh, with the occasional white bone peeking out.

***

Dov sat on a chair in the middle of the bakery. He had snapped back, leaving the body of the vengeful golem, after Ari took his last fiery breath. It was done. He was done. Dov held Sarah's bandana to his nose, breathing her in. He closed his eyes, picturing her. Seeing her at every stage, from her birth to her first steps, first words, and even her first cinnamon rugelach. He cried...hard. His baby girl, taken from him in the most vicious of ways, by a pack of monsters. Well, they got to see a real monster, to feel the fear she felt and the pain she'd endured. Tears fell, wetting the fabric, but still, he smelled her. The sweat, her shampoo, and just the slightest hint of cinnamon.

The door to the bakery opened, and heavy, yet soft footsteps sounded on the floor. Dov didn't look up, just kept his eyes down, smelling her. The hulking mass moved closer, its shadow engulfing the small man. Dov prayed, smelling the scent of Sarah...and then it was gone. Replaced by the smell of dough and cinnamon.

HOMEGROWN COMEUPPANCE

ROWLAND BERCY JR.

Homegrown Comeuppance
by Rowland Bercy, Jr.

Prologue

"Take a hiking tour through the rainforest, he said. It'll be fun, he said," Scott taunted as he and his boyfriend, Brandon, cautiously made their way through the dense foliage, keeping well away from the murky waterway they'd stumbled upon which they knew was teaming with a variety of deadly predators. During their adventuring, the couple had somehow drifted off the main trail and was now hopelessly lost somewhere deep inside the tropical landscape.

"Relax, we'll be fine," Brandon comforted. Judging by the panicked look on Scott's face, Brandon's attempts at reassuring his life partner failed miserably.

"Relax? How the hell do you expect me to relax?" Scott replied worriedly. "We've been walking for hours and haven't seen a soul. Hell, I don't even know if we're headed in the right direction." He glanced at the sun shining through the thick canopy of trees overhead. "The sun's going to be setting soon and I'm not thrilled at the prospect of spending the night getting eaten by a plethora of small, buzzy, bitey, burrowing, nipping things…ewww," he said while waving away a small swarm of gnats circling his head.

"I'd be less worried about the tiny, buzzy, bitey things and more so about the huge, slithery, snakey things that I heard can get so large, they can swallow a man whole," Brandon teased, but immediately regretted his attempt at levity when he saw the look of worry flash across Scott's face. "I'm just kidding," Brandon comforted, slinging his arm over Scott's shoulder and pulling him close.

"Not funny," Scott pouted, unable to conceal the slight smile tugging at the corner of his mouth as he playfully pushed Brandon away. "Seriously, what the hell are we going to do?"

"We just gotta' keep moving," Brandon encouraged, taking hold of Scott's hand and urging him to follow.

The couple resumed their trek but halted almost immediately when Brandon spotted the most bizarre looking tree he had ever seen. "Whoa, check it out," he remarked, motioning to the strange plant. Curiosity piqued; the two men walked up to the odd-looking tree which stood just over ten feet tall. The girth of the trunk was significantly wider than any of the surrounding trees and the crown was unlike anything they'd seen before. The upper branches looked less like branches and more like thorny, amber-colored vines or octopi tentacles.

"What the hell kind of tree is this," Scott inquired, "and how the hell did we not see it sooner? It's like the damn thing just appeared out of nowhere," he finished, bending down and picking up what looked like a baseball-sized seed, or some strange fruit produced by the odd-looking plant. The upper branches quivered and swayed aggressively, which Scott thought odd, considering the day was humid and breezeless. He tossed the seed to Brandon right before one of the branches whipped down and raked him across the face. It left a ragged, three-inch-long gash running lengthwise down his cheek. Scott screamed in agony and slapped his hand to his ravaged face, thinking that one of the branches above had dislodged and accidentally hit him in the face on the way down. Brandon, who stood a few feet away while examining the pod, looked up just as another thorn covered branch reach down and wrapped itself around Scott's chest. The appendage lifted Scott into the air with ease, holding him high above the ground as yet more thorny tendrils wrapped around him and began to constrict.

"What the fuck!" Brandon yelped, looking up in confusion at his partner who struggled in vain to free himself from the branches. Brandon began to move towards the tree in attempt to help Scott free himself, but one of the limbs whipped out towards him. Falling and dodging the appendage, Brandon quickly rolled out of reach as two more tentacled-branches made a grab for him. He shot to his feet and looked up at Scott in a panic. Brandon tried another advance towards the tree, but froze when he saw Scott, unable to speak due to the amount of pressure being inflicted by the squeezing branches, aggressively shaking his head from side to side. Blood ran in a steady stream down Scott's legs as thorns from the creatures' branches punctured deep into his body. Another aggressive constriction by the tentacles was followed by a sickening crack, as all of Scott's ribs broke simultaneously. His eyes went saucer wide before his body went limp with death.

"Nooo!" Brandon screamed, tears streaming down his face as another, slimmer tentacle shot forth from the center of the creatures' trunk. The tentacle wrapped itself around one of Scott's arms and savagely ripped it from his lifeless body. It was then that Brandon caught movement out of his peripheral vision. He once again managed to dodge a tentacle as a second, smaller tree creature he'd failed to notice, made a grab for him. He ran in a blind panic, still clutching the seed-like pod Scott had tossed to him earlier. Harmless bushes, branches and vines snatched at his clothing and bloodied his face and arms as he plowed through the rough terrain. His terror-stricken mind convincing him that the foliage was more of the horrid tree creatures.

Before long, the waterway that he and his partner had so meticulously avoided, came into view. Terror-struck, Brandon fled from the attacking trees and recklessly dove into the murky waters. He surfaced almost immediately and glanced back at the gloomy forest. Brandon managed to breathe a short-lived sigh of relief moments before the jaws of a thirteen-foot Black Caiman savagely clamped down on him and promptly dragged him beneath the surface. Seconds later, the pod bobbed to the surface and floated downstream.

***

Business was slow, as usual, so Angela decided to close early for the day and do a bit of shopping to cheer herself up. As of late, the small bakery she owned had experienced a financially devastating loss of patronage, brought on by a more modern bakery which had recently opened in town. She remained in business on a wing and a prayer, but if something didn't give soon, Angela was positive she'd have to permanently close the bakery in search of a more stable source of income.

"Interesting, isn't it," Lucas, the shop keeper whispered, startling Angela, who was in the process of inspecting the mysterious, baseball-size seed she'd found sitting on one of the shelves. It was just collecting dust in the back of the small antique shop. The seed was the color of red clay and wrapped in what looked like thick, vine-like tendrils. It was completely unique and unlike anything she had ever seen before in her years of gardening; her favorite pastime, second only to baking.

"What kind of seed is this?" Angela inquired as she continued her scrutiny of the strange pod.

"I found it floating along the riverbank and thought it looked interesting," Lucas responded, smiling. "I actually forgot I even had it. But now that I'm seeing it again, I do recall what a resident elder told me it was rumored to be," he continued mysteriously.

"So, what is it?" Angela asked curiously.

"You're a local," he stated matter-of-factly. "Well, I'm sure you've heard tale of the Ya-Te-Veo. The carnivorous, man-eating trees rumored to inhabit the surrounding rainforest. Well, this, so I've been told might be a dormant seed of that legendary tree."

Angela rolled her eyes and scoffed. "That's silly," she retorted. "There is no such thing as a carnivorous, man-eating plant inhabiting the forest. That was a senseless story parents use to tell their children to keep them from venturing too far into the jungle. Without boasting, as you know, I'm a bit of a plant enthusiast, and one hell of a gardener. I'm well-versed in and have studied the local flora for years now. I've never seen anything remotely resembling a Ya-Te-Veo."

"Neither have I," Lucas responded, "but then again, I never had the cojones to go looking for one," he finished with a smile.

"Well, I'm curious to see what type of plant this seed would produce, if it'll even grow at all. How much do you want for it?" Angela asked, reaching into her purse.

'You give me what you think it's worth, and we'll see if what you offer is sufficient," Lucas stated slyly, allowing Angela to feel as if she had the upper hand in the transaction.

Pulling out a denomination of Brazilian real, she held it out to him. Satisfied with what Angela offered, Lucas took the money and slipped it into his pocket. "Consider it yours," he announced, walking towards the counter. Angela followed, bagged her merchandise and thanked Lucas as she left the shop. She headed towards her car, which was parked a few blocks away, and rolled her eyes when she saw Juliana approaching from the opposite direction. Juliana, the bane of Angela's existence, was the owner and operator of the new bakery in town. She was a shrewd businesswoman and had no problem letting Angela know that she and her bakery were here to stay.

"Angela, querida, como você está?" Juliana greeted sarcastically. "Fancy seeing you out and about this early. Shouldn't you be at your bakery?" she finished with a contemptuous smirk on her face.

Angela crinkled her face in response and replied "Whatever, Juliana, you're so fuckin' fake. Almost as fake as that horribly botched boob job you got there. Who the hell did your surgery, Freddy fuckin' Krueger?"

Juliana's' eyes narrowed in response to the insult, but she was quick on her feet with a comeback.

"Better to have botched boobs than a broken-down bakery," she spat back nastily. "You should probably give up the ghost and accept the fact that you're holding on to your dated, run of the mill bakery by the skin of your teeth. Might as well just throw in the towel and bow out gracefully, while you still can. Who knows, maybe once your doors are closed for good you could come and work for me...as a dishwasher," Juliana laughed wickedly as she turned and walked away, completely dismissing Angela in the process.

Flustered, Angela's mind ran in circles in attempt to conceive of a witty retort, but it was pointless. Juliana was right, at the rate things were going Angela would soon be forced to close shop, permanently. Crestfallen, she continued to her car and headed home.

Angela lived about 10 miles away from the historic city of Morretes Brazil, in a modest two-bedroom house, situated on a small piece of land, adjacent to the Mata Atlantica Rainforest; a biodiversity hotspot known for its high species richness. Instead of heading into the house, she walked around back to a large greenhouse and retrieved a large, empty planter. She filled the container with fresh soil and buried the seed at a depth of approximately two times the width of the seedling. Then, she soaked the soil with a generous amount of fast-growing, experimental fertilizer she was in the process of developing. She had no real hopes of the seed germinating properly, but it was worth a try.

"Good luck, little buddy," she said as she left the greenhouse to retire for the evening. "I'll be back to check on you in a couple of days."

Two days later, Angela walked into the conservatory and froze when she saw that the seed had indeed sprouted. A slim, brown trunk had grown from the soil and stood about three inches above the lip of the pot. Standing at attention atop the trunk were what looked to be finger-length, thorny, vine-like branches, which were beginning to bow outwards.

"Well, I'll be damned. Even after sitting neglected and forgotten you still had a bit of life left in you," Angela exclaimed, pleased as she examined the sapling from afar.

Once the leaves relaxed fully and fell away from the trunk completely, Angela could imagine the tree bearing a slight resemblance to Salix babylonica, a species of willow native to the dry areas of northern China. Or even a large, underwater sea anemone. Whatever type of plant this turned out to be, it was exceptionally rare, perhaps even an endangered species. She could imagine how someone who happened upon this tree in the wild, when fully matured, could mistake it for the fabled Ya-Te-Veo tree. Especially if the wind was blowing wildly. In a situation like that, its branches would be swaying frantically to and fro, and could easily be mistaken for malicious, man-snatching, tendril-like appendages.

Anxious to get a closer look, Angela walked towards the pot in which the mysterious plant had taken root and haphazardly tripped over the watering container she'd left on the ground. Falling forward and reaching out instinctively for something to break her fall, she knocked over the planter in the process. After the tumble she sprang up immediately, worried that she had damaged the plant during her fall. Her concerns were confirmed when she saw that the sapling had indeed snapped off at the bottom of the trunk and was lying broken and useless in the dirt.

"Fuck, fuck, fuck...," Angela whispered, scolding herself for her clumsiness. Reaching down and picking up the broken stem, she was pissed at herself for potentially fucking up the opportunity to re-introduce what had to be a rare, possibly endangered species of flora back into the local eco-system. Her mind raced frantically, trying to conceive of a way to possibly save the sapling. She considered stem propagation: Replanting the trunk into the soil to see if it would once again take root. But Angela had no idea what sort of tree she was dealing with and was doubtful of a successful outcome utilizing that technique.

Looking around the greenhouse for other possible solutions, inspiration struck when she saw a popular palm tree native to the rainforest known as Socratea exorrhiza, or the so-called Walking Palm Tree. Which many locals believed could walk around, aided by the trees' strange, stilt-like roots which grew outward from the base of the trunk, several feet off the ground. Giving it the appearance of multiple legs, which are rumored to enable the palm the ability to relocate from a shaded area to sunlight. By growing new roots in the direction, it wants to travel, and then allowing the old roots to slowly lift into the air and die, permitting a slow movement toward the side where the new roots have grown.

Angela had been experimenting with a horticultural technique known as grafting, most used in asexual propagation of commercially grown plants for horticultural and agricultural trades. In which vascular tissues of two plants are joined to continue their growth together. For successful grafting to take place: the scion; the upper part of one plant must be placed in contact with the rootstock; the lower part of another plant. If both are kept alive and growing, the grafting would be a success within a few weeks. She had no idea if it would work, but for some reason she had the insane idea to unite the mysterious new tree with the Walking Palm.

She scooped up the broken plant and reached for a pair of pruning shears. With a swift snip, Angela evened off the bottom of the mysterious tree before heading over to the Walking Palm tree and snipping off its crown. She used Parafilm Grafting Tape to secure the two halves together. Then, she pushed a wooden stake into the soil of the potter, trying her best not to damage the roots of the Walking Palm, and secured the new plant to the stake using twine. Angela stepped back and admired her handiwork. "Well, looks like the rest is up to you guys. I'll do my best to help you along the way, but I've got to be honest; the outcome is looking pretty grim."

Over the following days, and much to Angela's surprise the hybrid tree seemed to flourish. Three weeks into the process, the plants' merger was complete, and she knew without a doubt, that it would survive, which was unbelievable in and of itself. Even more incredible was the rate at which the newly fused trees matured, along with its odd appearance. Whatever category of tree the seedpod produced was of an unknown origin, and was, without a doubt, what fueled the local legend of the Ya-Te-Veo.

The thing grew so rapidly that it outgrew its original planter, so Angela relocated it to a pre-selected space in her backyard. Placing the tree outside seemed to spur its growth even more. She was well versed in various plant life and knew of some - such as bamboo - which could grow up to 36 inches in twenty-four hours. However, a tree growing as fast as the one Angela had cultivated was unheard of.

After only five weeks, the tree stood a little over 8 feet tall. The trunk was already significantly larger and perched atop the high root system of the Walking Palm, which grew outwards from the base of the tree, several feet off the ground. The leaves, which resembled tentacles, sprouted every-which-way from the apex of the trunk, were marvelously beautiful and hung almost to the ground. They had grown to about 7 feet long, were brightly colored, covered in thorns and tapered to a sharp point.

***

Startled from a peaceful sleep, Angela sat bolt upright and looked around in confusion. "What the hell was that?" she whispered. Chills ran down her spine as the screaming continued. It sounded like a baby crying at the top of its lungs, which further increased Angela's anxiety. Whatever it was, it was obviously hurt and in tremendous pain. She hesitantly threw back the covers and made her way to the bedroom window, which faced the backyard. Cupping her hands around her eyes, Angela tried to see if she could locate the source of the commotion, but it was impossible to make out anything in the perfect darkness enveloping the yard. The screaming continued for another ten seconds before abruptly cutting off.

Angela considered going out to investigate the disturbance, but reconsidered when she remembered a news story, she'd heard about a man being attacked in his yard by a jaguar. It had ventured out of the rainforest and wandered into the city in search of food. "Fuck that," she said aloud. Whatever it was had either escaped from, or was being devoured by, whatever had attacked it. Whichever the case, she decided to wait until morning to investigate. Decision made, she jumped back into bed and fitfully drifted back to sleep with nightmares of mutilated, wailing babies chasing her into the darkness.

The following morning, Angela stood in shocked silence as she peered out of her bedroom window. She could hardly believe what she was seeing, so she decided to go outside and get a closer look. Somehow, one of the many goats that she had on her property, had gotten itself tangled within and impaled under the prominent, stilt-like root system of the hybrid tree. If the beast had just gotten itself trapped within the cage-like roots, it wouldn't have surprised her. But the fact that it had somehow gotten impaled by a root through the middle of its stomach completely baffled her. The soil surrounding the root system was loosened and dug out, almost as if the tree itself had been uprooted. Probably a result of the animal digging around the roots looking for food, but that hardly explained how it had gotten skewered.

"Well," Angela stated, "regardless of how you got yourself in this situation, there's only three options at this point. Either I cut the root and pull you off, or I cut you open and pull you out, or I leave you there and let my wondrous new tree utilize your decomposing flesh for nutrients." She gasped in surprise and retreated as the decision was made for her. Several smaller, intertwined tentacles at the cap of the trunk, which went unnoticed earlier due to the height of the tree, sprang to life.

Staring wide-eyed, Angela watched as the smaller tentacles parted and a longer, slimmer tentacle shot out from the center of the trunk. It swayed in the air for a few seconds, like a cobra poised to strike. Then it slithered down the outside of the textured trunk until it reached the body of the dead goat. Without hesitation, the thing coiled around one of the creatures' hind legs, ripping it off with ease. Then it retreated into the center of the trunk, taking the severed limb with it as it did so.

There was a small splash of liquid as the tentacle disappeared with its prize, some of which leaked down the side of the trunk. After a few seconds, the tongue-like tentacle emerged from within the center of the trunk and repeated the process. This time, it wrapped itself around the goats' horns before giving a savage twist. The animal's head and cervical vertebrae separated with a sickening squelch before disappearing into the trunk. This continued until nothing more than bits and pieces of the carcass remained strewn about the yard.

"What. The. Fuck?" Angela voiced aloud as she watched the tree collect and, she could only assume, store the carcass of the goat. "I guess the fabled Ya-Te-Veo tree really does exist," she exclaimed excitedly, appraising the thing from a safe distance, well out of reach of any of its tentacles. Her mind was spinning as she tried to figure out how such a plant could exist. She remembered one of the most fascinating plant species she had the opportunity to study, and even grow once, known as predatory flowering or carnivorous plants. They were a species of plant which derived most, if not all, of their nutrients from trapping and consuming animals, protozoan and insects.

One such variety of carnivorous flora, known as pitcher plants, would attract prey with bribes of nectar, causing the victim to fall into the fluid-filled pitcher. Within the pitcher, digestive enzymes would then break down the kill into an absorbable form of nutrients for the flower. That might explain the liquid Angela had witnessed splashing out of the center of the trunk. The largest of the pitcher plants, being endemic to Borneo, is called Nepenthe's rajah. It grew up to 41 centimeters high, 20 centimeters wide and was famous for occasionally trapping vertebrates and even small mammals, such as rats, frogs, lizards and even birds.

The thing before her was 10 times the size of Nepenthes rajah and considerably more destructive. Angela had never heard of a carnivorous plant this large, or this ferocious, but she knew it wasn't unheard of for plant life to evolve or genetically mutate due to changes within their cells. She also knew that some mutations could be triggered by temperature fluctuations, environmental instabilities, and insect or animal damage. Maybe this particular plant changed its physiology to dissuade predators or to more easily capture prey for nourishment. Whatever the case, this unknown variation of carnivorous plant life was remarkable. Deadly, yet extraordinary.

That fact was again reiterated when a beautiful Hyacinth Macaw landed on one of the thicker tentacles and started pecking at a cluster of, what looked like, tentacle-wrapped, baseball-sized seed or fruit pods of some sort she hadn't noticed earlier. A few of the pods fell to the ground, one rolling and coming to a halt at Angela's feet. The Macaw took flight, presumably in search of another food source. Suddenly, the tongue-like tentacle rocketed from the center of the trunk and swiftly grabbed the bird out of the air. There was a brief squawk of panic as the bird was snatched, mid-flight, and hauled back into the center trunk, all in the blink of an eye.

"Oh fuck," Angela shouted in surprise, retreating even further from the tree as a cascade of blue feathers floated down around her. "This is crazy!" she cackled, thinking about being responsible for the discovery of a lifetime. "Hell, who knows, maybe I'll receive some sort of financial compensation for my discovery." Pondering a possible reward, Angela thought about being able to make improvements to her bakery… something to give that bitch Juliana a run for her money. Her eyes widened at the thought of the bakery, which should have been opened an hour ago.

She'd gotten so caught up in the discovery of what the marvelous plant was capable of, that she had completely forgotten about work. She may be on the verge of closing down, but she still prided herself on her work ethic and had a responsibility to her remaining customers. With this, Angela ran back into the house, showered quickly and got dressed. Prior to leaving for the day Angela went out to the yard again and cautiously retrieved one of the pods which had dislodged and rolled away from the tree, and also to snap a few quick pictures of the tree, from several angles, with her cell phone.

***

The day seemed to drag by at a snail's pace. There were a few customers now and then, but not nearly enough to keep Angela's mind or time occupied. Hell, there weren't even enough customers to cover the overhead of Angela coming into work for the day. Luckily, her mind was preoccupied with thoughts of mutated, carnivorous trees as she studied the pod, resting on the counter in front of her, while also casually flipping through the pictures of the tree on her cell.

"How's business," a voice asked, startling Angela from her scrutiny of the photos. She looked up to see Juliana standing in the doorway, smiling smugly.

"Ugh, must you always be so damn annoying?" Angela sighed in frustration.

Though the bakery was immaculate, and the air heavy with the fresh scent of rising yeast and sweet bread, Juliana curled her lip in mock disdain, strolling in as if she owned the place. Juliana would never admit it, but she was impressed with Angela's establishment, and with how

Angela was dealing with the impending closure. If she'd found herself in the same predicament, she would be freaking out trying to conceive of a way to prevent the inevitable.

Angela, though, endured the termination of her life's dream with unbelievable fortitude. Another admirable trait Juliana would never admit to appreciating in her competition. Truth be told, she worried that Angela would somehow manifest the resolve to keep her popular, albeit tiny, bakery up and running, and Juliana would not rest easy until the doors of said bakery were closed, once and for all.

"What are you doing here?" Angela asked, irritated at the unwelcome intrusion. She wanted to jump across the counter and choke the smug off Juliana's face. Simultaneously extinguish the life from her body, hence by saving her bakery in the process. However, Angela was a lady and would never sully her hands on the likes of Juliana. Looking at Juliana and then down at the photos on her phone, inspiration struck. Perhaps, if she played her cards right, she could get rid of her competition and save her bakery, without getting her hands the least bit dirty

"What do you have there?" Juliana asked, stepping up to the counter and motioning to the pod. Angela covered it with both hands, slowly sliding it off the counter, concealing it from view.

"Oh, you'll find out soon enough," Angela replied shrewdly. "You see, while you've been busy prancing around town, doing your best to undermine me and my place of business, to which I have wholeheartedly committed myself, I've been busy, trying to think of a way to save it. I've created a recipe for the most delectable, most mouth-watering sweetbread you have ever tasted, using an unknown fruit from a tree only I know the location of."

Juliana laughed. "Nice try. I've used just about every fruit, berry and seed within a hundred miles of here. I'm sure whatever exotic produce you think you've discovered, I'm already aware of it."

"Not this one," Angela smirked, slowly shaking her head from side to side while cunningly relaxing her hands, temporarily exposing the gourd. Juliana glanced down at it, but Angela once again cupped her hands around the object, concealing it from sight. She turned her back to Juliana, walked away from the counter and into the kitchen. In a move that would have earned her a standing ovation from the shrewdest of conmen, she left her phone, which still displayed a picture of the tree and its mysterious fruit on the screen.

"Don't you need to be getting back to your shop?" Angela called from the kitchen, making as much noise as possible in an attempt to let Juliana know her whereabouts. Unable to resist the temptation, Juliana quickly picked up Angela's phone. Hurriedly swiping through the photos, she came across one showing the tree with a cluster of the pods clearly visible. In the background stood Angela's house, which Juliana had visited a few times in the past, when the two had been more cordial with one another.

Juliana stealthily placed the phone back down upon the counter and promptly left the shop, without saying another word. With no further provocation from Juliana, Angela exited the kitchen and smirked nefariously when she glanced at her phone, lying face down on the counter. "Here's to hoping that curiosity kills the cunt," Angela laughed devilishly and decided to close shop and go home to await the inevitable, uninvited visit from Juliana, which she was sure would happen sometime after nightfall.

***

A little after midnight and Juliana was driving to Angela's home. She wasn't sure if the cryptic new fruit Angela had spoken of was the one pictured on the tree she'd spied on Angela's phone, but she was determined to find out. She figured that if it was some previously unknown drupe, she could swipe a few from the tree and use the seed within to germinate and grow her own crop. Then, she could harvest the new ingredient of which Angela had boasted, assuring the continued success of her bakery and the inevitable closure of her competition. Deciding it best to approach the property on foot, Juliana abandoned her car well away from Angela's home and continued the rest of the way on foot. She navigated to the home undetected and with ease, the full moon above providing ample light by which to traverse.

Arriving just before one in the morning, she surveyed the residence while concealed behind a cluster of bushes next to the home, on the opposite side of the street. Upon inspection, Juliana discovered that all lights within the house were turned off, suggesting that Angela had already retired for the evening. From where she crouched, Juliana did not have a clear line of sight to the back of the property, where she knew the plant, she sought was rooted. Giving the home a final once-over to look for any movement from within, Juliana made her way across the street, confident that she would not be spotted.

Sticking to the shadows, Juliana stealthily made her way to the rear of the house. When she rounded the corner, she froze when the odd-looking tree came into view. The thing looked like some twisted version of a weeping willow. It had beautiful, yet wickedly spiked, amber-colored, drooping branches, which hung to the ground, and resembled tentacles.

The trunk seemed to be multi-hued and stood atop a weird outcropping of stilt-like roots. Even at a distance and with minimum lighting, Juliana could tell the tree was quite the sight to behold. But there would be time for gawking later. Right now, her only concern was obtaining a few of the pods and making her escape. She checked the windows along the backside of the home that faced the tree. All was still. Juliana hesitantly stepped away from the safety of the shadows, making her way towards the tree.

The vicious looking thorns covering the drooping branches glinted in the moonlight. The branches hung protectively around the center trunk, where a cluster of the seed pods that Juliana had come in search of dangled. Lifting her hands and holding them out in front of her with palms facing outward, she warily pushed them into the drooping branches while trying to avoid the wicked spikes. She hesitantly spread the hanging branches as if parting a portiere, when they seemed to pulse and throb against her skin.

Juliana almost snatched her hands away in surprise and would have probably sliced her wrist open in the process, but she steeled herself when she looked up and saw the prize, she sought only a few feet away. Resolve to obtain the mysterious fruit renewed, she continued deeper into the drooping mass of branches. Upon reaching the trunk, she looked around at the branches surrounding her and was astonished that she had made it through the tangle unscathed. Face tilted up, she reached for the pods hanging temptingly overhead. Movement at the apex of the trunk made her freeze, as smaller, foot long tentacle-branches rose into the air. They swam languidly through the air, as if searching for something.

Unbeknownst to Juliana, the tree was utilizing receptors in cellular membranes within the tips of the appendages atop the trunk, to generate and sense different forms of long-range electrical signals. Anything ranging from light perception to temperature variations, wounding, and water and salt stress, by which it could transduce relevant environmental information. Upon sensing Juliana's body heat, all the smaller tentacles seemed to focus their attention on her in unison.

Juliana's eyes went wide when she saw the tree's odd behavior. Keeping her eyes on the tentacles, which tracked her movements, slowly she began to back away from the trunk, but winced in pain as her back contacted a thorn protruding from one of the branches. Responding to her touch, the branch whipped up and gouged deep, ragged furrows along Juliana's back.

She howled in pain and whipped around, pressing her back against the trunk to retreat from the multitude of hanging branches which sprang to life around her. Thrashing spasmodically, they whipped in and out. One after another the branches lashed towards Juliana, who crouched against the trunk of the tree, holding her hands over her face in a feeble attempt to protect herself.

With each blow, the tentacles mercilessly shredded bits of skin from Juliana's exposed flesh. One blow was so violent, it sent her crashing into the trees raised root system. The impact made the entire plant shake, causing digestive liquid to splash out of the hollow trunk. Juliana screamed louder when the blistering liquid saturated her. The digestive fluid burned as it ate its way into the deep tissue layers of her flesh.

To her dismay, Juliana looked up to see where the caustic liquid had rained down from, when more drops fell from above, directly into one of her open eyes. The resulting damage was immediate and severe as the digestive fluid ate its way into the socket. She slapped her hand to her face but was unable to hold back the discolored pool of flesh and blood oozing from her orbital cavity.

The branches continued their assault, brutally flaying the skin from her body as she tried to crawl on hands and knees through the mass of whipping tentacles. She was almost free of the tangle when a light shone in her one good eye, temporarily blinding her. The light retreated and when her vision cleared, Juliana saw Angela standing well out of reach of the tree. Her good eye widened as thoughts of salvation entered her mind, until she saw the malicious smirk plastered across Angela's face. "Help me," Juliana mouthed, reaching out a pleading hand in Angela's direction.

"Help meee," Angela repeated mockingly. "Bitch, I wouldn't piss on you if you were on fire."

A tentacle whipped out, snaked around Juliana's out-stretched arm, and snatched her into the air. Angela angled the flashlight upward, illuminating Juliana as she floundered about, kicking and screaming. Juliana wailed like a banshee when the tentacle tightened and drove its thorns deep into her wrist. Angela looked around worriedly, fearful that some passer-by would hear Juliana's panicked cries, but her concerns were laid to rest when another, thicker appendage wrapped itself around Juliana's face. Her eye widened in shock and pain as thorns from the tentacle stabbed multiple holes into her skull, one puncturing a gaping hole into her left cheek. The tentacle tightened, dragging the tip of the thorn along the base of her tongue, shredding her mouth to pieces in the process.

Blood poured from the savage wound and the left side of Juliana's jaw dangled, frayed, and broken, when the tentacle withdrew from around her head. As the one wrapped around her face retreated, the slim, tongue-like tentacle within the trunk's center emerged, dripping digestive fluid, and snaked itself around one of Juliana's legs. She shook her leg aggressively, trying to free herself, but it was useless. The thing was far too strong, and Juliana was growing weaker by the second. The tentacle began to withdraw back into the center of the trunk, dragging her along.

Though the trunk was not wide enough to accommodate the entire width of Juliana's body, it was more than wide enough to admit the one leg entangled by the tongue. Her leg disappeared into the creatures' *maw* and Juliana began convulsing violently when her foot contacted the digestive liquid within. The next moment she was submerged up to her ankle, then her knee, and then her thigh, until she found herself straddling the top of the trunk. The tongue pulled again but was met with resistance and could drag Juliana no further into its' center. With one last, aggressive pull, there was a sickening snap as Juliana's other leg; the one hanging on the outside of the trunk, broke and twisted upwards at 180 degrees.

Angela turned away from the macabre scene as one last agonizing scream bubbled up from Juliana's throat. Tendrils, one after another, like serpents with ferocious energy and infernal brutality, wrapped about Juliana's lifeless body. Ever tightening, and with the cruel swiftness and savage tenacity of anacondas fastening upon prey, they viciously dismembered Juliana and deposited her body parts into the digestive enzymes within the creature's trunk.

"That'll teach you to fuck with me," Angela muttered, making her way home. Though there was no body to dispose of, she was concerned about the amount of blood left behind by the tree's savage attack on Juliana. Luckily, a ferocious storm was forecasted to hit tomorrow afternoon, promising a torrential downpour that would wash the tree and the surrounding area free of any lingering carnage.

The following morning, Angela woke and went out to check on the tree. Maybe there was something she could do in advance of the approaching storm to assist with removal of any possible evidence of the previous nights' event. She exited her home and froze when she rounded the corner to the backyard area. The tree was nowhere to be found. Angela walked over to where it had been planted, thinking that someone had uprooted and stolen the plant as she had slept, but that theory was dispelled when she noticed a trail from where the tree once stood, leading off into the thick forested area surrounding her yard. Kneeling to examine the empty hole, she recalled the grafting technique she had utilized to save the sapling weeks ago.

"The Walking Palm Tree," she whispered aloud, her eyes once again following the trail leading off into the rainforest. "*Merging the Ya-Te-Veo with the Walking Palm must have modified the root system at a cellular level, creating a hybrid tree, capable of kinesis. Just as the creatures' branches can move and act independently of one another, so too now could its root system. Permitting the tree to uproot and relocate itself,*" she thought aloud

She remembered the goat, and how it had been impaled by one of the tree's roots. The root must have eradicated itself from the soil and attacked the goat, piercing the animal through the stomach before re-planting itself. She caught movement in her peripheral vision. Looking to her right, she was shocked to see a five-inch tall Ya-Te-Veo sapling. A beautiful, laced-wing, iridescent dragonfly landed on it. In the blink of an eye, a slim tongue-like tentacle shot out from the saplings center, wrapped itself around the body of the dragonfly and dragged the buzzing insect back into the tiny trunk. Angela tore the sapling out of the ground and ripped it to shreds.

She stood slowly, staring off into the rainforest. She thought about the town which was surrounded by the forest into which the Ya-Te-Veo tree had escaped. Thought about the residents of the city who still used the surrounding lands, and the children who still ventured deep into the forest to play, and whispered to herself, "Oh God, what the fuck have I done?"

COUNTY CONTEST

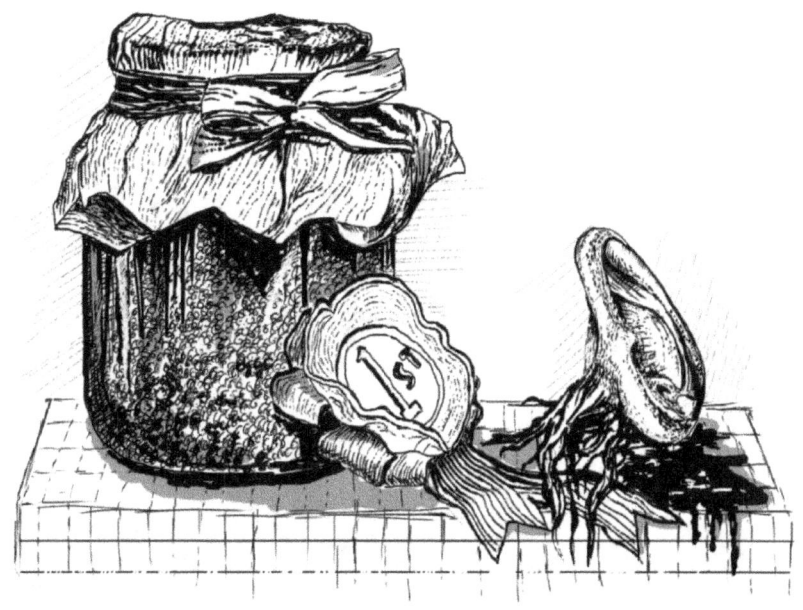

CANDACE NOLA

County Contest

By Candace Nola

Horace Jenkins was a quiet man. He kept to himself and ran the small bakery in town, with his one assistant, Trevor. Trevor was a bit of a loser; a mis-guided stoner that had done jail time for petty crimes and was wandering through life living off odd jobs and hand-outs. Horace took pity on him one winter, giving him a job and permission to turn the spare rooms in the basement of the bakery into a small living area. It wasn't much to look at, but it was livable and warm, and Trevor kept it neat as a pin.

Trevor was clean and sober now, grateful to be off the streets. Horace sometimes caught a glimpse of a haunted look in his eyes, a bit crazed, but he chalked it up to his years of drug use and hard living. Trevor was good at his job, kept Horace company and did all he could to help.

Horace and Trevor got along very well, despite their differences. They kept different hours at the bakery, with Trevor, being a night owl, baking all the different pastries and cookies throughout the night and helping Horace with donut duty in the mornings. Horace ran the place during the day, one person more than enough for the small stream of business that they did in the small town. Horace kept the bakery going in his wife's honor, the late Mrs. Jenkins had passed on seven years before, after a long battle with breast cancer.

Jenkin's Jams and Jellies were well-known for their homemade preserves, jams, and jellies of all kinds. Mrs. Jenkins won the county fair canning contest every year that she had been alive, her cherry rhubarb jam being declared one of the best combinations ever. Their jams and jellies graced the insides and tops of their donuts, strudels, pastries, cakes, and pies, with every flavor you could think of. The buttercream icing is made fresh every day, blended with only the finest and freshest fruit purees that Horace prepared during the day. Trevor would take over the process at night, letting the thick fruit blends simmer and bubble for twelve hours, stirring, sugaring, and tasting to ensure only the best quality.

Horace took great pride in maintaining the bakery just like his dear wife had, but Horace was troubled. He had lost the canning contest the last few years and feared that he was letting his wife down. He took home ribbons, of course, but not those royal blues with the big number one stamped on them. He took home second and third, runner-up and honorable mentions, but he was losing his touch and not winning that big blue.

He spent hours testing new fruit combinations, and old ones, trying to get them just right, just tart enough and slightly sweet. It was all about balance, see? Balance, and richness, color and texture, it all had to balance just so, to have that certain pop upon the tongue. To tease the taste buds into exploding with flavor, to cause chills to dance along the spine, as the taster consumed something divine.

Trevor joined him in his efforts, bringing ideas from the old cookbooks he scoured during the night. They talked, they brainstormed, they tasted, and they canned. It was safe to say that they were both obsessed with bringing the blue ribbon back to Jenkins Jams and Jellies. They became consumed by this singular task. The town was rooting for them and relishing in their new attempts. Each new pastry thick with berries and cream, tarts full of jelly and fresh fruit, donuts so heavy with jam, the dough could barely contain it. The cake flavors were incredible and sold out nightly. Lemon cake with blackberry cream, Almond torte with cherry filling, cheese danish with strawberry rhubarb jam, vanilla cake with raspberry coconut cream, the list went on and on.

The farmers in town, those not concerned with contests and ribbons, often dropped by with extra fruit from their farms, recipe cards in hand from their wives or mothers-in-law, all ready for a chat, a pastry, and an idea to win the blue. Horace listened to each idea with enthusiastic grace, each recipe card stored and tried out later that day, judged, rated, and often kept for pie or cake, but none fit the particular taste that Horace had developed over the years. Some fruits preserved better than others, tasted better as they aged, rather than weakening into an unidentifiable blend of sugar.

Horace kept smiling, determined to succeed and basking in the success of the small bakery. The canning contest was a personal pursuit, but his attempts at creating new flavors had put new life into the bakery. People were raving all about town and soon they began to come from towns nearby. Jenkins Jams and Jellies were becoming a big deal and Horace was pleased. He knew this year, he would win that blue ribbon for his canning jam. He would make his wife proud, once again.

He continued his days like this, working side by side with Trevor in perfect unity. He served up coffee, donuts, and teas, and jotted down new recipes in-between. One quiet Wednesday, when the bell chimed, he looked up to greet a new customer and was startled to find a stern woman glaring at him.

"Hello, Welcome to Jenkins Jams and Jellies, May I help you?" He greeted her in his normal cheerful tone.

"Well, I'm not sure. I'm new in town and in need of the finest pastries that you have to offer. I was told that you were the best bakery in town. I was just so rudely informed that it is my job to bring the pastries for the ladies' library tea, as if they pay me enough to do so. I've only just gotten here, and they are already trying to rob me." She spoke snidely, her nasally tone becoming more condescending as she spoke. As she looked around the small cafe setting, the gleaming oak floor, the rustic wood shelves full of canned preserves and the delightful help-yourself coffee bar, she sniffed as if offended.

"I see, well, we are the only bakery in town, but I can assure you that we are one of the best in the county, everyone says so. What type of pastries were you interested in? Do you need to place an order, or do you want to pick out a few from the case? Everything was baked fresh today."

"Hmph. Fresh, you say? I'll be the judge of that. I suppose I will just need to take whatever you have available now."

Her rude tone was beginning to grate on Horace, but he just took a deep breath and reminded himself that perhaps she was just having a bad day, that we all have bad days. He stepped over to the cold case of pastries and donned a fresh pair of serving gloves before he grabbed a bakery box to prepare it with several waxed sheets of paper. He looked up at her expectantly.

"Ma'am, were there certain ones that you wanted to pick?" Horace gestured at the full case of treats, each oozing with filling, icing or cream.

The woman bent over a bit, glaring into the case, studying each baked good as if they had sprouted horns or flies. After a few minutes, she straightened up and began tapping on the glass, barking her order at him.

"Two of these, two of these, no, not those, these!" Tap. Tap. Her long finger sounded almost indignant as it tapped the pastry case.

"Two of these over here, give me one of this, one of these, and one of those. No! The other one." Tap. Tap. Tap. The finger tapped, all the way through her order. It was the most annoying sound, but Horace smiled and continued filling the box.

"There, that makes a full Baker's Dozen." Horace added a thirteenth treat to the box and closed it with a flourish.

"What? I didn't order that, put that back!" She admonished him in her shrill voice.

"It's on the house, ma'am. One of our best recipes. My wife's recipe in fact, God rest her soul. It's the cheese danish topped with her famous cherry and rhubarb jam. County contest winning recipe, right there!' Horace smiled at her and continued tying up the box with his signature red and white twine.

"On the house, you say. It better be. I will not be paying for baked goods that I did not order, sir!" She snapped as she took the hefty box from him. She stepped over to the register before glancing to the delectable looking coffee bar.

"I suppose you charge for your coffee too?" She asked, looking down her nose at him, her round glasses making her look a bit owlish behind the frames. Horace tried not to smirk as he rang up her purchases.

"No, Ma'am. We sure don't charge for coffee or tea. Old house custom. We honor the Bakers Dozen round here and we don't charge for good old-fashioned coffee or our many loose-leaf tea combinations. We pride ourselves on our hospitality around these parts. Go on and help yourself."

Horace watched as she clopped her way over to the coffee bar, watching the way she inspected and studied each item. It infuriated him and intrigued him, who was this woman and why did she behave so rudely? Most of the customers here were nice, friendly folks; people he had known for decades. The folks he knew would not take kindly to this woman's behavior. He watched her sniff the coffee that he had just brewed fifteen minutes ago before inspecting and sniffing each canister of tea. He waited patiently and watched.

Trevor appeared from the back with a basket of jams to put on the shelf, startling Horace from his observations.

"Boss. Got some more jam to stock. Got 30 jars from the last recipe, the new one." Trevor called over to Horace as he began setting the ribbon topped jars on the shelf with the others.

"Thank you, Trevor" Horace replied, still watching the woman as she ogled Trevor. Her owlish expression grew haughtier by the second. Horace was relieved to see that Trevor had his hairnet on properly for once. The man's long hair was pulled back in a tight bun, secured with an elastic band and the hair net was properly pinned in place. Something told him, this woman would pounce on that oversight like a lion with a chew toy. Her glare could have roasted the man on the spot.

She looked Trevor up and down as she stood there, preparing her coffee before turning to read the labels of jam that he was placing on the shelves.

"New recipe, you say?" She picked up the jar and held it up to the light, observing the rich red color in the sun.

"What blend, may I ask? It simply says, 'Wild Berries'." She turned to show Horace the jar that she was holding.

"Oh, yes, Ma'am. New recipe. We are dead set on winning that County Contest this year. My Mabel used to win it every year. Her cherry rhubarb jam just makes the taste buds dance! Least, that's what the judges used to say, before she passed away.

"The Wild Berries blend includes blackberry, raspberry, elderberry, and blueberry. A bit of rhubarb gives it that deep red color and the elderberry really sets off the flavors. Would you like me to ring that up for you?" Horace asked her, as she approached the register again with her coffee and the jam jar still in her hand.

"I suppose. As if you haven't made enough money off of me today." She said, setting her purse on the counter to retrieve her faded wallet. She pulled out two twenties and handed them over.

"That'll be $37.75." Horace said kindly, counting out her change and handing it back to her. "May I ask what brings you to town, ma'am? Why our little neck of the woods?"

She snatched her change from him before she spoke again.

"Nosy lot, aren't you? I suppose one cannot expect privacy in such a small town. My name is Dr. Katherine Rutabaga, LMNOP and I am the new librarian in town and rightly so. That little hovel you all call a library is a disgrace. I'm glad I got here when I did. Is there anything else you would like to know, sir or am I free to go?" She spoke with so much disdain in her voice, Horace was reluctant to ask anything else.

"No, ma'am. Just wanted to know who I had the pleasure of serving today. I do hope you enjoy the pastries. Come back soon, even for a coffee. Everyone is welcome to stop in for free coffee throughout the day. Welcome to town, ma'am."

"Well, with riffraff like that around," she shot more daggers at Trevor as he stocked the jam, "I can't say how often I'll be back." And with that, a haughty sniff and a quick turn, she was gone, marching severely down the sidewalk with her bag held tightly in her right hand, swinging stiffly at her side.

Horace watched her go, parting the dainty red and white checkered curtain as Trevor came over to watch too. A low whistle left his lips before the woman had crossed the street followed by a strained chuckle from Horace.

"What a piece of work, eh, boss?" Trevor whistled again while shaking his head. "I ain't seen such rudeness since I left the Big Apple."

Horace sighed and went to lock the front door, happy that it was closing time for the day. He didn't think he could handle another dose of Dr. Katherine Rutabaga, LMNOP, or whatever the fuck she said.

"Well, Trevor, even rude people eat pastries." Horace turned the sign to "Closed" and took off his white apron, heading to the back.

"Come on, let's try out the black elderberry jam, see how it's going." Horace donned his black rubber apron and gloves, suited to the high temperatures of the boiling jam and the canning process and handed a set to Trevor as he came back through the curtain.

"It's bubbly and thick, been simmering for a couple of hours now. Should be time for sugaring if needed. If not, I can do it later tonight, once the elderberry cooks down a bit more. The skins tend to be bitter as they cook." Trevor picked up the long wooden paddle and stirred the giant pot as Horace got a clean tasting spoon out, a small slice of fresh bread and a fresh square of glazed pastry, then he cut each of those in two.

He liked to taste each recipe three times to ensure the perfect levels of tart and sweet, since bread and sweet pastry each have their own balance. That's how his Mabel taught him and that's just how he did it. He watched Trevor stir the thick mixture, so deep red it almost looked black. He had his notebook handy, ready to jot down their thoughts on this recipe. He couldn't help being a bit excited as Trevor finished his stirring and handed him the tasting spoon.

Horace reached into the giant pot with the long-handled spoon and got a small spoonful of the thick liquid. He set it down gently on the steel worktable before they both took small tasting spoons and spooned a bit onto each bite of bread and pastry before putting a bit more on the small spoon. They tasted it from the spoon, on the bread, and on the pastry, and shared their thoughts. Trevor thought it needed more sugar. Horace agreed but something else was still missing, some unknown flavor that he just couldn't name. He wasn't crestfallen but something close to it. He thought they had a winner with this one. He was failing his Mabel and he didn't understand what he was doing wrong.

Trevor sensed the mood change in Horace and went back to stir the pot, gently suggesting that a few more hours of simmering and sugaring would deepen the flavor and texture. Maybe they just give it a few more hours. Horace agreed and busied himself cleaning up the rest of the kitchen and prepping the pastries for Trevor to bake that evening. Trevor felt bad for his boss and his friend, hell, his only friend. Horace gave him a chance and a home when no one else had. Most people looked at Trevor the way the lady had looked at him this afternoon. Trevor wasn't a bad guy, just had a rough life and fell in with the wrong crowd.

Horace and Mabel took him in, helped him get clean and sober and taught him job skills. They gave him something he never had before, a bit of confidence in himself. He was almost as good of a pastry chef as Horace was, although he would never admit it. He was going to help Horace win the blue ribbon for canning, if it was the last thing he ever did. He swore that to himself, silently as he stirred the pot, watching his troubled boss go about his evening routine.

The night ended quietly as Horace finished and went upstairs to his small apartment. Trevor made himself comfortable in his basement apartment, taking the kitchen timer with him. He went about his evening, making a small dinner, popping pastry trays in and out of the basement ovens and checking on the simmering jam upstairs every 30 minutes or so.

Morning came and went, donuts were made, the early risers came in for breakfast and coffee and small talk was made. As the morning slowed, Horace and Trevor tasted their jam again, declared it finished and as good as it would ever be. It was downright delicious, but Horace still felt it lacking. Trevor knew not to argue and set about canning the jam for the afternoon and reserving several large jars for the week's pastries and baked goods. New flavors were shared early and often. If they sold well, then they would be put into regular rotation.

Several days had passed and they were working on a new creation, strawberry, basil, rhubarb jam with a hint of lemon. The entire bakery smelled sublime. Customers were raving about it as they came in to pick up orders or just to impulse buy. Late in the day, on another Wednesday, Dr. Katherine Rutabaga (LMNOP) darkened the door once more. Horace looked up, stifled a sigh and greeted her like any other customer.

"Ah, Dr. Rutabaga, how nice of you to drop by. How can I help you today? I hope you found the last batch of pastries to your liking?" Horace stood near the register, pair of gloves in hand, ready to serve the frowning matron.

"My liking, indeed, Sir. Please use my title when you address me. It's Dr. Katherine Rutabaga, LMNOP, if you please." she practically snarled the words at him. "And your pastries are much too sweet, almost everything I tasted was much too sweet. It's no wonder the little brats around here are out of control, having that much sugar in anything rots the brain! Who taught you to bake anyway? I certainly hope you have some type of degree behind you, selling this drivel to decent folks."

Horace felt his face begin to flush, a hot red flare in his chest that raced to his neck and beyond. He silently counted to ten before he attempted to speak, pretending to ready a bakery box instead.

"Well, I am sorry to hear that you were not pleased. How can I help you today? Would you like a refund, did you not consume any of the baked goods? I do have a degree and I do conform to classical baking standards. I realize that not everyone consumes a lot of sugar, perhaps that is why you found them too sweet." Horace replied as patiently as he could muster.

"Refund? Ha, as if you'll give an old lady a refund on a box of week-old baked goods. No, sir. I am not that naive nor am I that broke. I do not need your charity; however, I did find the jam to be adequate. Not as good as my mothers, mind you, but adequate. I will take another jar of the Wild Berries Jam and two other kinds." She smirked and turned on her heel, towards the back of the cafe.

She clomped over to the wooden shelves where the pretty jam jars waited for customers to browse and sample. She sniffed and sneered at the small, covered platters with their bites of bread and pastry and tiny tasting spoons. Looking at the jars, she took down a Wild Berries Jam and handed it to him. Then she spotted the almost black jam on the middle shelf, Black Elderberry, the label read. She picked it up and showed it to him.

"Do you have a jar that I can taste? Your display does say that all jams can be sampled." She pointed to the small sign in front of the tasting display. She went back to looking at the jams, browsing, turning them this way and that, before she settled on the cherry rhubarb jam.

"I'll take this one too." she thunked the jar on the display case and waited for Horace to come around with the sample jar. Horace retrieved a small sample tray from the small refrigerator behind him and handed her one of the small cups. Each small cup was covered with a small plastic lid and Horace motioned to the spoons and small plated bites behind her.

"Help yourself to bread or pastry and let me know what you think. The samples are prepared fresh every morning and kept cold until requested. We do not leave open jars on our shelves." Horace took the other jars over to the register as she busied herself with her sampling of the Black Elderberry.

Horace found his hands shaking as he wrapped the jam jars in white paper, tying them with the red and white twine, wondering where things had gone so horribly wrong that he was now dealing with this shrew. Not many people make his blood boil, but this woman was just downright mean. Not like his Mabel at all. Mabel was a saint compared to this entitled, nasty, vile creature.

He could hear Trevor come up the back stairs into the kitchen and he hoped he would just stay back there. Trevor was much more outspoken than he was, and he had already had his fill of her. Talk all over town was that many had already had their fill of her. She was quickly making enemies. Horace shook his head sadly, reminding himself that life is often hard for many, and it can make some people hard to deal with, hard to like. Maybe life had done her wrong and she just didn't know any other way. He took a deep breath, bagged her jam jars and walked back down to the display case where she stood sneering at a fruit tart.

"Was there something else that you wanted?" he asked, his quiet voice restrained but even. "Did you want the Black Elderberry jam?"

"Yes, I'll take the jam, it has an interesting texture to it, good woodsy flavor. Not fabulous, mind you. But it'll do for a bit of toast. Wrap up this fruit tart too, it can't be too laden with sugar. At least, I hope not, you'll be hearing from me if it is. I'll take a plain cheese danish as well and two of those raspberry scones. Those library ladies do enjoy an afternoon treat, this will suffice, I suppose." She looked down her nose at him as he prepared the box of treats, silently judging his every move.

She moved over to the coffee bar and made a fresh cup of tea as he rang her up. After she paid and clomped out of the bakery, Trevor all but burst from the back room.

"That bitch!" He almost yelled it as he stomped over to the front door, locking it behind her. "How dare she insult you, how dare she even come back in here. I swear, boss, we don't need to serve her. We can refuse her service. It's your bakery, how dare she talk to you like that?" Trevor was fuming, pacing back and forth on the wooden floor.

"Now, Trevor, we must treat everyone with kindness. The customer is always right, remember? Maybe we did over sweeten the last batch of pastries. I have been distracted with the canning contest, perhaps I did add too much to those. I've been working so hard to bring back the blue ribbon for my Mabel, maybe I didn't pay enough attention." Horace shrugged and looked down at the floor, just looking for something to do with his hands. Trevor's' intense gaze was disconcerting, he had that slightly crazed look again.

"Now, we both know that is not what happened. Those baked goods were perfect as they are every time. She is just a bitch! She's a shrew and a lunatic. Someone needs to put her in her place." Trevor stomped over to the coffee bar and made a lavender chamomile tea. The absurdity of the furious man choosing such a calming blend amid the heated situation struck Horace as comical and he began to laugh.

Trevor gave him an odd look as he kept stirring honey into his tea before cupping his skinny hands around it. Horace continued to chuckle as he went into the back where the latest blend was simmering. It smelled heavenly and he couldn't wait to taste it. Trevor followed, sipping on his tea and they set about their routine for the night.

Weeks passed as the county fair posters began to appear in the windows. The town began to whisper with excitement as preparations were made, committees were formed, and contests were announced. All the usual country fair stuff, biggest vegetable, biggest flower, best pie, best cookies, best cake, danish, best jam, etc. So many things to judge, so little time to prepare. Not to mention making time to see the horse pulls, and the demolition derby, both exciting events for the small town.

Trevor began to sense the urgency in Horace, as he still didn't feel like they had a winning recipe. Seven new recipes had been created, tasted and rated by the town.

Winners, each in their own way for new favorite flavors for cakes, pies, tarts and pastry but just not quite a contest winning jam. A blue-ribbon County Contest Jam, that Mabel would be proud of. Trevor really felt bad for his boss. He was depressed and sad at his imagined failing of his wife and Trevor couldn't stand to see him like this. Horace truly felt like he couldn't rest until he had done this one last thing to honor his wife. He had not won the contest since she passed.

Even more disheartening was that word had reached Trevor that Dr. Katherine Rutabaga, (LMNOP, mind you) had big plans to enter the jam and jelly contest, using her momma's recipe, as folks would tell it. The same recipe she had been judging Jenkins Jams and Jellies with for the last few months now. Word had it that she had been carefully deconstructing the baked goods she bought from Horace and analyzing the ingredients, especially the jam and jellies. Comparing flavors and different combinations all while trying to manipulate old Horace into not entering the contest simply by making him feel inadequate and unworthy.

Trevor was sick over this news. Horace was a kind, gentle man that only wanted to restore his wife's beloved blue ribbon to her jam display. Horace felt like he was failing her if he didn't win it at least one more time. Dr. Katherine Rutabaga, (LMNOP) needed to be dealt with quickly. Trevor was not about to let her ruin the contest for Horace. If he saw her again, he would be having his say, Horace or not.

The Sunday before the fair judging began, Trevor and Horace were hunkered down in the back room of the bakery. On Sundays, they closed early, after serving the church crowd, then they took the day to prepare for the week but today was special. Today, they were trying out two variations of an old recipe and Horace was excited. They had one more week to enter their jam into the contest and Horace was sure that one of these recipes would be the winner. He had found the recipe tucked away in his wife's old photo album and he was sure it would be the one, an old marmalade recipe that called for fresh ground ginger, fresh blackberries, lemon, orange and a few other herbs. It sounded divine and Horace did not recall his wife ever making it before.

Both batches were simmering in huge pots in the back room, as the men cut, chopped and ground other ingredients that still had to be added. Massive amounts of fruit, herbs, and nuts were prepared for both batches. The smell was heavenly, and the men continuously chuckled as their stomachs rumbled repeatedly throughout the day, even as the industrial fan in the back window sucked most of the scent outside. Horace finally put on a big batch of stew for them to eat as they chopped, simmered, boiled, and sugared the thick batches of fruit, rinds and herbs. As the day wound down, Horace took his leave and headed upstairs to his bed. Trevor had napped much of the late evening hours and would take over.

Several hours after Horace retired for the evening, Trevor was in the basement kitchen removing trays of baked goods from the ovens when he heard a noise overhead. It sounded like the utensil drawer being sorted through. He chuckled to himself, thinking Horace had come back for one final check. Then he heard it again, this time it was like steel on steel, and that gave him pause. Horace only used the long-handled wooden spoons to stir and taste the jam batches. He would never use steel because of the high temperatures.

He quietly crept up the stairs to see what was going on. He had a bad feeling that it wasn't Horace in the kitchen. When he heard a soft female voice cursing as he reached the top landing, his suspicions were confirmed. He peeked around the corner to see Dr. Katherine Rutabaga, (LMNOP, don't ya know?) ladling scoops of the jam mixture into a small glass jar but the spoon was too hot and too big for her to handle, and she was making an awful mess.

"Well, well, well, what do we have here?" Trevor sneered as he stepped out into the kitchen. The woman, startled, quickly turned around, knocking the glass jar over. She gasped as the hot mixture streamed over her hand and poured to the ground.

"You?" She almost shrieked. "What are you doing here?"

"I live here." Trevor snarled. "Now, what are you doing here? I'll only ask once before I call the cops." Trevor crossed the room to pick up the glass jar, only to have her jump back and strike at him with the hot spoon.

"You stay away from me, you hooligan. I know what you want. What all men like you want. I'll scream. I'll tell the cops you assaulted me. You best give me that jar and let me go." She spat the words at him, sneering, as if she expected her threats to work.

"Lady, you broke in here. I live here. My boss lives here. You are the one with no business here. I suggest you leave now, before Horace wakes up and before I call the cops. Just what are you trying to pull?"

"Horace doesn't deserve to win that contest. I do! He's a dried-up old has been. It's my turn!" Dr. Katherine Rutabaga, LMNOP, screeched at him and lunged for the jar.

Trevor was bending down to pick up the half-full jar of boiling sugar just as she rushed at him, trying to snatch the jar. She wrapped both hands around the top and tried to tug it from his grasp, not realizing her mistake in time. She barely had time to gasp as Trevor let go and the boiling sugar exploded from the jar into her face, searing and blistering it as it slid down her pale skin. Her skin blistered and bubbled and began to slough off in chunks as the molten sugar stuck to her skin and cooked it.

Trevor scrambled back in horror and could only stare at her as she clawed at her face, trying to wipe the boiling mixture from her eyes and mouth. She was making a horrid gurgling sound as her wide eyes screamed at him for help, but Trevor was paralyzed. He backed up against the wall as she made it to her feet, blindly seeking the sink but slipped on the jam mixture that was still steaming on the floor. She fell hard, splitting her head open on the side of the boiling steel pot. Thick crimson blood spilled out and into the bubbling mixture below as she hung there, before the weight of her body gave in to gravity and she slid off to the side.

Trevor stood there in shock, blood and jam coated the floor, the sink and the steel pots. Dr. Katherine Rutabaga, LMNOP, was dead; bleeding out from a split skull with half of her face skinned down to raw muscle and bone while the other half was burned to a bloody pulp. He looked around the room in a panic, the crazed gleam back once more, muttering to himself. With a pale face and wide eyes, his gaze fell on the industrial meat grinder they had set up to grind the nuts and rinds and he felt his heartbeat slow down. Sure, he could fix it. Make it like it never happened. Horace would never know how this bitch tried to ruin him. He stepped over to the knife block and took out the cleaver, an odd grin on his face.

Setting it down on the worktable, he bent down and lifted the dead woman under her arms, hoisting her into the large sink. Stripping her, he set all of her clothing aside to be burned later. He donned the safety goggles, rubber gloves and apron and picked up the cleaver.

Whack! Whack! Whack! Three solid chops severed the head from the neck. He followed with her arms, then the legs, first at the knee, then at the hip. He took the filleting knife and sectioned her skin, pulling it loose from each section with strong rapid tugs, like pulling the skin off a chicken drumstick. He chopped each breast off, and tossed the fleshy mounds into the grinder first, followed by thick slabs of meat from her thighs, belly, calves, and torso. While it fed through the grinder, he removed the remaining skin from her back, and buttocks, and pubic region. In went bloody mounds of rump and fleshy labia, ten little toes with the nails pulled off.

He scalped the head, and pulled the remaining flesh off, tossed her ears into the grinder, the fleshy part of her cheeks, chin and neck followed the rest of the parts, along with her heart, kidney, and liver. All tossed into the grinder, all while he tried to stave off his own hysteria.

"Just a little more, gotta protect Horace. I can save the jam. I can make the blue-ribbon recipe. He'll see. Just a little more and it'll all be fine." Trevor kept muttering to himself as he cut, chopped and ground up the Rutabaga remains until nothing, but bone and hair remained. His eyes gleamed with a fresh insanity as he muttered and cut, cut and muttered. The grin on his face pulled his cheeks taut and pulled his lips back slightly from his teeth. He looked like a madman complete with rubber gloves and goggles. Bits of blood and gore spattered his face and dripped from the black apron.

The meat grinder whined and ground away, as pound after pound of pulverized flesh met with bloody blades. Blood sluiced from the grinder as the meat splattered into a bowl. Trevor caught it all, and put it back in, turning the blades to a lower setting, running the meat back through before doing the same, once more, grinding it on the lowest setting. The final texture was pudding in the bowl, creamy, rosy, pink, pudding with a few crimson drops of blood swirled through it.

This was added to the batch of bloody jam that Dr. Katherine Rutabaga, LMNOP, had bled into, as she hung on the steel edge, slipping from this life to the next. Trevor really had done nothing to injure the manipulative shrew, the killing she had done herself. He merely cleaned it up. And clean he did. The floors were bleached, mopped, bleached again. The big fan in the window was turned on high and the back door opened wide, once the blood was gone.

The mop was bleached and rinsed and bleached again. Her clothes were taken downstairs to the old pizza oven and burned, along with the remaining hair, skin, bones and other bits and bobs that would not grind. The pizza oven would burn most of that to ash and then he would go bury it far away when the ashes cooled.

Sugar, blackberries, oranges, and more lemon rind was added to the jam, along with more fresh ground ginger root. The deep red bubbled and boiled as the fruit mingled with the sharp tang of copper and citrus. Trevor stirred and tasted, tasted and stirred. Even knowing what was in it, it was ...good. Delicious even, he began to grin. This was it; this would win the county contest; he just knew it would. He could barely wait for Horace to wake up to taste it, but it had to cook down for several more hours.

He went back to cleaning and baking, finishing the pastries for the morning like nothing had happened. He hosed the bakery floor down again and again, bleaching every surface, took apart the grinder, scrubbed it, boiled the parts and scrubbed it again before he put everything away. He burned his clothes in the bottom of the pizza oven and donned fresh ones. Then he baked half a dozen loaves of bread and a small pizza in the still burning oven to explain away its use. All his bases were covered, he was in the clear. Trevor sat on the back step, eating pizza, grinning from ear to ear. Kitchen timer in his hand, he waited for pastries, for morning and for Horace to come downstairs.

When Horace came down to open the bakery a couple of hours later, Trevor was ready for him. Tasting spoon in hand, bites of bread and golden pastry on their plates, and the heavenly smell of blackberry and ginger in the air. He eagerly called for Horace as soon as he heard his footsteps in the bakery. Horace came into the kitchen with a smile on his face, although it didn't quite meet his eyes. He looked tired and haggard, more despondent than Trevor had ever seen him before.

"Boss, I think we did it." Trevor said to him quietly, his dark eyes gleaming in the bright kitchen light.

Horace looked at the simmering pots, stirred them both, one just slightly thicker than the other. His eyes widened with pleasure as he took a deep breath, inhaling the aromas surrounding him.

"It smells divine." Horace replied. "Do you really think we've done it?"

"Yes, Yes, I do." Trevor replied, "but you be the judge, you must taste it. I've got everything ready for you." Trevor gestured at the steel worktable. He handed Horace the long-handled spoon.

Horace smiled and took the spoon from him, stepping to the first pot, he stirred a bit, then a bit more before bringing a careful spoonful out and pouring it into the waiting bowl. He tasted it, he smiled, pleased but then sighed.

"It's very good, Trevor, just as good as the others but something is missing, the texture or something is still just not right." Horace sighed as he watched Trevor finish his taste of the first batch of jam.

"Perhaps but try the second batch." Trevor urged. "It's a bit different, I had an idea, and I added a few things. I really think we've got a winner, boss. Trust me." Trevor grinned, clearly pleased with himself.

Horace accepted another spoon, stepped over to the second giant pot of jam and stirred the much thicker blend, inhaling deeply of berries, citrus, ginger and something more. He looked quizzically at Trevor before stirring the pot once more and withdrawing a ladleful of the crimson jam. He poured it into the fresh bowl, prepared his small bites to taste and blew gently to help it cool. Trevor was almost beside himself as he watched, preparing his own bites to taste, grinning, as Horace took his first bite.

Horace closed his eyes as he took his first bite, savoring the flavors, really letting them meld together on his tongue. The jam was heaven at first bite, absolutely divine on the glazed pastry bite. A tear escaped his eye as he stared at Trevor, and back at the pot.

"What did you add? This is magnificent! I think you might be right. This could win. This is amazing, tell me, what else did you add? How did you get that texture so perfect?" Horace's voice broke as a sob of pure happiness threatened to overtake him.

His Mabel, she would be so proud. This would win for sure, that blue ribbon was coming home. He knew it. Trevor was still grinning at him, from ear to ear. He was thrilled with himself, and he deserved to be proud. He had found the missing element.

"What did you add to it, Trevor?" he asked again, taking another happy bite.

"I put a little rutabaga in it." Came the cheerful reply.

DEATH, AND A DONUT

MICHAEL ENNENBACH

Death, and a Donut.

By M. Ennenbach

"Order up! One-twenty, one old fashioned and eleven glazed!" the man behind the counter announced over the low din of the surprisingly packed donut shop.

Death rose, black robes billowing eerily, the wickedly sharp blade of his scythe catching the wan yellow light. The crowd stopped what they were doing and stared at the grimmest of reapers as he seemed to glide across the black and white checkered floor. A cold air permeated him; the touch of the grave radiated out.

"Hey, your goddamned robe got in my coffee!" a voice cried out.

The crowd, somehow, at one time, managed to remain motionless, gasp, and were now facing the angry bald man in a newsboy cap who, in turn, was staring at the very Spectre of Death, Thanatos, with a defiant glare.

Death, a literal force of nature and unstoppable being, ignored the outburst and continued to the counter, where he set down his ticket. The clerk swallowed audibly in the silent room and picked up the ticket with a shaking hand. Verifying it was indeed number one-twenty, he robotically grabbed the white box and two white bags and set it on the counter. "Uh, it's on the house. There are a dozen donuts holes in the bag too. Glazed."

It is impossible to tell the expression on a bare skull, but if it were possible to infer an expression, the vacant eyes and perpetual smile seemed happy. Death nodded once and picked up the parcels and turned to leave. As the gaunt figure went past the angry man, he casually tapped him with the handle of his scythe. The man's eyes suddenly liquefied and ran down his stubbly cheeks, a soft gurgle coming from his throat, followed by a small gout of blue flame. He fell forward, spilling his coffee onto the table to drip onto the checkered floor.

It wasn't until the bells had sounded and the door swung closed again that the room erupted into screaming and chaos.

Everyone else died as scarabs crawled from the rapidly putrefying corpse of the bald man and swarmed throughout the shop, leaving nothing but pristine skeletons in piles. The clerk would live to be 114. He was never even sick once in his long life, though he would never understand the gift truly as he was driven quite insane.

Death was indifferent to the entire ordeal. A skeletal hand reached into the bag and popped a donut hole into the open jaw. The teeth mashed it into crumbs that fell through the empty ribcage and eventually tumbled onto the sidewalk from beneath the smoky robes. Pigeons darted down and pecked at the morsels of sweetness before stiffening and falling over. Maggots fell from the beak as the tiny tongue lolled out.

Death stopped next to a hearse parked in a handicapped spot. The car was a nightmare of chrome in angles that gave migraines if contemplated for too long. Death set the box and bag on the roof of the monstrous machine and pulled a set of keys from the voluminous ebony robes. The lights flashed a sinister red as the locks popped and the grim reaper set the scythe on back seat and the donuts on the rear floorboard.

A police officer stood in front of the hearse with a ticket pad in her hand. "Excuse me, you cannot park in a handicapped spot without a placard or special plates. I am going to have to write you a ticket." Death strode silently to the front of the car and stood patiently as the officer asked without looking up, "I need your license and proof of insurance."

She looked up and her eyes grew to the size of saucers. Death ran a bone finger gently across her cheek and turned towards the car. Where the finger had touched on the officer's cheek was now red and slightly swollen. She reached up and touched it and the skin burst open. The raw edges of the wound consumed the living flesh in a slow wave that ended in gurgling screams from a fleshless face as the hearse door slammed shut.

Death slid the key into the ignition and turned it, the engine of hellfire and torment roared to life causing every candle in a three-block radius to flare deep purple. Emerald smoke oozed out of the exhaust pipes and sparrows fell from the sky as they flew overhead, and squirrels convulsed on the grass.

Death turned on the stereo and Hank Williams began singing as a tinny guitar played behind his sad voice. Without looking in the mirrors, the car suddenly burst backwards into traffic, crushing the side of a gray Jeep, as a spray of blood suddenly painted the interior of the windshield. The hell beast vehicle leapt forward into the wrong lane sending a blue sedan into a parked car. The body of the sedan driver was crushed by the steering wheel that was now resting two feet further back.

Death paid no heed to any of it, phalanges tapped the steering wheel along with the drums, the donuts not shifting a bit.

***

The park was quiet for a warm summer day, some joggers ran along the manicured trails that wound through the trees and eventually alongside the lake. One, a red-faced man, puffed along making slow progress but steadily moving forward. A near fatal heart blockage luckily found during an examination gave him a new lease on life. He may not be breaking any records, but he was doing what he could to extend his life. Lionel Richie sang about Sunday mornings, and he wondered if maybe his choice in music was part of the problem.

He stopped and stared at a group of joggers that were running as if their lives depended on it. They looked at him with frantic wide eyes. He shrugged after a moment, then forced his feet to begin slapping the concrete.

"Know it sounds funny, just can't stop the pain"
He found the rhythm in the mellow seventies jam.

"Why in the world would anybody put chains on me? Yeah"
A calm came over him as he saw the sun over the waters of the lake, glistening.

"I just want to be free, just me, oooh baby"
And then he found himself stumbling forward, his foot hit something solid, and the ground came rushing up to meet his hands. Both wrists snapped at the impact, and he screamed in pain as he rolled onto his back. He squinted through the pain and looked to see what it was that had inexplicably caused this agony.

It was a dead goose. He looked around and saw dead geese and ducks all over the ground between the waterline and the jogging path. Confusion warred with the pulsating misery flaring up his arms as he tried to make sense of it. The other runners running past him, the dead birds littering the ground, the gears turned but nothing made any semblance of sense.

Then he saw Death tossing pieces of something from a white paper bag. Donut holes?

It was as if the ducks didn't see the black robes that seemed to shift like the smoke from a fatal wreck. The fight or flight instinct was extinguished by the temptation of sugary dough. The jogger's mouth twitched, and he tried to scramble backwards but his wrists gave out and he let out a yelp of pained surprise that startled the ducks.

The skull of Thanatos snapped to stare directly at him. Again, it is impossible to gauge an exact expression based on a faceless skull, but disapproval and anger seemed to smolder in the empty eye sockets. Death snapped the thumb and middle finger of the skeletal right hand. At first nothing happened.

The man stared in abject terror, frozen by the hooded skull's unflinching stare. Then the bodies of the dead waterfowl twitched, convulsed, and made their way back onto their webbed feet. They turned their unblinking dead eyes towards the man and began to awkwardly shamble towards him.

Death sighed from the bench, a hollow breath rattling through a birdcage of yellowed ribs, as the screams and sound of tearing flesh exploded from the trail. The hooded figure stood up, the grass shrank and curled up, first brown, then brittle, then dust, as the reanimated birds fell still, one by one, beneath the lessening arterial sprays. The now empty white bag carefully crumpled and tossed into a garbage can, Death strode across the carefully manicured lawn and through a small flower garden of desiccated blooms, on the way to the parking lot.

***

"Just let me run in here for a second. You can sit on the bench and wait for me, I'll look for something sexy," a petite brunette said with a knowing smile.

Her husband sighed, arms already over laden with bags. "Fifteen minutes. The baseball game starts at three and I need to grab cigars."

She kissed him on the cheek and walked into the garish pink store. He turned and carefully maneuvered through the shambling zombies of consumerism with a scowl. He managed to find a bench and let the bags slide down his arms to rest between his legs as he slid the earbuds in to listen to the pregame. He let his mind wander as they talked on-base-percentages and the pitches certain batters would chase, finding calm in the statistics. Then he saw a white box open in front of him with three rows of glazed donuts. He assumed this was a free sample to try and convince him to buy a dozen, but he was far too crafty for that. He didn't look up, just snatched a donut, and muttered his thanks before closing his eyes and falling into the numbers.

It melted on his tongue with sugary goodness, and he smiled, really smiled, for the first time in hours. Too many people, too close and too loud.

A crowd began to gather as he let out his first, and last, strangled gasp. It seemed as if the fluids were just suddenly evaporated from his system, going from normal skin tone to gaunt and then to gray in a matter of seconds. His ear buds fell out and the tinny sound of voices called in the silence as onlookers stared in horror. Then a crackling sound as a goiter formed on the now dead man's throat. It undulated the papery skin and slowly worked its way to the gaping mouth.

Maggots, thick and writhing, poured across the blackened tongue and onto the faux marble flooring, more and more, an incomprehensible number of larvae washed out and against the shoes of the panicked crowd.

The writhing maggots popped, releasing clouds of green spores that floated along the upper mezzanine and everyone that inhaled it broke out in sores and fell screaming.

Death stood patiently on the escalator, the donut box balanced on one hand, his scythe resting on a boney shoulder, the empty-socketed gaze transfixed on one store on the lower floor.

It was Natalie's first day at Build-A-Bear. She prided herself on her preparedness, always ready for any situation, head on a swivel. Now, she pumped the button on the floor and forced back tears before saying softly, "Now put the heart to your, ummm, mouth and whisper your love into it then place it in the body of the owl." She nearly fainted as the cold of the grave swept along her tan arms. The robe seemed to hunger to touch her but stayed a millimeter off her. She added a little more cotton and gulped. "Is that cuddly enough?"

Death reached down and gave a tentative squeeze in the pudgy tummy of the mischievous barn owl before nodding briskly. Natalie shook as she carried the stuffed bird to the counter, where she avoided looking at the skeleton in wispy black, packing the happy rabbit into a white box that looked like a little house. "Does the owl have a name for the birth certificate?"

Death's head cocked at an angle a flesh and blood skeleton could never hope to achieve due to ligaments and the laws of reality. One finger pointed out and neatly tapped the name tag on her vest.

"Aww. That's sweet," Natalie said, briefly forgetting who it was she was talking with. She remembered and had to look down at her name tag twice to spell her name correctly as fear drove rational thought from her head. A small spot of cold seemed to radiate from the name tag where the plastic blackened and cracked. She didn't look at the bodies of the two middle-aged women that sniffed a little rudely when Death cut in line. One of the heads stared up from the floor behind the counter by the cash register. Natalie was on autopilot. She put the birth certificate in a small cardboard frame and set it by the little house.

Death offered a donut, but she declined with a forced smile and muttered *no thank you*. Death shrugged and balanced the boxes and left silently. A group of mall walkers marched in various toddler-faced sweatshirts, arms swinging fiercely, eyes down on the shiny white sneakers who walked right into Death.

Later, when she could articulate what she saw fully, Natalie would describe the scene as such.

The five old women marched forward, and it was like one of those car washes, the kind where you sit in the car and the big straps of canvas smack the car as purple and green colored foam hits the windshield. Except not. The robe seemed alive as it wrapped itself around the bodies of the walkers, the billowing fabric slapped rhythmically against the glass window at the front of the shop. The bears fell off the stands as the sentient fabric pounded harder and harder against the window and then, boom. The robes stopped flailing and a spray of assorted innards sprayed against the glass. Natalie could describe the various viscera as it slid slowly down. She turned in her two weeks' notice immediately.

Death walked on unconcerned, the boxes still both pristine white even as the rest of corridor was not so fortunate. Onlookers stood frozen, gore-soaked, as Death waited for the doors to slide open before stepping out into the light of the day. Hell had come to the mall as affirmed by the guttural yells of terror.

***

Kristoff stood staring at the glass doors to the grocery store, his service revolver clutched in his sweaty hand. The news had been going on and on about the different scenes of carnage and death throughout the city. It started with a donut shop. As his shift began, he listened to the reports about a mall.

"Goddamn terrorists," he muttered as he tried to will his stubborn feet to move.

He flinched back as a woman slammed headfirst into the glass door, it slowly slid open, and her limp body fell forward. This kept the doors open and the sounds of screaming soon rang out into the parking lot. The terrorists were dressed in long black robes, and the few survivors described them as Death itself. Kristoff pulled his belt up over his prodigious belly with a shimmy and a grunt and raised his weapon, using his other hand to settle the slight tremor.

He took his first steps through the open door, stepping over the unconscious, stressing the word even though her head seemed to hang at an angle that looked quite unnatural. The body of a cashier hung, torn open as if something huge had crawled out, on the slowly rumbling conveyor, a sick slapping as his innards, now outards, oozed along the black rubber.

Kristoff felt his breakfast, three sausage biscuits, roil in his guts. A drip of sweat fell into his eye and he blinked furiously at the stinging. He ducked low and tried to survey the scene. Something, something big, had torn down the aisles, leaving shattered jars and torn boxes of food scattered all over the half-eaten bodies that lay strewn among the discarded goods. Carts lay on their sides, packages sent all over, filthy wheels hanging limply or strung with strips of flesh and thick mucus.

Kristoff could not think of a single act of terror that left a mess like this behind. He tried to think back to his training and took a deep calming breath. He had been through scenarios like this. Admittedly in virtual reality, but he held two distinct speed running records in the remakes of Resident Evil One and Two.

The thought occurred to him that he was indeed playing a game. Or dreaming. Either or, he was in his element. He crept along, past the body on the belt, great attention to detail, the way the torn skin hung looked as real as a high-end graphics could manage.

The noises went from wails to wet chomping sounds as he crept through chemical enhanced, sugar-coated bits in bright colors aimed at children's imaginations. A muffled sound caught his attention, and he froze in place, a sustained hissing followed by a rubbery squeak.

Kristoff choked down a scream as something touched his leg. He spun, sending a wave of pastel marshmallows skittering as he pointed his weapon in front of him and felt his finger grow tight on the trigger.

"Help me–" a faint woman's voice moaned, buried under boxes of oatmeal and toaster pastries.

Kristoff made a noise he hoped passed for calming and grabbed the hand and squeezed it. "Can you make it to the front door? The path is clear."

The hand went limp, and a ragged exhalation came from the bloody mouth of the woman. That was when Kristoff noticed her legs farther down the aisle, a thick pool of blood making the spilled oatmeal swell and take on a pink color. Kristoff sucked in his gut, held back the bile, and crawled forward to the end of the aisle. The hissing and squeaking still coming faintly and itching at the back of his mind.

At the end of the aisle, he peered out and wished he hadn't. The meat section had been ravaged, strips of raw beef and pork, and other cuts he tried not to discern, were cast everywhere as if an orgy of feasting had occurred. A butcher was slumped over the deli slicer, his arms thinly sliced in a soupy pile on the other side of the gore encrusted machine that still spun, sending a spray of red to run down the window between him and the counter.

At the far end, at the floral section, Kristoff saw a figure in a long black robe and cursed under his breath. He got to his feet, adrenaline surging through his legs, giving them a teetering effect like a toddler. He pulled every bit of false bravado he could muster and held his weapon in front of him. He paused slightly as he tried to comprehend what was happening.

A figure that appeared to be the Grim Reaper, identical to the figure immortalized on heavy metal covers and bikers' arms, stood surrounded by blackened flowers that drooped towards the floor, petals drifting like a tepid grey snow, stood filling balloons with helium. A half dozen brightly colored balloons were tied around the handle of an intimidating looking scythe. As Kristoff stared, Death pulled the balloon off the hissing tank and wound the sphincter of the balloon through skeletal fingers, then quickly tied a green ribbon around the balloon knot that was wrapped around the wooden handle.

Kristoff took a steadying breath and set his finger gently on the trigger, aimed and ready to fire as he spoke.

"Put the scythe down and turn around with your hands in front of you!"

Death put a balloon on the nozzle, yellow this time, and it inflated quickly.

"No habla Española, Senior Dias la Muerte, so turn your robe-wearing ass around, right fucking now!" Kristoff yelled.

Death plucked the balloon off the tank and turned around to face Kristoff, who immediately pissed himself as he squeezed the trigger and the gun barked and lurched up. The bullet flew down the aisle and hit the balloon, right above where Death was holding it. The now free balloon shot up and began to fly erratically through the store. Death managed, again, with a face devoid of skin or eyebrows or even lips, to look annoyed. The robed figure turned, grabbed another yellow balloon, and put it on the tank of helium.

"You on drugs, motherfucker?" Kristoff yelled. "I have a fucking weapon! And by the power vested to me by the Union Allied Security Company, I demand you surrender yourself to me until other authorities arrive!"

Death raised a hand and snapped once; it was the sound of a coffin lid locking in the still store. Kristoff opened his mouth to say something but went still when he heard a sound behind him, a wet slithering sort of sound. He turned slowly, for a second got a glimpse of the thing that had torn itself free from the cashier at the front. A skinless slug demon with an impossibly large mouth that opened slowly to show spiraling rows of razor-sharp teeth like the inside of a turtle's mouth; somehow more terrifying for the single finger impaled on one of the vicious looking barbs.

Death left the grocery store, seven balloons bobbing merrily on the handle of the scythe as Kristoff shrieked in agony.

**

The hearse rumbled, the sound of a thousand souls being smothered by the inevitable hand of eternity, as Death sped down the toll road southbound in the northbound lane. The stereo crackled a bit, an old song obviously recorded off vinyl began to play, an ethereal hollowness to the guitar. Robert Johnson began to sing about the crossroads as Death looked to the left at the darkening sky.

Horns blared and cars swerved lanes, careening off the concrete barriers and each other as the chrome hell chariot raced along the toll way. A large blue semi with a long white trailer jerked, smashing the car on its left directly on the driver's side, the impact causing it to bounce over the right side into an empty yellow school bus that crumpled before teetering over on top of a red sports car trying to zip past on the shoulder.

There was no place for it to go as the hearse hit it head on. From the side, had anyone been alive to see it, the cab of the truck swallowed the hearse. In slow motion, the driver found his bottom half on the windshield of the hearse that came tearing through while his still conscious upper half was propelled through a hailstorm of shattering glass from the truck's windows. A ripple ran down the side of the trailer, solid matter forced into a mercurial state until the hearse burst out of the back of the trailer in a stream of ice cream and intestines as the laws of physics caught up to the trailer and it exploded, the shrapnel cutting through vehicles and concrete alike.

The windshield wipers did little but smear the chocolate and feces with a marshmallow bile swirl across the glass. Death didn't see as the car barreled through a jack-knifed eight-wheeler with a windmill blade strapped to the back. The halves of the trailer swung pendulously and destroyed the barriers on either side crushing vehicles on the southbound side and frontage road. Death turned up the radio to drown out the screeching metal and explosions before wrenching the wheel left and heading into the night, eschewing roads for the fields and errant cattle.

***

Death watched as the last rays of Helios fell behind the horizon before stepping out of the vehicle to stand beneath the field of twinkling stars. Carefully, the blade of the scythe carved a crescent moon into the soil, the outline crackled with purple light that flared brightly, and in the skies above the stars winked out, one by one, until only darkness swirled above.

What is it, Thanatos? A voice, sinuous and smooth, spoke from the dark.

Death held out a paper plate, the old-fashioned donut sitting in the center with a lone candle swaying in the breeze.

This foolishness again? The voice sighed, a note of disbelief ringing coolly.

Death stood implacable staring into the night.

Fine.

The inky blackness detached itself from the sky and coalesced, moving the same as the robes that clad the gaunt horseman to form a figure of perfection that stepped down from the heavens to stand in front of the reaper. Her beauty made everything else lesser simply by her proximity, yet it was balanced by coldness that spoke more of warnings of danger than poetic odes.

Nyx, one of the first beings, the personification of darkness, stood with her hand on her hip and a note of inconvenience set on her perfect face.

We have existed since long before Kronos himself, stepped forth from Chaos before time existed. Why do you insist on this charade every year?

Death held the donut in front of Nyx silently. She made a sour expression before leaning forward and blowing out the tiny flame. Death plucked out the candle and reached into his robe and pulled out a blanket that he spread carefully on the ground.

Nyx sighed and sat down and carefully inspected the donut.

This looks horrifying.

Death just pointed and Nyx broke off a piece of the golden dough. She sniffed it hesitantly before popping it into her mouth. Her eyes widened and she smiled, albeit against her will.

Oh my. This is truly ambrosia.

Death went back to the hearse and returned with the seven balloons and white cardboard house and sat down next to her.

Nyx arched her eyebrow at the colorful balloons.

More theatrics, Thanatos?

Death released the balloons, one a time, red then orange then yellow. Green, blue, and two different shades of purple slowly drifted into the night.

Nyx stared at them in confusion for a moment.

This is lost on me.

Death placed both hands together above his head and slowly spread his arms down until they were parallel to the ground.

A rainbow?

Death nodded and looked away from her. Nyx gasped softly and watched the balloons, a rainbow in the darkness, an impossibility made real. The stars reflected off the years that formed in her black eyes as she followed them higher and higher. Her cold hand slid over to rest in top of the skeletal one sitting on the blanket. They sat silently until all that remained of Nyx's rainbow was the memory of it floating into eternity.

Death passed the final box over to Nyx who looked at it with an odd expression. She popped open the top and pulled out her owl and tried to hide her bewilderment. She pulled out the piece of paper and looked it over.

Natalie?

Death shrugged.

Nyx looked at the owl for a long while before finally pulling it in to her chest and squeezing it.

I believe that I love it.

Then she leaned in and brushed her lips against the cheekbone of the skull.

Thank you.

Nyx rested her head on the shoulder of Death, her owl squeezed close to her chest and sighed happily. And Death, even though there was no real way of telling the expression on an expressionless skull, seemed content., if not downright happy, as they quietly sat on a blanket, under the stars, together.

A Closing Word from Uncomfortably Dark...

This is my personal thank you to all the contributing authors for taking part in this project and for helping a new author find her way in this industry. For helping me along the way, advising on my stories, my ideas, and my endeavors, for helping me become a better writer, a better editor, and a better interviewer; each of you have helped push me out of my comfort zone, into a better version of myself, a stronger and more confident version.

I cannot thank you or this community enough. I look forward to many more years of interviews, reviews, stories, and good times with each of you.

Without further ado, on to the supporters of the Baker's Dozen, this would not have been possible without all of you. We thank you, from the bottom of our Uncomfortably Dark hearts.

Brass Supporters:

Katrina Nola * Johann Thorsson * Giusuppe Lo Turco * Allie Mosser

Bronze Supporters:

Julia Messina * Dara La Rue * Ashante' Harris * Chelsey Sirmons, IV

Silver Supporters:

Christina Pfeiffer * Michael Mueller * Bear McCoy * Matthew Clarke * Raquel Bercy * Frazer Lee * Shawn Scott * Joan Pichon * Juliet DeVirgilio * Debbie Alder

Dark Dozen Supporters continued...

Ruby Supporters:

Darc Rose * Brandon Dziedzic * Karla Kay Peterson * Brett Evans * Eric Butler * Alan Aspinwall * Katrina Nola * Matthew Henshaw * Ben Freeman, III * Bob Waldron * Chelsey Sirmons, III

Gold Supporters:

Jamie Brown * Donna Latham

Platinum Supporters:

James Smith * Darcy Rose * Karen Catrelle * Linda Nola *

Vickie Logsdon * Kristine Prais * Ben Freeman, III * Earlene Green * Ruthann Jagge